Champagne Book Group

Presents

Camouflage

By

Ivy Keating & Scott Spotson

Champagne Book Group
www.champagnebooks.com
Copyright 2019 by Ivy Keating & Scott Spotson
ISBN 978-1-947128-55-2
Print January 2019
Cover Art by Robyn Hart
Produced in the United States of America

Champagne Book Group
2373 NE Evergreen Avenue
Albany OR 97321
USA

Dedication

From Ivy: Dedicated with love to my family: Sean, Drew, Brandon, Katie, and Emma.

Dear Reader

Standing on the edge of a New England forest, I found myself wondering what could be in there that we couldn't see. Then I wondered, if we discovered something extraordinary, what would we do with it?

Join Scott and me on our quest to discover if science and sentiment can win out over fear and the instinct and determination to destroy.

One
Breathe

Vanessa arrived early to her stationery store, carrying her favorite brewed coffee from the shop down the street. After unlocking the door, she placed her belongings on the counter and returned to the cool air outside to crank open the forest-green awning with beautifully scalloped trim. Droplets trapped after the heavy rainstorm the night before trickled down the canvas and over the elegant font which read "Sun Pressed Greetings." A pile of local newspapers stood against the large storefront window, and she scooped them into her arms to take inside.

Collecting her designer pocketbook and warm beverage, she walked to her office at the back of the store. At her desk, she admired the display of greeting cards featuring prints of paintings created by local artists. When she placed her coffee on the marble coaster on the antique desk, the sight of a spider creeping with its tiny long legs over the scribbled-on notepad made her jump. At arm's length, she held the pad in front of her in one hand, opened the window with the other and shook it off outside before settling in her chair.

The first sip of robust coffee invigorated her as she savored the bitterness of the warm beverage. Vanessa turned on her computer and sighed as she looked over last week's sales. *Ugh.* A fresh realization— the final balloon payment for the loan she'd taken out to renovate the store was due in two months.

The familiar sound of a woman's low-heeled shoes came closer. Vanessa continued to focus on the tally.

"Going over the books? I know that look," said her assistant Jenny, a pleasant, middle-aged woman whose talkative nature entertained the customers.

"Good morning," Vanessa replied. "Yes. But it's not just that."

"Oh," Jenny stammered. "You read the article?"

"What article?" she asked, turning to give Jenny her full attention, wondering why the gentle wrinkles around her assistant's eyes looked more pronounced.

"It's about Jason. A front-page article," Jenny said glancing at the newspapers stacked on the floor by the desk. "Do you want to read it? I can come back." She bent and pulled a copy of *The Daily Villager* from the pile.

The headline on the front page read: *Popular High School Coach Missing.*

For a moment, Vanessa didn't answer, then she nodded. "Yes, if I can have a moment."

"Of course," Jenny said and quietly shut the office door on her way out.

As she skimmed through the article, Vanessa's heart beat rapidly as she scoured the story like a sleuth, carefully deciphering anything new on the case. The piece contained everything she'd told Detective Ryan Lewis at the Wilton Police Station last Wednesday and now, the reality was crystal clear. Her friend had disappeared!

Jason Kenner was her next-door neighbor growing up; the messy haired ten-year-old who dared her to climb into the "boys only" treehouse in his backyard. She thought of him like a younger brother. He was one of her only friends who knew her family's secret that her dad was an alcoholic. When Jason came by her home after school, Vanessa's father often reeked of liquor and used to curse at him. Jason didn't stop coming. And he promised her he'd never tell.

During their twenties, they lost touch when they both went out of state to college, and then two years ago, it shocked her when they bumped into each other in Wilton's town center.

She gripped the paper as she thought about the last time she saw him. She had gone over to his home to finalize a design for a jersey with his winning basketball team's logo. As head coach of the Wilton High School basketball team, he had taken the opportunity to arrange for the sale of the shirts at her store, and the profits would go to the school's athletic fund.

When Vanessa had to leave their meeting to return to work, he planned to go jogging in Quarry Head Park. He lived close enough to walk there, but she gave him a ride instead so they could chat a little longer. She vividly remembered his charismatic smile as he said goodbye.

Now, more than a week later, she experienced an emptiness in the pit of her stomach as she digested the bleak news and the reality that she might never see him again. She looked up from the paper, recalling how he came to her home the night she and Richard, her boyfriend of three years, broke up after he accepted a job in another state without consulting her. Her mood lightened thinking about how Jason kept her busy with movies and yoga classes. They even played tennis again like they did when they were teenagers. The warm feeling faded as she considered that he might be gone for good.

After tossing aside the article, she tried to continue working, but an hour later she realized she'd forgotten to return a call to an important client and was struggling to enter the new inventory on the spreadsheet, Jenny came back and asked if she could start putting the newly received order of scented candles on the shelves. Vanessa hadn't even opened the boxes.

Unable to concentrate, she asked Jenny if she could run the store by herself until their other employee joined her in the afternoon.

"You've had a difficult time lately. I can't imagine where Jason is, and I could tell you were just getting over Richard. That bum. Who does he think he is leaving and expecting you to follow along?" Jenny asked.

It wasn't a question that needed to be answered. "I know, but it's better that I found out what he was really like. I deserve someone who thinks of me and not just himself." Easy to say; hard to admit.

When she told Richard she was not ready to give up running the store, he berated her for choosing "that silly shop" over him. Those three words crushed her. She had put a lot of effort into building a business she could be proud of, despite the recent downturn in sales, and his belittling attitude toward it really stung.

Jenny's voice broke in. "That's right, you deserve someone better. Where are you going to go?"

Vanessa didn't answer right away, but over the last few days she'd kept thinking about when she dropped Jason off at Quarry Head Park. She even had a nightmare about it. She was in the forest and heard him crying out in pain. She kept running through the undergrowth getting thrashed by brush and saplings but could not find him.

In reality, the dream made no sense. When a friend of his from work filed the missing person's report, Jason's car could not be found. Since he lived alone, this led the police to believe he'd made it home from the park.

Even so, it was the last place she knew for certain that he'd been. Maybe something had fallen from his pocket and she could find a clue as to where he might be. "I need to go back to the park," she said.

She'd only visited the park once before, the previous autumn, and that was with Jason. Visions of the path they jogged on entered her thoughts. The landscape had exhibited the most striking seasonal colors, when the leaves on the trees turned to hues of yellow, orange, and red. The brightness of the memory now dampened by his disappearance. *I have to go there.*

"Of course," Jenny said. "And don't worry about the store. I have it covered."

Vanessa sighed with relief. "Thank you. I'll be in early tomorrow."

She walked outside, her pace resolute. A quick check of the storefront window made her smile. She took pride in the display: a rocking chair made from white paper birch, a side table with a few of her personally selected greeting cards next to a set of three different size white pillar candles. *Elegant-country style.*

Anxious to get on with her search, she hurried home to change into her workout clothes. She tied her long brown hair up in a high ponytail and headed out.

Why am I going to the park? Because it's the last place I saw him. Maybe I'll find something or think of something new to tell the police.

She knew that was wholly unlikely, but she couldn't shake the sensation she should return to Quarry Head.

The clear blue skies created an inspiring view for the fifteen-minute drive to the park from her house. Fifty-nine degrees out and glowing sunshine bounced off the brightly colored canopy of trees. Unfortunately, the radiance of the day did nothing to lighten her distracted frame of mind. She looked around the entrance and stretched in preparation for a jog. She didn't know which path Jason chose that Saturday, so she walked past the stone benches and started down the first trail she saw.

Her steady pace soon became a jog and then a run. There was so much to consider. *Where can he be? If he's not hurt, where did he go? Maybe he decided to take some fantastic adventure and didn't tell anyone. It would be just like him to go on safari in Africa, but not to tell me or to miss work and worry his family.*

She had so many unanswered questions. Far down the path her breath didn't keep up with her fast pace. Her nerves somewhat soothed by the physical exertion, she eased into a slow, steady jog.

She didn't know how much time had passed, but the sky darkened as some clouds moved in. State officials had meticulously painted color-coded shapes on the trunks of the trees to help visitors stay on the path, but Vanessa did not know where each trail ended or how much further she had to walk to return to the entrance. Alone in an unfamiliar place, she shuddered as a cold shiver swept up her spine. The denseness of the forest allowed her to see only a couple of yards in any direction. Her heart pounding, she found the next trail marker.

Even with no idea where it led, she had to keep moving. The branches on the trees swayed with the wind, causing the leaves to rustle. She walked swiftly, desperately searching for any familiar sight, hoping it would lead her back to where she entered.

A rumbling sound in the woods behind her set her nerves on edge.

What was that?

For a second, she thought the ground shook under her feet. *What now? An earthquake?* Not likely in Connecticut, and she detected no further earth movement.

Maybe I just imagined the vibration. Get a hold of yourself.

In full flight mode, she clenched her fists, but before she could bolt, an antlered buck raced by. She gasped as she saw the look of terror in its big dark eye. The noise behind her intensified, and two fawns dashed by. With no safe direction to take, she cowered to the ground, holding her hands to her ears.

Then, silence came once again. Trembling, she stayed low to the path, attempting to regain her bearings. Slowly she lifted her head as she listened.

Breathe… Breathe…

Vanessa's gaze darted back and forth.

Now it's safe to go. I have to get out of here!

Run!

Two
Quarry Head

In an all-too-rare moment of quiet at his desk in the Wilton Police Station, Chief Sean Dermott pored over the Jason Kenner missing person case file. With chestnut-brown hair, warm russet brown eyes, and a slightly larger than average muscular stature, he always surprised new acquaintances when introduced as Wilton's police chief. At the age of thirty-six, they always thought he was too young to have such a senior position.

When he read the entry about Quarry Head, he thought about when he visited the area after becoming chief of the department. On that clear day, he stood on a ledge near the entrance and caught a glimpse of the Long Island Sound nearly thirty miles away. He felt like king of the world with his new title, up high on a boulder looking out over valleys of preserved land with no other people in sight. The park was open to the public, with no admission fee. Occasionally a visitor could pull into the entrance and find he was the only one there.

Near the end of that day, Sean stood on the ledge and watched the orange and golden hues around the setting sun disappear behind the mountain. It hadn't been that long since he thought he would never see the true colors of daylight fading again.

Five years back, a robbery suspect fleeing an apartment building had struck Sean on the left side of his head with an iron crowbar. He managed to tackle the perpetrator to the ground but sustained an injury that damaged his retinal nerve, resulting in a mild degree of red-green color blindness.

He'd have been unable to do his job if he could not properly identify things like the color of a perpetrator's clothes or getaway car. Yellow, orange, and red became tinted by green. He also found that different shades of blue looked more violet.

During his time-off to recover, he found an ophthalmologist who suggested a possible solution. The doctor gave him special tinted contacts. With the lenses, Sean could see colors with accuracy again. They blended with the natural color of his eyes allowing him to keep his condition a secret. He feared if his peers knew, they would still question his abilities. He also worried he'd be overlooked for promotions and other opportunities even though he was allowed to return to duty.

Now, as Sean paged through the Kenner file, he contemplated the issue of jurisdiction when it came to Quarry Head Park. He knew this park to be a state-owned facility, under his management because it sat within the borders of his town. This meant Colonel Frank Gunner, head of the Connecticut State Police Department, had to be notified. A task he believed required his delicate diplomacy and could therefore not be left to anyone else.

Thinking about that call, Sean took in a deep breath. With over thirty years of police experience, the colonel made it quite clear that he believed Sean was too young and inexperienced to be promoted to chief despite the landmark case that had catapulted him to the position. It also did not help that Frank had unsuccessfully recommended one of his own officers for the job.

Concerned that anything he filed would be closely scrutinized, Sean pulled out all the information he could find on Quarry Head Park and the adjoining property, the Tribol Preserve. The three-hundred-acre park was once a quarry, producing millstones for grinding corn. Now the land had been allowed to return to its natural state except for two stone benches near the entrance and the hiking paths that were cleared for visitors.

He spoke directly to Frank about why the area needed to be investigated. Then he assigned Detective Ryan Lewis to search the location for any clues Jason may have left behind.

When Ryan's team did not come up with any leads, Sean made sure he read the written report twice before signing off on it.

The moment he closed the file, police administrator, Marcy Charter, paged him. "Chief, a woman named Vanessa Strauss is asking for Detective Lewis. She's here about the Kenner case but Ryan's out."

"Did you ask her why she wants to see Ryan?"

"She said she was just in Quarry Head Park, and she wanted to report something that happened there."

"Okay, I'll see what I can do. Send her in."

In front of Marcy walked Vanessa Strauss, dressed in black lycra running suit bottoms and a bright pink top, her breathing agitated. Alerted to her obvious distress, Sean snapped to attention. He glanced twice at her delicate features. Her long, shiny, dark brown hair swept away from her face drew attention to her hazel colored eyes.

"Good afternoon, Ms. Strauss is it? I'm Chief Dermott."

"Good afternoon, Chief, and please, call me Vanessa."

"Then you must call me Sean," he replied, gesturing to the chair across from his. He could sense her urgency from the nervous fidgeting of her hands and her inability to stand still. "Please, take a seat. Are you all right?"

"I just had a really scary experience at Quarry Head Park," she exclaimed setting herself into one of the two chairs in front of the desk.

"Why don't you tell me what happened?"

She inhaled deeply before she began. "I was jogging on one of the paths when I heard an unusual rumbling sound, and the ground seemed to shake. A moment later a huge deer ran right in front of me, and then two more deer. I thought for a moment that there had been an earthquake, but it was this rumbling sound that really frightened me... I felt surrounded."

"Could this sound have been a motorcycle?"

"It didn't sound like one. No, it sounded like something extremely large dragging on the ground."

There had been a murder in Lakeside Park in nearby Pound Ridge, New York. The suspect left the scene on a motorbike. "Can you tell me which path you were on, and how far in you'd gone when you heard the sound?"

"I was on the yellow path, about three quarters of the way around it, I think."

"I'll make sure another search of the area is done today."

"Will you be conducting it?"

Sean paused. Typically, he would not get involved on that level, but after reading the Kenner file again, it bothered him that no one actually saw Jason drive his car away. Plus, if there was a remote possibility that a murder suspect was hiding in the area, he wanted to be more hands on. This was his community after all.

"Normally I wouldn't be personally involved in the search, but as Detective Lewis is out for the afternoon and I don't want this to wait, I'm going to call in the K-9 unit and have them meet myself and another officer there.

Vanessa's expression softened. "Can a police dog track a person even so many days later? Do you think Jason's still nearby even though his car is missing?"

"He could be, and yes, dogs can pick up on a scent for weeks depending on conditions like the weather and how well traveled the path is."

"Thank you," she said, sounding grateful. "Oh! Will you need a piece of Jason's clothing? For the dog, I mean."

"Yes," he said, "I'll have to go into his house. If I hurry—I can get the warrant for today still."

"I could meet you there and let you in. I know where he hides a spare key."

"Fine, you can meet us at his house, but we'll go to the park alone."

"Of course, but I'd like to go into the house. I haven't been there since he was reported missing. Maybe I'll see something that can help find him. Something you might've missed."

Vanessa wrote down her cell phone number, and he agreed to call to let her know what time to meet later that day.

Sean took the slip with her number and gave her one of his cards with his direct line on in case she had any questions. He wanted to assure her everything would be all right and Jason would be found, but he could not make that promise.

"Do you think you'll find him?"

He looked her in the eyes. "He's our number one priority."

Three
Old Times

Sean made the call to Colonel Gunner regarding the new search of the park, then went to get the search warrant. When he returned to the station, Marcy informed him an officer from the state department was on his way to see him about the case. Sean gritted his teeth at yet another demonstration that Gunner had no confidence in his abilities. When Marcy told him the person coming was his best friend, Detective Ethan Roberts, Sean's mood lightened.

He first met Ethan on the Tri-State Wrestling Team in high school. They bonded over playing sports and watching football. When Ethan shared his decision to enroll in the police academy after college, Sean knew that was the right career path for him as well. Though before now they never worked in the same office or together on a case, they remained friends, watching sports or going to bars, when their schedule allowed.

Sean entered his office and read over messages while he waited. An update on the Lakeside Park murder flashed on the screen. Immediately he opened it:

"The victim in the Lakeside Park homicide has been identified as Alfred Biderman. The suspect is a Caucasian male, approximately forty years old. He was seen leaving the park on a black off-road motorcycle with no license plates, wearing a black helmet, worn-out gray jacket, and blue jeans. A sketch of the suspect is attached."

Sean studied the drawing. Marcy paged him breaking his concentration. "Detective Ethan Roberts and Officer Steven Cole are here. Should I send them to you?"

"Of course."

Sean looked at the doorway as Ethan, Steven, and a very large German Shepherd entered the room.

"Hey man, glad they sent you." Sean stood and embraced Ethan who reciprocated by slapping him firmly on the back. Then he introduced himself to Steven. "So, you're the new officer with the K-9 unit," Sean said as they shook hands.

"It's an honor, sir. You have quite a reputation," Steven said.

"I hope it's a good one." Sean laughed. He knew there were rumors about how he got the promotion to chief. Some of the more senior officers felt they deserved the position more than he did which had resulted in bad feelings and malicious gossip. "I see you have Baso with you. Is it okay if I give him a pat?"

"Go right ahead," Steven said, standing tall.

Sean bent to stroke the dog's back. "How have you two adjusted to working together? I know he was close to his previous handler."

"Took a bit of getting used to, sir, but I took him hiking with me for a few weekends and between that and a bit of jerky, we seem to have come to a good working agreement."

Sean smiled and patted the dog fondly on the head before standing. "Have you had a chance to look at the Kenner file?" he asked.

"Yes. I'm up to date on it," Steven said.

"Good. So, then you know I have a missing person and no leads except he was last seen entering Quarry Head Park. We have reason to believe he made it back home, but his friend Vanessa was jogging in the park and heard some unusual noises, so I want to do a more thorough search."

"Baso can pick up the scent of a person over a quarter mile away. He's trained in tracking and cadaver retrieval. If your man's anywhere near where we're working, he'll find him," Steven said.

"I have the search warrant so let's get to this guy's house and pick up something for Baso to sniff."

"I'll meet you at the park in, say, thirty minutes?" Steven asked.

"Sounds good. Vanessa, asked to go into the house, so I'll have her meet us there with the key."

Ethan adopted a more serious tone, one which held a hint of suspicion as he said, "What's your take on the girl?"

Trying to steady his tone, Sean said, "She's not a suspect. She originally came forward on her own and has now offered us keys to Jason's house. She seems genuinely worried by his disappearance."

"If you say so," Ethan mumbled.

They left the station, and Sean got into the passenger seat of the cruiser. Driving with Ethan reminded him of the time they spent together at the police academy. He grinned as he remembered how Ethan coaxed him into driving a dragster on a course in New Jersey, saying it would be good practice for pursuit training.

Ethan glanced at him. "So, are you going to call Emily?"

"Not a chance," Sean said.

He had asked his long-term girlfriend Emily to move in with him when he purchased his house in Wilton six months ago. He quickly became frustrated with her berating him for choosing work over spending time with her. After two months or more of constant fighting, she left him.

"Aw, man. She gave you hell, but all that make-up sex was worth it. Heck, she could do it to me!"

"Don't go there and, no, you can't call her."

"Just messing with you."

"What about that girl you were hanging out with in the bar the other night? You never told me what happened," Sean said jokingly. She had looked much too young for him.

Ethan laughed. "She was talking about her final exams. And doing tequila shots at the bar."

"Get out of here!" Sean roared with laughter.

"Very funny."

They were nearing Jason's house. As they pulled into the driveway, Sean saw Vanessa waiting by the front door, watching them. "What?" he asked, as Ethan turned to him with a poorly concealed leer.

"Are you kidding? You didn't tell me she's fucking hot," Ethan said in a low voice, barely moving his lips.

"Back off," Sean growled.

He and Ethan exited the cruiser. Sean's cheeks warmed as he scanned Vanessa, clad in an off-shoulder sweater and fitted jeans that did little to hide her attractive figure.

"Thank you for calling me," she said as she greeted him.

For a moment, it appeared as if she was going to grasp him by the hands, but she stopped short. Ethan darted an envious glance at him, but he ignored it.

"No problem," Sean said. He introduced Ethan and asked if she had the key.

"I do. I was wondering if anyone had reported seeing the car…but I guess no one has.

"No. Not yet," Sean said.

"Well," she said, looking skyward for a moment. "I'm just hoping we hear something soon."

"I hope so too. I have to ask you for the key, so I can enter first." Sean held out the warrant.

"Of course." She handed it over and explained where it had been hidden, pointing to the shrub.

Taking command, he took the lead and walked up to Jason's small ranch-style home. She followed, then Ethan. Sean unlocked the door and entered the premises.

He immediately noticed that no one had been there for days. The mail, delivered through a slot in the front door, lay in a pile on the floor. Vanessa went ahead into the living room. He picked up the letters and went through them.

"Hey," he said quietly to Ethan, who was also searching around. "Isn't this an awful lot of bills?" Vanessa was by the couch, out of earshot.

"Yah, I think so."

"There are at least seven letters from credit card companies, and this one's addressed to a Marsha Phillips. Of course, he rents the house and it could be for the owners, but I don't recognize the name."

"Yeah, that's odd."

"I'll check it out." Sean tucked the envelopes into his jacket pocket.

They joined Vanessa in the living room. On the floor by the couch was a basketball adorned with dozens of signatures. The end table had an empty glass with a moldy film at the bottom.

Sean felt sorry for Vanessa. He could see her brow furrow at the sight of the unopened letters and filthy glass.

"If you could point me to his bedroom I'd like to take a look for a shirt or something," Ethan said to her.

"It's the one on the left," she said in a somber voice.

Sean followed her into the small kitchen where there were a few dirty plates, glasses, and utensils sitting in the dry sink. He glanced at her to decipher her reaction. Her face had paled.

"Are you okay?" he asked, concerned.

"Everything looks just the way I last saw it that Saturday I drove him to the park. When I came in he was finishing a bowl of cereal. There it is—in the sink. We sat at this table, and this is the sweatshirt that was hanging over the chair—just like this."

"It doesn't look like anyone's been in this house for some time," he said, careful not to jump to any further conclusions.

Vanessa walked over to the drawer to the right of the sink. She hesitated before opening it.

"These are his car keys." She picked them up to show him. "Jason tossed them into the drawer the day I drove him to the park."

"Are you certain?" Sean asked.

"Yes. He unclipped his house key from this keychain, said he didn't need his car, and I guess they were too bulky to put in his running belt."

"Do you know if he had another set?"

Vanessa paused then said, "I'm not sure. Maybe. I guess he could have used another."

"Let's leave them where you found them for now."

"It doesn't look like he's been in the house—but surely he must have come by to get his car? Otherwise where is it? I'm really confused."

"That's why I'm here. To figure this out and find him."

"I know." She sighed.

Sean followed her out of the kitchen. He could tell she knew the layout of the house, but she didn't open any other cabinet or look for anything in particular. She exhibited a distant familiarity which made him think their relationship was sincerely a friendship and not a romance.

Jason used the second bedroom like a den. There was a small worn-out leather couch with scrape marks revealing its age, and a thirty-inch plasma television on a bridge table.

"Did he just move in? The rooms look empty," Sean asked, seeing no shelves, lamps, or pillows. None of the creature-comforts of a lived-in home.

"Not really. I guess he just liked it this way."

"I have what we need," Ethan called out. In a clear plastic bag he held a blue and white striped T-shirt taken from the bathroom floor.

"We're coming," Sean replied

"It doesn't seem like he's been back," Vanessa said in a low tone.

"Well, if he contacts you, let me know right away."

"I will. And will you call me if you find anything on your search of the park? Even if you just find out where his car is."

He promised he would. Then he watched her leave before walking to the police cruiser with Ethan.

"What do you think?" Ethan asked as he backed out of the driveway, then drove off down the street.

Sean stopped thinking about Vanessa and reverted to his police chief mindset. He frowned ahead at the open road. "I have reason to believe he may not have made it back to the house. Vanessa found his car keys in the kitchen drawer."

"Could've used a spare set."

"True." Sean thought for a moment. "If we don't find him in the park, I don't think we'll find him nearby, because he would have tipped someone off. But we do have these credit card statements, and the car's missing. It's time to do a more thorough background check."

"Agreed," Ethan said and then jumped right in with, "So… are you going to ask her out?"

"Who?" Sean smirked.

"Vanessa, of course. I think she's into you."

Sean scoffed. "Oh, you got that from the way she walked past me in the house?"

"No, but when you locked the door, I heard her say you should call her."

"That was just for information on her friend," he said with a laugh. "If you're done, the park's just up ahead."

Four
Search

Ethan steered the police car into Quarry Head Park and drove down the dirt road leading to the parking area. Sean zipped his jacket anticipating the cold air. Low, gray clouds darkened the day.

He turned his head away in order to discretely remove the prescription contact lenses and place them into the tiny plastic case he kept in his pocket. The only two people he was comfortable sharing his condition with besides his parents were Ethan and Emily, but he still preferred to take them out discretely.

When he chose not to share the damage to his eyes with other friends and colleagues, he also kept secret the advantages it gave him. At night, or in very dim light, he could see better than a normal, sighted person without the lenses. He also gained the ability to distinguish camouflaged objects from their surroundings because his vision naturally focused on the outline of things over color.

He planned to look through the woods and knew he'd have the advantage of seeing if there was something in the brushy undergrowth. The memory of plucking a friend's missing earring from a gravel driveway crossed his mind.

Another cruiser pulled into the lot. "Come, Baso," came Steven's voice.

Sean waved him over. He waited with Ethan observing how Steven handled the large police dog which was so obedient the leash was always slack.

"Vanessa said Jason went to the park for a run, so let's start by one of the trails," Sean said. The three officers headed toward the entry point to the paths.

"This is good," Steven said.

Ethan handed him the bag with the shirt and the tongs. In response, Steven extracted the clothing for Baso to sniff. Panting with excitement, the dog put his nose to the ground and took off.

He led them to another tree with a green, painted triangle signaling to Sean that Jason may have taken this trail. The impending rain may have chased off the "fair weather" visitors, but they passed one jogger who raised his eyebrows at seeing the spectacle of three uniformed police officers and a large German Shepherd running by. About one mile into the green path, near a tree trunk with a painted yellow square indicating the paths crossed, Baso slowed. Then the dog stopped, and started barking.

"The scent ends here," Steven said, a bit confused. A few raindrops hit their heads.

Cursing, Sean looked up at the sky. "Think the rain will throw off the scent?"

"Not necessarily. The rain can actually help bring the scent closer to the surface of the ground," Steven said.

"But how could Jason's trail just end in the middle of the path?"

"I don't know. Let's try it again." Steven held the shirt under Baso's nose, but the dog didn't budge. "That's it. I don't know what to say." He looked puzzled. "I'll walk Baso around some more, but then I'm going back to write up the report."

"Be sure to send me a copy. Thanks for your help today."

"We'll split up, and I'll meet you at the entrance," Ethan said.

The further Sean went from the trail, the denser the forest became. Due to the abundant leaves, brush, and undergrowth, it became more difficult to see the ground, but he used his vision to his advantage. The outlines of objects stood out like the piece of brown paper on top of leaves the same color. Nothing worth collecting as evidence yet.

He approached an old stone wall. Nearby he could make out a depression in the soil. His instinct kicking in, he wondered if a motorcycle could have left it.

Earlier, Vanessa mentioned she heard a strange noise when she was jogging here. It made him think of the Lakeside Park suspect. The track seemed very wide, but a bike could have been ridden back and forth over the area. A soil sample could be tested for traces of rubber or metal which could indicate the presence of a motorcycle.

Bending, Sean pulled a rolled-up plastic bag out of his trouser pocket. He flipped open his switchblade, dug up a few tablespoons worth of dirt, and deposited it into the container pressing along the seal to securely close it.

On the way back to the path, Sean squinted as the cold misty rain tapped his face. He stumbled on a thick tree root, bracing himself against a pile of large rocks from the remnants of a different stone wall, less structured then the other. Wedged between two boulders he saw a distinct pattern. *Snake skin?*

Yes, scales, unmistakably from some kind of reptile. The

material looked about a hand's width and an arm's length. He could not determine if a snake shed it or if it was a clothing accessory like a belt worn down by the elements.

As the trees rustled, he snapped to attention. *Jason?*

Five
Video

Sean focused on the area of forest where he heard the sound.

Tree trunks, low branches, scrubby understory—he could see it all in perfect detail but nothing that would make that crunching noise. He pushed his way through the brush, picturing the missing man dragging himself along the ground.

What the...?

His eyes opened wide. There before him he found a very dirty looking mutt, whimpering as it looked at him.

The shabby dog didn't run away as he approached. It lay on the ground, then rolled onto its back and lifted a paw in Sean's direction.

"Aww," he said in a soothing tone. The animal looked like a mixed breed, at least part golden retriever. Carefully, he bent to pick up the hound, hoping it wouldn't turn aggressive.

To his relief, the dog lay quietly in his arms. Walking back to the parking lot, he cradled the animal to make sure it stayed comfortable.

"Where the hell did you get that?" Ethan asked, his brows raised.

The dog came alive in his arms, wriggling and yapping. Sean looked at it, surprised at its new-found strength. "Where do you think? You're the detective."

"Funny. We'll drop him off at the pound on the way back."

"Not so fast. I'll take him with me to the station and talk to animal control in case someone reported him missing. He might also need medical care."

"Seriously?"

"It's my duty to handle this properly," Sean said in a tone that was final.

"Softy," Ethan retorted, but the scowl turned into a grin as he turned away.

They trudged through what had now become a downpour, and soon seated themselves in the dry car with the dog on Sean's lap. Mud covered Sean's jacket, but he didn't mind. The mutt picked its head up and licked Sean's face while thumping his tail on the seat.

"Well, we know Jason was there," Sean said, frowning. "Baso picked up his scent."

"Did you doubt it?"

"No, just being thorough."

"Can't make a connection with the Lakeside Park murder, but we can say for certain that Jason's not in the park anymore, or Baso would've found him."

"Yeah, you're right."

"While I was out there I found an area of soil with a long straight depression about thirty inches wide and four times as long. I'm having it tested for traces of rubber, metal, anything that could indicate a motorbike."

"Sounds wide for a bike but let me know if the soil analysis shows anything," Ethan said, stopping the vehicle in front of the station. "Hey! Want to try that new sports bar in Fairfield?"

"Sure. How about this Friday?"

"That works for me."

They gave each other a hearty goodbye. Sean started for the door, with the dog still in his arms.

"Hey, Sean," Ethan called after him from the car. "You're never going to take that mutt to the pound, are ya?"

"Don't worry about it. He'll find a good home."

He smirked. "Yeah, I think I know exactly whose home that will be. That mutt's got you suckered. You're a lost cause." Then he chuckled and saluted Sean. In a moment, he was gone.

Sean took the dog to the waiting room.

"Oh, how cute," said an officer walking over to them. "He's adorable." She stopped to stroke the top of his head. "He looks hungry, and a bath wouldn't be a bad idea."

"Can you get him a bowl of water and see if you can dig up some food? Then get a leash from the utility room."

"On it, Chief," she said. "What's his name?"

"Scout," Sean said, surprising himself. The name just came to him—and he liked it.

He washed his hands and face in the sink. From his pocket he removed the contact lens case and the sample size bottle of solution to sterilize the tinted lenses before putting them back in his eyes.

Now to get more comfortable. He shut his office door and hung his wet jacket on the coat rack. Sitting at his desk, after he sloughed off his muddy boots, he grunted with exertion as he removed his damp socks. His bare feet touched the polished tile floor. *Ah, much better.*

Still cold but drying off at least. Content, he mulled over the events of the last few hours. *What do we have? Not a whole lot. A man gets dropped off in the park. Sets off down a trail and disappears into thin air.*

He paged Detective Ryan Lewis to his office. Time for another meeting on the case.

A sturdy man with jet black hair neatly swept to the side entered the room carrying a large notepad.

"Have a seat. I wanted to update you on the Kenner case. How'd it go in court today? Did you finally get a chance to testify?" Sean asked, referring to the case that had kept Ryan away from the office.

"Yes. Sorry I couldn't be there for the search today. I keep hearing how good Baso is, and I really want to see him in action. Did you find anything new?"

"Baso did pick up Jason's trail, but it stopped in the middle of the path. Don't know what to make of it yet. And here's something interesting. There's a set of Jason's car keys in the kitchen drawer of his home. Vanessa says that's where he left them the day she dropped him at the park."

"That's strange considering the car is gone, but I'll look into it and see what I can come up with."

"Good. I also want you to go back to the house and do a complete search. I found multiple credit card statements." Sean handed him the opened letters. "Take a look at the address on this one."

"Marsha Phillips? Doesn't sound familiar. Who is she?"

"I'm hoping you can find out. She's not the owner of the home."

"Will do. Am I searching for anything in particular?"

"No, but most of the charges on the statements are for cash advances. I want to know what he's spending the money on. You've been to his house when he was first reported missing—it looks empty and the furniture's old and worn-out. Oh, and do a background check. See if there're any police records, even a traffic ticket."

"I'm on it, Chief. Anything else?"

"Yes, deliver this to the lab," Sean said, handing him the soil sample. "We're looking for anything that would show if a motorcycle was there, like rubber fibers. They'll know what to test for."

Ryan leaned forward to get up, but Sean held up his hand to stop him. "Yes?"

"Could you please have someone from the South Wilton Veterinarians Clinic check out the dog in the waiting room and see if anyone reported him missing with animal control? With any luck, no one will claim him."

"Sir?" said Ryan, looking confused.

"I want to keep that mongrel," he said and smiled.

Ryan grinned. "I'll take care of it."

~ * ~

The following week on Monday, when Sean returned to work, he found new information on the homicide in Lakeside Park in his inbox.

"The fingerprints lifted from the evidence belong to Marcus Branca. He is now the number one suspect. He's also the prime suspect in a robbery caught on tape in Litchfield. The security video from the drugstore robbery and a mug shot are attached."

The next paragraph got him thinking.

"A current address for the suspect is not confirmed. His mother, Evelyn Branca lives at 201 Daleview Circle in Norwalk, Connecticut. A transcript of her statement is attached. She stated the last time she saw her son was two years ago in October when he asked her for money."

He's robbing close to home. He has no confirmed address, and he last called his mother two years ago.

Sean's gut told him—*she's lying*.

He closed the email to focus on the open cases within his department.

The results of the forensic tests from the soil samples should be in.

He placed the call to the lab. The receptionist told him the tests were completed and transferred him to a technician who gave him the results. "The soil samples you sent over came up negative for synthetic and natural rubber. No trace metals either. We found nothing man-made in it."

Sean thanked the woman. *Nothing then.*

He glanced at the time on his computer screen. In one hour, he needed to attend a seminar on emergency protocols as outlined by the Department of Emergency Services and Public Protection, given at the University of Connecticut. He turned off his computer, preparing to leave when he saw Ryan standing in the doorway.

Sean waved him in. "What's up?"

"I have the report I promised on Jason Kenner last week."

"Including what happened to the car and the credit card statements?"

"Yes. And some information from recent bank records," Ryan

said, handing Sean a hard copy.

"Have a seat."

"Remember the name on the account, Marsha Philips?"

Sean nodded.

"She's an old girlfriend who lives in Albany, New York, about two hours away. I was able to speak with her."

"What did she say?"

"They lived together, and she was crushed he's missing. It sounded like Marsha cared very deeply about him, so I asked what the nature of their relationship was today. She said they're just friends. They broke up because he has a gambling problem."

"Is that why he has so many credit cards?"

"Yeah. He uses cash advances to get money. Marsha said he's been doing that for years. He wanted her to open a card in her name and take out an advance for him. She refused and gave him an ultimatum. Get help for his addiction, or it's over. He never got help."

"Does she know there's a credit card statement in her name going to his house?"

"She does. She knows he opened a card in her name illegally, but she doesn't want to press charges. Two months ago, Jason told her that he owed someone money and they're after him. He asked Marsha if she could loan him two thousand dollars, but she refused. He opened the card without her permission but then called her to confess what he'd done and closed the account. She feels terrible for him. She said he's a good man; he just has a problem."

"That's very forgiving considering what he did," Sean said.

"Yup, but the story checks out. I followed up with the credit card carrier, and they did receive a request to close the account. And there's more. Marsha said when they first started dating Jason owed someone $11,000 for betting on football games. He was so scared they would come after him, he told her if he didn't get the money he'd have to leave town. She gave him a small loan, and he took a second job to cover the rest. Marsha said he would tell her he stopped gambling, but she knows he never did. He was always short of money the entire time they were together."

"I'm a little surprised none of his friends said anything. There's nothing in the file about it," Sean said, wondering if Vanessa knew about Jason's addiction.

"From the way Marsha spoke—he was good at hiding it. He held a steady job, and for the most part they had a good relationship."

"I can see that. Jason's very popular around here. He was working with kids coaching the winning basketball team. Looks like a model citizen. Any idea who he owes money to?"

"Not yet, but his landlady said he hasn't paid his rent in two months. I did some checking, and he's behind on all his other bills. There are some illegal gambling operations in neighboring towns that local law enforcement is building cases against. I could contact them."

"Yes. Do that."

He nodded. "Right away."

"Oh, did you find out what happened to his car?" Sean asked, standing and gathering his things.

"As a matter of fact, yes." Ryan followed Sean to the door. "The car was repossessed for non-payment. He hadn't paid in almost six months. It was pure coincidence it was taken away now."

"See what else you can find and keep me updated."

Ryan returned to his office, and Sean left the station. On the way to his police car, he detoured into the building next door which housed the Animal Control Department.

After exchanging greetings with Officer Benjamin Gibson, the head of Animal Control, Sean asked if anyone claimed the dog he found.

"No such luck. No one's called, and the poor creature's been staying at the animal hospital since you had him brought in," Ben said.

"How come?"

"He tested positive for Lyme disease. He'll be okay, but they wanted to start him on antibiotics so they kept him there."

Sean rubbed his chin. *The dog's been through enough.* "If no one calls you today, I'm going to pick him up and take him home."

"Good for you," Ben said with a smile. "Hey. Since you're here, a video just came in of a mutilated animal in Quarry Head Park. Want to take a look?"

"Someone filmed it?"

"Yeah."

"I don't have much time. Is it long?"

"Not at all. Just shy of two minutes."

"Sure. Let me see."

"I just want you to be prepared. It's pretty gross."

"I appreciate the warning," Sean said, even more interested.

Ben pulled the file up on the computer and turned the screen toward Sean.

The camera caught every angle of the gruesome sight. Sean flinched. *What the hell?*

The body in the footage looked like a deer. The features on its face were squashed; the eyes no longer clearly defined. The neck of the animal was bent in the middle—the head lay flat on the ground twisted to one side. Two stumps, which were once the deer's front legs, jutted out just past its ears. Its back legs were crushed and wedged into position under its belly. Even more bizarre, the lifeless mass had a gelatinous looking coating over its entire body.

"Do we know what happened to it?"

"No. The footage was taken by a fifteen-year-old boy on his cellphone. He was riding his bike with a friend in Quarry Head Park. They went off the path, and his friend fell from the bike when he hit this dead animal."

"Who gave you the video?"

"His mother sent it in by email. She wanted to make sure someone cleaned it up before anyone else got hurt. She said her son's friend developed an itchy rash from the slime covering the animal's body."

Sean pointed to a marker on a tree in the video. "This is next to the yellow path," he said. "Hold off on removing the animal for just a few hours. I have to go to a seminar at the University of Connecticut, but when I come back I want to take a look at it myself."

"Sure. Hey, when you get to the school you should talk to Dr. Greg Mitchell. You can show him the video."

"Why? Who is he?"

"Greg's a professor at the University and the head of the Biology Department. He knows a lot about animals and specializes in herpetology."

"Herpetology? The study of reptiles?" Sean asked.

"That's right. Actually it's reptiles and amphibians, so he covers both land and water. Greg lives right here in town. Last year he helped us relocate a Bog Turtle found in someone's yard. They're endangered, you know."

"But even I can see this looks like a deer."

"I know, but he's very knowledgeable. He might be able to help. Anyway, it's just a suggestion, and you'll be there anyway."

"Okay, can you send me the video?"

"Not a problem. I'll email it to you now."

Sean thanked Ben and left for the University. Once in his cruiser he scrunched his nose, mulling over the grisly video. *Natural causes or foul play?*

Six
Evolution

In the midst of dozens of attendees in the cavernous lecture hall, Sean listened to the new protocols for handling emergencies and natural disasters. The information was vital for conducting department safety drills. Toward the end, his mind drifted to the many topics that distracted him lately, including the open cases back at the station, plus the tantalizing prospect of meeting Vanessa once again.

When the session ended, he sought out Dr. Mitchell. He asked for directions from the faculty receptionist who gave Sean an enthusiastic endorsement of the professor.

"Dr. Mitchell was given a grant for research to help stabilize the dwindling population of corn snakes throughout the state. He just finished building an enormous reptile terrarium, twelve feet long by eight feet wide and six feet high. You must go see it. I've seen the habitat—it's amazing. The professor's giving a lecture now, but he likes when people drop in."

He thanked her and headed off as per her instructions. He found the room and stood just outside the open door, his laptop case hanging from his shoulder. Lecturing from the front of the classroom, Dr. Greg Mitchell looked as if he was in his sixties, slightly overweight with messy gray hair. He dressed like a teenager in faded jeans and a long-sleeved worn out T-shirt.

The professor climbed a short ladder beside an enormous tank which must've been the one the receptionist raved about. He seemed surprisingly nimble, stretching to adjust one of the heat lamps under the hood, while he explained how the temperature had to be lowered gradually to mimic the outdoor conditions favorable for brumation, a less dormant state of hibernation.

The large reptile habitat featured vines running up branches. On its packed dirt bottom English Ivy, umbrella plants and several variations of leaf litter flourished. A sturdy plastic wall divided the tank into two sections. Both sides had water flowing from the top of a mound of soil. No doubt impermeable material lay under the surface. At the base of the hill, the water gathered in a stream that rushed around the tank where it was collected and pumped back to the top to renew the gurgling cascade. Erected amidst the brush in both sections were two rows of stone walls built to scale.

Greg displayed a dramatic teaching style. When he wasn't working on the tank he constantly moved his arms, gesturing wildly. He spoke fast as if he had too much information to impart and not enough time.

Questions were permitted, and he gave detailed responses. Interested in the lecture, Sean stepped into the room.

The professor stopped talking and looked at him. "Did you want to learn about the study?" he asked Sean.

"I didn't mean to interrupt. I was wondering if you had a few minutes after class?"

"Absolutely. Why don't you join us? I'll be done in fifteen minutes."

Sean took a seat in the back.

Greg clapped his hands. "Back to work," he said with a smile. "Who can tell me why we should care about maintaining our population of corn snakes? Yes, Alan." He pointed to a young man up front.

"Everything's connected. Ya know, you remove one thing and it affects the other things," the student responded.

"Good. Remember that. We're going to come back to it in a minute. I want to give a brief overview of the evolution of snakes and lizards before we get to why their existence is important to our ecology."

The room was quiet as he spoke, with everyone facing forward.

"The first scaled animal evolved from amphibians that spent time in both water and on land. This happened roughly three hundred and ten million years ago during the Carboniferous Period. By the end of this period, giant animals, such as the carnivorous dimetrodon roamed the earth."

Greg pointed to pictures of the dimetrodons posted around the room. They looked like large lizards with huge sails on their backs.

"Snakes and lizards appeared by the end of the Permian Period, between two hundred and fifty-two million to two hundred and ninety-eight million years ago. Unfortunately, at the end of the Permian period there was a mass extinction. Ninety percent of the marine life and seventy percent of the terrestrial animals were wiped out. Many of the earlier reptiles died out too. It took thirty million years before the earth would see anything near the diversity in species again. But what era was around the corner?"

"Mesozoic!" a male student called out.

"You would be correct," Greg said with a smile. "The Age of Reptiles. The Triassic, Jurassic, and Cretaceous periods, and we have actual fossils of scaled reptiles from the mid-Jurassic period."

Pointing to the wall behind him, he continued, "I put up some pictures of the creatures that roamed the earth during this time. Take a look around."

Sean glanced at the huge charts and posters adorning the walls.

He watched the students' delighted faces as they looked at images of plesiosaurs, the marine reptiles that could grow to fifty feet in size. The creatures looked like huge sea serpents. *Amazing.*

"So, where'd they all go? The giant marine lizards? This fine plesiosaur here?" Greg asked gesturing to a picture of the creature. "About seventy five percent of these animals were wiped out in the Cretaceous-Paleogene extinction, also known as the K-Pg extinction. But snakes and lizards?" Shrugging, he waved his hands. "Oh, they survived. They survived because they were able to adapt to their new environment. In fact, snakes and lizards are so amazing at adapting that we have snakes with features like lizards and lizards with features like snakes, for example the genus Ophisaurus commonly known as glass lizards have no limbs. Their bodies developed to suit their needs.

"The larger marine reptiles like the mosasaur and plesiosaur have all become extinct. Most scientists believe this was due to the limitations imposed by their enormous size. You see, the larger you are, the harder it is to live in a changing environment.

"Now, let's turn our attention to this tank. I'm hoping the study provides some information for stabilizing their deteriorating numbers. Let's go back to my original question. Why should we care about maintaining our population of corn snakes? Alan said it's because if we remove one thing, it can affect another." Greg smiled and nodded at the student. "He's absolutely correct. Now I want someone to tell me how that pertains to corn snakes. One less snake to worry about, right? So what?" he asked, shrugging.

A young woman toward the back raised her hand.

"Yes, Katherine?"

"Everything in an ecosystem performs a function. So, if you're asking specifically about the corn snake, well, they eat rodents. Rodents carry disease. If the corn snake population dies out, maybe there will be more rodents to spread diseases to other species, even humans can be hurt or get sick."

"Good answer," he said, "and there have been cases of ecosystems devastated because of the loss of one single species and the wave of effects afterward. We may get into that later this year in class too."

He stood with his hands on his hips, a glint in his eyes. His students looked up; the room was quiet. Sean straightened in his seat, feeling more like a classmate than a police chief.

Extending his arm toward the tank Greg said, "I have a challenge for all of you. Count how many snakes are in there."

"Can we take a look?" one female student asked.

"Yes. Come on up."

The young men and woman left their desks to gather in front of the enormous tank.

"I found one. Over the tree limb," a student spoke.

"Yep!" Greg replied.

"Two under the lamp on the large rock," another called out.

"Under the light is what we call a basking spot. That corner of the habitat is kept warm and bright by heat lamps. The snakes enjoy lounging in those conditions, so I have several areas just like it. Corn snakes are solitary creatures—I had to create many different resting places, so they wouldn't fight."

"Is that one back by the water in the other corner?" a student in front asked.

"That's four so far."

Another student interrupted. "There's one by the brush next to the stream. Five now."

"Yes, very good," he said, encouraging them, but then there was silence.

"How many are there?" a student close to the habitat asked.

"There are six. So far you've found five. Take your time," Greg said.

Engrossed in the demonstration, Sean knew if he removed his contacts he'd be able to clearly see the hidden snake. Even though the reptile's scales matched the orange colored leaves keeping it hidden, his vision would focus on the outline of its body.

Everyone stared for another minute until the last snake moved its head. The glimmer of its golden eyes caused some students to jump back. The professor let out a laugh. "That's the sixth one!"

"Wow, I was looking right there and didn't even see it," a student admitted.

"That tends to happen," Greg said. "They're masters of camouflage." He glanced at the clock on the wall. "All right everybody, that'll do it for today. What did you think of the tank?"

A few members of the class called out things like, "Awesome!"

Even after the class was over, Greg was the center of attention once again as three students enquired about being lab assistants on the project. He wrote down their names before they left and then walked over to Sean.

"I hope you enjoyed the lecture. I try to keep it lively. By the way, I'm Greg Mitchell."

"Sean Dermott, chief of police in Wilton. I wish I had more classes like this in college."

"I'll take that as a compliment. How can I help?"

"I have a video of a mutilated animal found in Quarry Head Park. Ben from Animal Control told me you might be able to tell me what happened to it."

"Well, it may be hard to tell from a video, but let's have a look."

Sean booted up his computer and played the video. Greg leaned in closer and asked him to run it again. A few seconds in, he asked Sean to pause the recording.

Pulling the chair out from the desk, Greg sat in front of the screen. He looked straight ahead at the image. Sean waited for him to comment.

"I've seen this before when Santini spit things up."

"I'm sorry, but I don't know who Santini is," Sean said.

Greg kept his attention on the image as he replied. "Santini was a gopher snake from one of my research projects. It developed an irritation in its digestive tract and regurgitated its food."

"But that's a deer! Any animal big enough to swallow a deer would have to be huge."

"I admit this is extremely unusual. I'm not really sure what to say."

"Is that what you think happened to it?"

"Could you start the video again and stop it at the full front view?"

"Of course. Tell me when," Sean said.

The footage ran for about ten seconds before Greg said, "Now." He pointed at the screen. "I agree we're looking at a deer. I'd guess it was attacked judging by the crushed and distorted limbs." He paused and scratched his head. "I'm curious about the slime covering its body. Have you gone into the park yet to see it?"

"I was going to head there after this. Why?"

"I need to see this gelatinous coating up close."

"You think some kind of animal attacked it?"

"I'm not sure," Greg admitted. "It looks like digestive mucous, but it can also just be rotting flesh. Certain infections can cause oozing. I'll be able to give you a better idea of what it is and what happened if I can see it in person."

"When can you go?" he asked, eager for Greg's in-depth analysis at the scene. "I have asked Animal Control to wait for me to investigate before they remove it."

Greg said he could meet at 4:00 p.m., and Sean agreed. He thanked him and left to return to the station.

A row of red maples brightened his walk to his vehicle. On his way he received a call from Ethan. Refreshed by the scenery, he answered with a light voice.

"Hey man. I have good news and bad news for you." His friend's tone was apologetic.

"Let's hear the bad news first." Steeling himself, he gazed at the bright red tree tops. His gut told him the bad news had something to do with Ethan's superior, Colonel Gunner.

"Frank received the report about the dead animal found in Quarry Head Park. It included a line that said they would remove it after you investigate. Frank's asking why you're holding things up."

Sean opened the door to his cruiser and sat at the driver's seat. "He's out of line. Did you see the video? I want answers as to how it died. I have an animal expert meeting me there this afternoon to give me his opinion."

"I saw it. Pretty disgusting. I was thinking ritual killing. It looked saturated in something, but who knows. As for Frank, I'm on your side. Honestly, I don't want to get involved, but I have to follow orders. So, when can I meet you?"

"I'll be at the park at four. You know it's a waste of your time," Sean said, his voice tight.

"I know, but what can I do? Frank says I have to be there. Listen, four is close enough to quitting time. After the park, I'll write up my report at your station, and then we'll go out for a drink. You can blow off some steam."

Sean couldn't help but crack a smile. "Yeah, I guess. Hey. I have a question. The animal specialist joining us; his name's Greg Mitchell. Do you know him?"

"I've heard of him. He's signed off on some environmental impact reports."

Sean filled Ethan in on Greg's speculation about the slime coating.

"Sounds far-fetched, but he's the expert," Ethan said.

"Now tell me some good news," Sean said.

"The suspect in the Biderman murder, Marcus Branca, was apprehended a few hours ago. They're interrogating him now, and if he cooperates we should know if he was in Wilton October 17th—the day Jason Kenner was last seen."

Seven
Piercing

Sean asked Officer Ann McKay, who had additional training in forensics, to go with him to Quarry Head Park. Ann was a short, physically fit woman who took boxing classes to stay in shape. He worked out with her at the gym. He was much taller and broader, but she liked to tap him with her boxing gloves and in her toughest voice say, "If you were in my weight class I'd kick your butt." At 3:45 they left the station together.

They met Greg at the park. He carried a bag in his right hand and a large zoom lens camera over his shoulder. Sean carried his own field kit packed with vials, gloves, syringes, a knife, flashlight, notepad, first aid kit, and a compact camera.

"We're going to wait here for a moment. There's a detective from the state police on his way to join us. In fact, I think he just pulled in," Sean said, looking across the parking lot.

Ethan hurried over to the group. He greeted Sean and introduced himself to the others.

"Sean, should we follow you?" Ethan asked.

"Yes. Right this way," Sean replied, indicating the yellow path. "Animal Control is coming to collect the remains around five, so we need to get done quickly."

He and the others walked the trail for about ten minutes, not saying a word to one another.

Deep in the woods, the group stopped as Greg pointed to a couple of hawks circling in the sky. "Something's up," he said.

"I think it's just off the path this way," Sean said after tilting his head up to view the large winged birds fanning the sky.

As they neared their destination, a foul odor wafted in. So pungent he was not the only one to hesitate to move forward.

"Whoa," Ethan said, cross-eyed as he mimed waving away the scent in front of his face.

"I think we're very close." Sean's eyes watered.

"I'm surprised no one noticed this scent." Ann cupped her hand around her nose.

"It may have become this intense only recently," Greg suggested. He looked less disturbed by the smell than the rest of the group.

"That, and the animal is away from the trail. Most people who come to the park don't really venture beyond the paths," Sean said, grimacing. "Let's keep going." He noted a familiar-looking tree a little past the rectangular, yellow marker. *Yes, the branches jutted off in these directions.* "I recognize this area from the video. It's this way," he said, confidently leading the group a few more steps over the rocky ground.

Then the four of them stopped abruptly.

They'd found the deer. The wretched, mutilated creature appeared to have suffered a violent death, its body distorted, and its face smashed leaving it barely recognizable. Unidentified gooey slime coated the body.

G`reg moved closer first. His frame was stiff as if he was on full alert. No one in the group spoke as he zeroed in, without hesitation or indication that the mind-numbing stench impacted him. His camera kit remained unopened; he would see the evidence first hand, without a lens in the way.

Sean, too, headed straight to the mucous-covered animal and bent to look closer. Holding his arm across his face so his elbow covered his mouth and nose to keep from gagging, he studied the body. His brows wrinkled, Ethan grabbed a long thin branch from the forest floor and dragged away some of the mucous from a small pile directly in front of the body. He reminded Sean of a kid with a stick examining a dead jellyfish on the beach.

After several long seconds, Greg spoke deliberately, as if trying to convince himself as well as the others. "This slime coating over this animal is the same as what you see when a reptile regurgitates its food."

No one said a word. Then Sean pointed out the obvious for the second time. "But it's a deer," he said.

"Yes, and there are no known reptiles in this area large enough to ingest a deer." Greg frowned as he stood to face the group while Ann snapped photos and recorded notes in her notepad. "However, I've been studying reptiles for almost forty years, and I can tell you for certain this animal has been regurgitated. The deer's still whole, but it's crushed around the shoulders and legs. It looks like the work of a snake."

The other three just gawked at the mutilated body and did not speak.

"But you said there were no snakes that large in this area," Ethan said.

Greg shrugged, his voice calm as he said, "You could have a situation where someone illegally released a large snake such as a python here. It's completely out of its natural environment, agitated and trying to survive. Sometimes an overly stressed snake can become aggressive and mistakenly attack something much bigger than its digestive tract can handle."

"Do you think that's what happened?" Sean asked, a little shaken.

"I can't make that determination. I just know what this looks like. What type of snake and why it's here, that I can't tell you," Greg said, scratching his head.

Sean took command. "I'll get a vial of the mucous and send it to our lab. The park will need to be closed until we can figure this out."

"Sean," Greg said, "is it okay if I take some samples too? I'd also like to analyze this mucous. I've done this many times, and then we can see if my findings match yours."

"Yes, good idea."

Sean took out a map of the park to mark the exact spot where they found this wretched animal, as Ethan spray-painted a boundary around the carcass. Bright orange lines on the forest floor now surrounded the body. Just in case the orange markings disappeared with the turnover of dead leaves and forest soil, Ethan also marked a large boulder nearby with a small "x".

"Ann, radio Ben. Tell him we're closing the park and get him down here with some ropes and signs. I'll call Doug who should be nearby on patrol and get him to guard the entrance."

"Yes, Chief. I'm on it," Ann said.

"Ethan, what do you think?" Sean asked. "Will the colonel have an issue with me closing the park?"

"I'm sure he'll agree. Right now, we can't guarantee the public's safety here."

With a flash of inspiration, Sean walked over to Greg. "The other day when I was here, I noticed something that looked like snake or lizard skin on some rocks. Maybe it's still there?"

Greg spun around, his eyes wide. "Perfect! Did you happen to take any samples to your office?"

"No, I didn't think it was important before." Sean winced, realizing such critical evidence might now be gone.

"C'mon," Greg said, putting his camera away in his bag and tightly sealing in the contents. "Show me where you saw it. Hopefully it's still there. I can analyze the DNA to find out what species it is. Maybe we found what we're looking for."

"Good. We can use your expertise."

Sean scanned the group's activity. The examination of the deer was coming to a close with everyone putting away equipment and notepads. They all gazed at him, awaiting his orders.

Although by rights Ethan would normally be in charge, it was obvious Sean was asserting command. "Ethan, you go with Ann and ask any visitors you come across to leave the park," Sean said.

"Yes. And I can take her back to the station when we're done, if you like."

"Good idea," he said. He could tell Ethan didn't mind letting him have his way. "We'll talk later when I get there."

Ethan and Ann nodded before they waded through the brush back to the yellow trail, scanning for any visitors as they went.

Now only Greg and Sean remained. They looked at each other.

"Ready to lead the way?" Greg asked lightly.

Sean took a moment to recall the spot near the trail where he saw the toppled stone wall. To boost his memory, he studied the map in front of him. "This way," he said, pointing ahead.

He and Greg strode up and down steep inclines. Bright red, orange, yellow, and rusty brown leaves along with fallen branches and scruffy plants covered the ground.

"Watch your step. It's just ahead," Sean said as they approached the stone wall he had visited the other day.

To his relief, the long strip of skin was still hanging there, just as he remembered. It hadn't blown away or been taken by a curious visitor.

Greg's jaw dropped when he saw the papery object. Squatting quickly, he worked his fingers around the rocks underneath it. His movements were fast and deliberate, but he didn't speak.

"What's wrong?" Sean asked.

"Wait one minute," he said, tossing aside some of the smaller stones before asking for help with the heavier ones.

"What are you looking for?"

"There's probably more of this," Greg replied. "You see, a reptile's skin doesn't grow with them, so they shed the old layer when the new one is ready to replace it. Sometimes to help remove the old scales, they rub against a rough surface like these rocks." At that moment, he pointed to another patch of molted skin near the bottom of the wall.

Sean closed in, ready to help him retrieve the other section of scales. After grunting and carrying away some of the larger rocks, they found themselves staring at an even bigger portion of the shedding, concealed under the boulders and dead leaves.

"Help me hold it open," Greg said. "But let's be careful not to tear it. Sloughed off scales are not that tough and can be torn if you go about it wrong. I'll let you know if we have to stop."

Working in tandem, he and Greg took a hold of the sample at opposite ends, then edged apart. The folds of the materials were stuck together, but slowly Sean and Greg coaxed the stubborn parchment-like sheet to straighten out.

Sean shook his head as he tried to comprehend the enormity of it. "This thing is just gigantic," he whispered to the herpetologist.

But Greg didn't respond, his gaze robotic.

A piercing scream rang out. Sean jerked. "Wait here," he ordered Greg, as he sped off toward the sound.

"Aghhh!" came the next blood-curdling cry that sounded like Ethan.

"Coming!" he managed to holler, despite the mad dash consuming his oxygen.

He ducked and weaved under low branches. More screams and loud swearing reverberated around him, propelling him forward even faster.

Now within visual range, fear struck his heart.

What the hell?

A colossal, slithering mass thrashed against the slender saplings. His mind reeled at its massive proportions. The ground shook as the creature surged in the direction of Ann and Ethan. In the distance, they raced for their lives.

Sean drew his gun and fired at the animal.

Gripped with terror, he saw it close in on his friends. The muscular neck swayed, giving him glimpses of its wide-open jaw and long, sharply pointed teeth. He looked for a better angle to shoot it, as they scrabbled up a hill.

"It's right behind you!" Sean yelled at them as he fired again.

Scrambling, they'd almost reached the top of the mound. Ann's foot slipped on the rocky soil, and Ethan spun around to grab her. The monstrous reptile jerked its head toward him, opening its mouth wider.

Sean screamed a protracted, "No!" helpless to stop its powerful jaws slam down around Ethan's legs.

Fuck! Sean tried to get a shot at its body but the distance between them, dense woodlands, and the constant motion of the creature made it hard to hit. The reptile braced itself upright on four flipper-like appendages, rearing its head back to ingest its prey—Ethan.

Ann crawled to the top of the hill and threw her body over to the other side, frantically reaching for her gun. The towering creature's teeth clamped onto Ethan. With a jerk of its head, he disappeared deeper into its mouth. In raging fury, Sean kept firing at the swaying animal. A bullet hit its body. The giant reptile recoiled and dropped back to the ground. Shrieking, it convulsed, slid backward, and choked out its hold on Ethan.

Sean's mind processed several split-seconds of rapid fire images. Flashes of prehistoric reptiles seen on posters in Greg's lab, a twenty-five-foot-long scaled body with a colossal neck, flat flipper limbs, and the massive tapering tail mowing down saplings as it disappeared into the forest.

Gripping the gun, he eyed the thick woodland to make certain the creature went away before he was jolted into action by an urgent thought. *Ethan!* He bolted to his friend's side, dreading what he would see.

Ethan's face was covered in blood from scratches and cuts. His eyes were closed. At first Sean averted his gaze from Ethan's legs, knowing that the sight would make him sick on the spot. *Don't let him die*, Sean begged of the Almighty. He placed his index and middle finger over Ethan's carotid artery to check his pulse.

With ragged gasps puffing from her mouth, Ann dashed down the hill to Sean's side. "Is he alive?" she asked, her voice unsteady.

"Yes, he's still breathing."

Ann buckled to the ground in pain, grasping at where her pants had a wide rip. Sean looked over; she had a deep cut above her knee that was bleeding. She grunted, squeezing her eyes shut as she looked skyward. "Don't worry about me," she commanded, her voice raw. "Take care of Ethan."

Another officer, Doug, rushed in, still about two hundred feet away. "What's going on?" he shouted across the distance. "I heard gun shots."

"Get an ambulance here, now!" Ann yelled back. "Officer down."

Doug sucked in a breath as he neared enough to get a look at Ethan's injured body, then he made the call.

Being careful not to move his friend, Sean removed his belt and tied it tightly around Ethan's leg, above the most critical gash as a tourniquet. "Ethan, can you hear me? Say something."

Ethan opened his eyes. Sean choked back tears while sizing up the damage. Blood soaked through Ethan's pants, trickling into a pool near his ankles. The crimson liquid surrounded several brightly colored leaves and intermixed with the dirt. Horror filled Sean at the sight of Ethan's twisted feet laying at unnatural angles away from his shins.

Invading the moment of silent agony, Greg appeared in Sean's line of vision. Without saying a word, he reached into his bag for a clean cloth and gave it to Sean to press on top of another huge gash on Ethan's thigh.

"Can he talk?" Greg asked.

"No. He's in shock, but he's still breathing."

A distant noise caught their attention. An ambulance wailed, speeding to the scene of the carnage.

Eight
Vitals

Pushing as far as it could past the trees and foliage, the ambulance screeched to a halt a hundred yards away. Two paramedics streamed out, bearing an empty stretcher. Doug led the paramedics to the spot where Ethan lay on the ground covered in blood. Sean knelt by Ethan's side applying pressure to try and stop some of the bleeding.

The paramedics bent to attend to Ethan. "The femoral artery may have been severed," one said, applying a tourniquet above the wound on his right leg and releasing Sean's belt. "You probably saved his life with this."

"The left femur looks fractured, but I can't be sure," the other said, while continuing to examine him.

In tandem, they worked to stabilize Ethan's vital signs, then secured him to the stretcher.

The ambulance driver, another emergency medical technician, examined Ann's leg. He put a temporary bandage over the cut and told her she needed stitches. She resisted going to the hospital for herself but agreed to accompany Ethan.

"What happened here?" the medic asked.

Sean steadied his nerves, choosing his words carefully as he said, "They were attacked by some kind of huge reptile. Just get them to the hospital now."

The medic reared back, his eyes wide. "Do you know what kind of reptile?"

"No. It's nothing I've seen before. The creature had him in its mouth. It was that large—over twenty feet."

"My God! We'll take care of them." The driver gave the signal to carry Ethan away. Then he put his arm around Ann's waist to help her walk.

"Hang in there, pal," Sean said as the paramedics transported Ethan to the ambulance.

"Greg," he said, still glancing in the other direction. "Would you meet me back at my office, so we can go over what I saw?"

"Yes, sure," Greg agreed as they walked to their separate cars.

Ben, from Animal Control, had just arrived. Sean focused on the details of what happened, keeping his emotions under control. Worried about Ben's safety while removing the deer from the park, Sean worked out a plan designating armed officers as escorts to help him collect the dead animal so it could be taken to cold storage for evidence.

His head whirled as he sat in his police car and took what felt like his first real breath in hours. With his friend's blood splattered over Sean's hands and the front of his uniform, he stifled a sob. Clutching the wheel, he started the engine then concentrated on the drive to block out the still fresh grisly images.

"Are you okay?" the attendant at the front desk asked, standing up from her desk with an astonished look when Sean walked in with Greg. Other nearby officers looked up, their mouths agape.

"There was an incident in Quarry Head Park. I'll be back in a few minutes to brief all of you. Don't go anywhere," he announced to his staff.

He escorted Greg to his office. Then he excused himself to clean up, grabbing the spare uniform he kept in the utility room.

He hurried to the restroom and washed the blood from his hands letting anger replace tears.

He's going to be okay. Damn it! He has to be okay.

After splashing his face with cold water, he took in a deep breath. He put on the clean clothes and returned to his office to speak with Greg. "Can you help me understand what that creature was and how we can protect the community from it?"

"I'll try. If you don't mind me asking, is Ethan a close friend of yours?"

"We're very close. I've known him since high school, and we went to the police academy together."

"I'm sorry, but you have to believe he'll be okay."

"I know," he said, wishing it was true.

Greg exhaled. "Now if you tell me what you saw, I'll take some notes, compare with what I observed, and try to identify it."

"Do you need paper and a pen?"

"No, I got it." Greg held up his hand. "I always carry everything I need in my briefcase."

He released the latch, and his bag exploded open. Piles of notes and diagrams spilled out of the attaché, but he deftly patted the fallout of papers back into some semblance of a pile while grabbing a pen and sketch pad.

"Try to describe it to me," he said, turning to a blank page.

As best as he could, Sean told him about the creature he had seen an hour ago. Greg took notes and attempted to draw it.

The animal took a shape somewhat like a dinosaur combined with a snake with unusual features; an oval-shaped body, thick tapering tail, with a very extended neck and relatively small rounded head. Its protracted triangular jaws contained rows of long, pointy teeth. Greg made a note about its movement being snake-like. He filled out the sketch with Sean's description of four flippers, two on each side.

"Incredible," Greg said in hushed tones. "Matches what I saw. How long do you think it is?"

"At least twenty-five feet."

"And you're certain you identified some kind of fin or flipper on its sides?"

"Yes, why?"

Greg looked down for a moment, then moved to the edge of his seat and stared straight at Sean. "This is extraordinary. I wasn't sure if I'd actually seen the creature or was imagining it. This large animal indeed looks like it's related to a reptile such as a snake or lizard as I suspected, but it has fins or flippers, which are distinct features of reptiles from the water. Could be a genetic mutation or an undiscovered species. It could give us new information on evolutionary biology, but no matter what, it's a very unusual creature and it would be beneficial to study it."

He spoke with hushed tones, his eyes large.

"Are you suggesting we capture it *alive*?" Sean asked, incredulous.

"Yes, we need to learn all about it, whether it's terrestrial or semi-aquatic, its diet, where it lives, especially if it's a surviving reptile and not a mutation. It could give us tremendous insight into how this creature and others like it evolved."

"We can't just keep it in Quarry Head! What would we do with it?"

"We'd have to move it out of the park to a protected area in a wildlife sanctuary or preserve, but you can bet scientists will flock from all corners of the world to see this specimen."

Sean pushed himself from his chair and walked to the window, gazing out before taking a deep breath. Willing himself to react with reason and not vengeance, it took a minute before he could answer.

"Okay, I can understand why you would want to study it alive. I still have serious reservations about public safety, but I'm willing to at least try to capture it."

"Thank you, Sean." Relief washed over Greg's face.

"Don't get too excited. That doesn't mean it will happen. Quarry Head is owned by the state so Colonel Gunner, the head of the state police, will have to make the final decision. But what makes you believe we'll be able to contain it or even find it again?"

Greg's eyes lit up when he spoke. "Well, the weather is getting colder. If it's reptilian and therefore cold-blooded, it will need to regulate its body temperature to stop from freezing. It may be searching for an area to brumate, which is a less dormant state of hibernation. I think we can probably draw it into a large container by using heat lamps. I'll create a proposal detailing how to capture it, and I'll locate a facility willing to provide temporary refuge."

Sean remembered the word *brumate* from Greg's lecture earlier in the day. His expertise would be crucial. "When I told Ethan you were meeting us at the park he told me he knew your name from environmental impact reports. Have you ever worked with Colonel Gunner before?"

"No, but maybe if he sees a workable plan it will help."

"I'm certain it will. I'll send officers over to guard the perimeter of the park, but do you think that will provide enough protection?"

"My guess is after what happened this afternoon the creature will seek a hiding place. It retreated into the forest, so I think that's where it's been living. I believe it will stay in the woods, but I don't know for how much longer."

"How soon can you write up the plan and send it to me?"

"I'll work on it tonight and send something first thing tomorrow," Greg said as he jammed his stubborn briefcase shut.

"Wait," Sean said, "I'm going to make a copy of the sketch." He scanned the diagram into his computer. He returned Greg's rudimentary drawing to him. "We'll talk later." They shook hands goodbye.

With Greg gone, Sean allowed himself to collapse into his chair. He could not put off calling Frank any longer. After dialing the colonel's private number and going straight to voicemail, Sean left a detailed message.

Detective Lewis was already peering through the gap in his door. "Chief, are you all right? Everyone wants to hear what happened. Marcy's saying we're getting calls from the local newspapers asking about officers being taken to the hospital. What's going on?"

"Tell everyone to go to the conference room. I have one more thing to do, and then I'll be there."

When Ryan left, Sean made the call to Norwalk Hospital.

Ethan was alive but in critical condition. The doctors were still performing urgent surgery, and the nurse told Sean he would have to call later for more details. Ann, having received stitches, was going to be discharged shortly. Taking a deep breath, he hung up.

A heavy burden on his shoulders, Sean walked to the conference room where eighteen of his forty-four sworn officers waited to hear from him. The other members of the department were either on patrol or currently off duty. He gazed out at the solemn faces staring back at him and began.

"Sorry to keep you all waiting. A few hours ago, we discovered a very large and dangerous unknown reptile in Quarry Head Park. I want to reassure you that we currently have the situation under control. Also, I wanted you to be ready to deal with the public when they have questions."

Most of the officers exchanged startled glances with one another.

"We're unable to definitively identify it at this time." Sean paused for a moment then continued, "Two officers have already been injured and were both taken to Norwalk Hospital. Detective Ethan Roberts from the Connecticut State Police has sustained critical wounds and is in surgery. We're waiting for an update. As for us, Ann has a cut on her leg that required stitches, but she's being released soon."

Agitated, Officer Nick Santos interjected, "Officers have been hurt, and we don't even know what we're dealing with? What's it look like?"

Sean thought for a moment. What should he say? "It looked like some sort of dinosaur with huge jaws and a very long neck. It moved with its body along the ground in a snake-like motion, but it could stand like a sea lion on flippers that were as big as me. Looked prehistoric and unlike anything I've ever seen except in movies."

Exclamations broke out all over as officer after officer expressed shock. Some scoffed at the preposterous suggestion.

"No way!"

"How big are you talking about?" Officer Ron Lamarre asked.

"Twenty-five feet long and about ten feet wide," Sean said.

Horrified gasps greeted his description. Further outbursts overlapped each other, making it impossible for any officer to be heard in isolation.

Finally, the room quieted when Officer Dana Langley spoke. "Chief, I don't mean to question you, but this is hard to believe."

"Yeah!" was the cry from someone in the back of the room.

"...and we must be very careful."

"Yes, I know," Sean said, straightening. "And you're worried that this sounds…crazy?"

"Exactly," Officer Langley said. "We believe you and all that, but…"

"But you're questioning it?" Sean understood their disbelief, but their doubt infuriated him when he considered the gravity of Ethan's condition and Ann's injury.

Dana fidgeted, massaging her arm. "No sir. Not that it happened. It's just hard to believe how something like a…a dinosaur could be in the park."

Sean took a deep breath to steady himself. "I don't know either. But I watched it almost kill Detective Roberts, and I'll never forget what it looks like."

More utterances and exclamations abounded from the assembly.

"I'm sorry, Chief," said Dana. "You understand, I just wanted to check."

He put his hand on the desk and leaned forward. "I know that what I just described to you does not seem possible. But it's out there, and it's dangerous." He scanned the room. Seeing no further response, he moved on. "Okay. Now as to our duties. For now, we're monitoring the park. For the safety of our citizens, we need to get the creature out as soon as possible, so we're working with a reptile specialist, Dr. Greg Mitchell. He thinks we can capture it and move it to a facility where it can be studied." He paused for a moment, then continued, "As you all know, Quarry Head is a state-owned park, which means we'll be working with Colonel Gunner."

Grumbling broke out even before he finished Frank's name. "Yeah, yeah, I know," Sean said, holding up his hand.

Suddenly, a heavy silence fell on the room. Many officers grimaced, their gazes darting past Sean toward the entrance doors. After a moment of confusion, he turned around.

A short, yet burly man in state uniform, with the wide-brimmed police hat symbolizing his executive status, Colonel Gunner stood in front of an assembly that had quieted in mere seconds. He removed his hat upon entry, revealing white hair trimmed in a crew cut. He hovered there, glaring at Sean.

"Colonel Gunner," he said, wondering if he overheard the response when his name was mentioned a few seconds ago. For his own sake, he hoped not.

"Chief Dermott," Frank said in a strained voice, with a nod.

Sean tipped his head back.

With his hat in one hand, Frank made a gruff gesture with the other. "Carry on," he said to Sean.

Attempting to keep his expression neutral, Sean turned back to his assembled officers. "Any questions?"

"How are we going to find this creature?" Nick asked, as Frank looked at Sean.

"Dr. Mitchell's going to work on that. Something about it needing heat because it's a reptile. We'll have to wait 'til tomorrow to see what he comes up with."

"How do you know it won't get into town and hurt someone?" Ron asked.

"Again, I'm relying on Dr. Mitchell's expertise. He says it's looking for a place to hibernate and shouldn't be straying too far from where we encountered it. We'll have officers on patrol in the park around the clock until it's captured just to be safe."

He paused, checking the reactions of everyone present. No one seemed about to ask further questions, which meant he'd achieved his objective of unifying the force on this sensitive matter. "The new schedule will be posted later. Thanks, everyone." He turned to Frank and asked him, "Do you have anything to add?"

"Not yet," said Frank, looking only at Sean. "If you're done, we need to talk. Your office, now!"

Gulping, Sean turned to exit the room, hurrying to catch up to the colonel.

The silence between them unnerved Sean on the way down the hall.

As he sat, Frank dropped onto the guest chair and placed his hat on the edge of the desk. His mouth clenched, the corners turned downward in a severe frown. He rested his elbow on the wooden armrest, pointing his finger up. His tone was like that of a hot coal; steady, but close to erupting in flames at any time.

This is not going to be good. He obviously rushed over the moment he got my message.

"What the hell is going on, Sean?"

Sean looked at Frank's incredulous expression. "There's a creature—"

"Yes. I heard your message. Did you do any back-up planning before you sent in this team to confront that dangerous animal in the park? How could you be so reckless?"

"Frank—"

"It sounds like you went in completely unprepared."

Now his tone sounded threatening. Frank glowered at Sean,

tapping his finger on his knee.

"I didn't *know* there was some enormous reptile on the loose. How could anyone?"

"That's not quite true, is it? Ethan informed me that a reptile expert told you he thought something tried to swallow the dead animal that was filmed. Was there anything else the expert said that you should have conveyed to my detective? You can't afford to make a rookie mistake like leaving out details when you're in charge."

Sean sat frozen. *Did I leave something out?*

"Nothing to say?" Frank retorted before Sean could reply. "Let me tell you about Detective Robert's condition."

Sean stiffened. "You were at the hospital?"

"No. I came straight here, but I got a call from his doctor just before I walked into this station. Want to know what he said?"

It was an edict, not an invitation. Sean knew what to say. "Yes."

Frank pulled out his police notebook. In a clipped tone, he read from it. "Six bones in his right foot were broken. Three bones in the left foot. Eight toes fractured. His left foot will require screws. Both ankles are severely damaged."

Sean felt the blood rush from his head.

Frank's brows furrowed. "Want to hear more?" Again, another throw of the gauntlet.

"Yes."

"His left leg is broken. Many puncture wounds and cuts. He needed over one hundred and fifty stitches. Right now, they're watching for signs of infection. They did a CT scan to confirm that all internal bleeding has stopped."

"Is he going to be okay?"

"Yes, he'll live, but we don't know if he'll walk again."

"Jesus," Sean said, shaking his head.

"Is that *all* you have to say for yourself?"

Sean did not have the will to argue. "I don't think we should be apportioning blame at this stage. Why don't we discuss how we can ensure the safety of the public?"

Frank slammed his pad down onto Sean's desk and glared at him. Sean waited for him to reply, his jaw tight. After a few tense seconds Frank sighed and said, "Yes, that's a good idea."

He was careful not to breathe out so deeply Frank would hear it. *Keep your cool.*

Frank's shoulders slumped as he sat back, shaking his head. "Crap," he said. "So it's real?"

"I saw it myself. It was terrifying."

"This sounds like one of these goddamn monsters shows I used to see as a kid," Frank grumbled. He straightened, the fire back in his glare. "All right, Sean, but from now on, this is my case. You report to me on this. Understood?"

"Understood."

"All right. I heard in there that you got officers assigned on a twenty-four-hour shift?"

"Yes."

Frank scratched the back of his neck. "Since Wilton Police has local jurisdiction, we accept your, uh, offer to supply resources. I'll send just a few additional officers from my department."

Yeah, right, thought Sean. He knew Frank would have arrived at the exact same decision, but he wisely let it go. "We're always ready to work together."

Frank raised an eyebrow, as if he knew Sean was putting on a façade. But if his professional demeanor unnerved him, he didn't let it show. "And what did you say back there about a Dr. Mitchell?"

"Dr. Greg Mitchell, a specialist on reptiles with the University of Connecticut. He will be here tomorrow to provide the information we need in order to capture the creature. Can you come back to the station to meet with him?"

"Given that you already have a good rapport with this reptile expert, it would be, uh, advisable for you to continue working with him, but I'd like to be here. Got that?"

"Yes." Now Sean was breathing easier. Frank was slowly letting out the leash inch by inch.

"What time tomorrow? I still have questions, and I'll need to clear my schedule."

"One p.m."

"Make it two p.m.," Frank snapped. "I already have a conference call scheduled for one. I'll take it on the way here."

"I'll call Greg and arrange it."

"Now, pictures, photos? Anything that shows what it looks like?"

He picked up a copy of the sketch Greg made earlier that was in a new file on his desk and handed it to Frank.

"Sweet mother of Jesus," Frank exclaimed. "We'll have to call in the Army to have it killed!"

Dread pooled in Sean's stomach. He was fighting his own instinct as well as Frank's. "Dr. Mitchell thinks we should preserve it at all costs."

"Why?" Frank's face exhibited total disbelief.

"Apparently it could be important for the scientific community. Dr. Mitchell said it's so unusual it would be beneficial to learn about its behaviors."

"Can't we study it dead?" Again, that incredulous voice. "I mean, I used to dissect frogs in science class way back in grade school. Why can't we simply dissect it?"

"He said scientists can gather more information on something that is alive. They can learn about its diet and how it lives. This is the only one of its kind so if we kill it we're limiting what we could learn."

"I'll speak to him about it myself tomorrow," Frank said, shaking his head. "Boy, these scientists are dreamers. They don't know what it's like to stand next to a crowd that's scared to death. He better know what he's talking about."

"Yeah," Sean said listlessly, having a feeling Frank might be right.

The colonel stood then and left without saying another word.

Sean waited for the footsteps to fade, then he looked at the clock. It was almost 7:00 p.m., and he wanted to get to the hospital.

He created a schedule for round the clock surveillance of Quarry Head Park, then checked his messages. Chief Miller from the Pound Ridge Police Department confirmed Marcus Branca was not in the area on October 17th. It didn't surprise Sean, who had arrived at his own conclusion that a connection with the Jason Kenner case was a stretch.

Before he could leave, the administrator at the front desk paged about a reporter that just called in asking to speak with him.

"Put them through." He would have to face questions from the press.

He didn't know how much they already knew, but they often inquired about things before he could put out a press release or announce it on the town's police website. While the media could be helpful in alerting the public, it bothered him when they sensationalized a story for ratings.

"Good evening, Chief Dermott, I'm Emma Barnes with the *Wilton Daily News*. Can you tell me why Quarry Head Park is currently closed?"

"We recently discovered a large reptile living in the park and have closed it to the public for safety reasons."

"What kind of reptile?"

"I can't tell you at this stage as we haven't yet confirmed exactly what it is. Officers are stationed in and around the park as a security precaution. As soon as I have more information, I'll let you know."

"Is it something like a boa constrictor or a python? One that could have escaped from an owner?"

"Not likely."

"Did you see it? Can you describe it to me?"

"We're gathering more information before we put out a statement."

"Do you think someone released it intentionally?" Emma said, her voice becoming more insistent.

"I don't think so, but we will be looking into every angle."

"The people deserve to know what's going on. Can you tell me if anyone was hurt?"

"An officer and a detective were hurt, but I can't give any more details on their condition at this time," Sean said, choosing not to hide the attack.

From his experience, he knew the truth would inevitably get out, and the public backlash for choosing not to reveal it would be a blemish on the department, fair or not. He could hear the reporter scribbling on her pad.

"What sort of injuries?" she pressed.

It irked him that she spoke so calmly when he told her officers were injured, even though he'd acted the same way while working on many a case. "I can't give out any information until their families have been fully informed. I'm sure you can respect that."

"Can you at least identify the officers for me?"

"I'm not ready to release names at this time. Not until I'm certain both families have been contacted."

"Will they recover?"

He put his hand over the receiver for a moment and then attempted to keep his voice steady. The reporter didn't ask if she could tape the conversation, but just in case he didn't want her to have a recording of him sounding emotionally vulnerable. "As I said a moment ago, I will not be releasing any medical information at this time."

He could hear her suck in her breath.

"I hope it's not too serious, and that they'll be all right."

"Thank you."

"Can you at least tell our readers what you're planning to do about this dangerous creature?"

"I didn't say it was innately dangerous, but it does present a threat. We are working on a plan to remove it from the park," Sean asserted. He had to keep control over the conversation and avoid being misquoted in the press.

"Fine," she groused. "Is there a warning you'd like to give our readers?"

"Don't go into Quarry Head Park."

"Anything more?"

"No. I have work I have to get on with. I have your number."

"Would it be all right if I follow up with you tomorrow, then?"

He agreed, and she thanked him before ending the call.

Sean dreaded seeing the headlines on the local news websites tonight. To that effect, he alerted the central police media department to keep tabs on what was being reported.

The folder labeled "Quarry Head Reptile" needed to be locked in his desk drawer. He filed it away and glanced at the memo he'd written to himself as a reminder to pick up Scout, the dog he found in the park. Scout was at the vet, but it was most likely closed by now, plus he could not wait any longer to go to the hospital to see Ethan.

As Sean climbed into his civilian Jeep, his phone rang. He glanced at the caller ID. To his surprise the display read: *Vanessa.*

Nine

Sunroom

"Hello, Vanessa? Sean here."

"Sean," came Vanessa's breathless voice. "I heard it on the local news!"

He knew exactly what she heard. "Yeah?"

"There's some dangerous creature in the park. Are you all right?"

"Yes. I'm fine."

"Can I see you right now? I'm sorry to impose, but…"

Distress tinged her voice. "I'm sorry, but I don't have time to see you now. I just left the station."

There was silence on the other end.

"Sorry," he mumbled. Yet, his longing to see her pricked at him, and he knew he couldn't shut her out. He sighed then said, "Actually, I'm on my way to visit Ethan at Norwalk Hospital."

"Oh, no. The news was saying an officer was in critical condition. Is that him?"

Sean grimaced. "Yes, but it's not as bad as they say." He refused to give into any dire predictions.

"Thank goodness. I hope you don't mind me asking, but could I meet you at the hospital? I've been there for my dad. There's a solarium on the first floor of the main building, and it's very nice."

"Sure," he said, strangely elated at the idea that he'd soon see her again, despite the circumstances.

"Thank you!" The relief in her voice was unmistakable.

"I'll go see Ethan first then I'll see you there in an hour?"

"Yes, I'll be there."

He hung up. As he drove to the hospital, he hesitated to listen to the local stations, but forced himself to stay informed. The bad news greeted him the moment he clicked the radio on. "…Connecticut State Police have closed Quarry Head Park in Wilton…"

"Chief of Police, Sean Dermott, has been quoted saying that a monstrous-sized creature is roaming the park, and we've received confirmation from Homeland Security that it has not been asked to intervene at this time…"

He swore at the babbling voices.

"Meanwhile, Colonel Frank Gunner, head of the Connecticut State Police Force, has called for calm. The colonel has met with the chief of the Wilton Police Department and has assured him that officers from the state department will be dispatched to assist in protecting this town."

He shook his head. Frank knew exactly what to say to handle the media and look like a hero.

Sean switched off the radio as he parked the car at the hospital. After checking in at the front desk, he took the elevator to Ethan's floor.

"He'll be sedated until tomorrow, but you can go sit with him for a few minutes," the nurse said.

Sean walked into the quiet, white room.

Ethan lay flat on his back in a hospital gown under the pristine, freshly laundered sheets. The IV bag hung on its metal stand near the wall pumped antibiotics and pain medication into a peripheral vein along his left arm. The stark purplish color of hours-old stitches on the right side of his face, looked darker against his pale skin. The sheet had been folded back from his left leg, which was in a cast and elevated on top of a pillow. Draped over his right leg, the covers looked raised. Thick bandages from his thigh to his toes made them bulge.

Sean took a chair from the corner and sat next to his friend. He felt as if the breath had been knocked out of him. "Just hang in there. You're going to be okay," he said in a soft voice. *Fucking hell. I should've gotten to you sooner.*

Ethan did not move. A nurse came. She looked at the monitors. Then she turned the plastic IV bag toward her. "It would be best to let him sleep," she said, her voice soft.

Sean nodded.

After sitting for a few minutes more he whispered to his friend, "I'm going to leave you to rest. I know you're going to get better. I'll be back again tomorrow."

Wistful, he took the elevator down to the first floor and followed the signs to the solarium. He walked through the hall in a fog of sadness, his shoulder slumping.

"Sean?" came the gentle female voice, full of warmth and instantly recognizable.

He raised his head. *Vanessa.*

A wave of calm enveloped him as he looked at her. She wore a white angora sweater and a pair of light-blue, faded jeans. In comparison, he still had on his uniform but wished he'd changed into civilian clothes. Anything to give him more distance from this tragic day.

Trying to shake the haze that still enveloped him, Sean joined her.

"You okay?" she asked, voice heavy with concern.

He rubbed his neck. "Yeah, yeah."

"How is Ethan?" she asked. Her voice sounded kind.

"Resting. The nurse said it was best if he slept through the night."

The small, empty sunroom was cheerful and cozy. A dozen large, potted plants accentuated a rock wall fountain in the center with benches carefully placed around the room to give visitors as much privacy as possible.

They entered the area together, and he gestured for her to take a seat, before joining her. "I can see why you liked coming here, especially if you had to be in a hospital. It's very calming."

"Yes, it's especially nice during the day when the natural light comes in. I apologize for insisting that we talk. It's not like me to be so pushy, but I didn't know who else I could speak with. Can you tell me what's going on? I can't bear thinking that Jason could have been killed by that horrible creature."

The sound of Jason's name snapped Sean back to reality. He had been so caught up in his own grief over Ethan being injured that it was only now, as he took a close enough look at her, that he realized she was pale, and her eyes were red and puffy from crying. And now she wanted answers to what might have happened to her friend.

He filled her in on what took place in the park a few hours ago although he did not give her exact details about the reptile or Ethan and Ann's injuries. Vanessa's face showed her horror at what he told her, but her most terrified expression was reserved for the revelation that he himself came face to face with the giant reptile and could have been injured too.

"Do you think Jason was killed by this animal?" she asked.

"Right now, we have no evidence to suggest that. In fact, we've found out some things about him that leads us to believe he may have intentionally left town."

"What types of things?"

"First, do you know if he had any financial problems?"

"He was always a bit odd with money. But well, maybe he…"

"What is it?"

"Sometimes he would spend money on something and then sell

it very quickly before he could enjoy it. Like when he moved to Wilton he bought a very nice pair of skis but sold them right before ski season started. And a few times he said he forgot his wallet when we went out to dinner. I didn't mind paying, of course. He could also be very generous. He bought me a beautiful handbag for Christmas."

The trail was getting warmer. "Did he ever ask to borrow money?"

"Yes, from the moment we bumped into each other in town. He borrowed one hundred and fifty dollars for the used couch in the second bedroom. As time went on, he didn't pay me back…but he kept apologizing about not having the money, so I told him not to worry about it."

"Anything else?"

"Yes. He felt so guilty because my shop…"

Vanessa brought her hand up to her mouth. He wondered what was wrong.

Sean leaned in.

After avoiding his gaze for a few more seconds, she shrugged. "Oh, what the heck. I can tell you, but I don't want people in the area to know. It's about my store. Jason knew it wasn't doing well. I even spoke to him about the possibility that I might have to sell it. I was surprised when he still asked me for a few dollars here and there, but as I said, it really wasn't a problem."

"I'm sorry to hear about your store."

"Thank you. But why are you asking me all these questions about Jason and money? What's this all about?"

"We've found out he may have had financial difficulties. Sometimes people leave their home to get a fresh start."

Her eyebrows ticked upward. "But Jason wouldn't do that! Not without telling his mother or his father. Not without telling me. He had to know we'd understand."

Sean just nodded, eager to say more but held back.

"What about the car? Do we know if he took it?"

"I'm not able to give you those details now, but I *can* tell you he no longer owns that car, and where it is currently does not help us locate him."

"Sorry if I'm putting you on the spot."

"No. That's all right. Jason's your friend, and you're just trying to figure out what happened to him."

"There's something that's still troubling me. Maybe you can help me understand it."

"I'll try."

"Remember when you called me after you searched the park? When you went in with the police dog?"

"Yes."

"You said you could confirm Jason had been in the park, but you said his trail stopped in the middle of the path. How could that be?"

"It puzzled me too, but then I gave it some more thought and came up with a few possible reasons. He could have decided to just turn around and go back the way he entered. Or the scent could have just deteriorated at that point."

"I guess that makes sense." Then she shuddered. "I wonder if that noise I heard when I went jogging could've been the creature?"

The thought horrified Sean, imagining her in danger. "We can't know for sure, but I'm glad you're safe. Do you have anything else you wanted to ask me?" He didn't want the conversation to end.

"No, but I'll try to avoid the news," she said with a smile.

"Good idea."

Her grin slowly faded. "You're not going back in there again, are you?"

"I most likely will have to, but don't worry."

"Well, I can't promise not to worry, but I don't imagine you'll change your mind. You're very brave. I'm terrified of that park now."

"Try not to think about it. When it's over and done, I'll take you back there."

He pictured himself walking into the park with his arm around Vanessa. The thought caused his heart to beat a fraction more rapidly.

"I'd like that."

He grinned. *Think of something to say.*

She sighed. "I still have some paperwork I have to finish at home. Are you going to stay?"

"No. I'm going to come back tomorrow. Hopefully he'll be awake by then."

"Would you give him a message from me, that I hope he gets better soon?"

"Of course." The thought of telling Ethan that she met him at the hospital made him laugh inside. Ethan would tease him about having the hots for her or feign jealousy.

"Where are you parked?" Sean asked.

"Right out front."

"Me too. Come, I'll walk you to your car."

Vanessa put her jacket on. "Didn't you bring a coat? It's pretty cold out."

"No, I don't need it," he said.

He looked down at his fresh uniform, recalling the one that had been saturated in Ethan's blood this afternoon, the one he had chucked into the large bin at the back of the police station. No dry-cleaning in the world, or any deep cleanse of Sean's guilt-ridden memories, could rid his discarded clothes of those stains.

Ten
Heat

Dr. Greg Mitchell dashed about the conference room in the Wilton Police Department checking out the audiovisual equipment. Although he arrived an hour early with his two colleagues, Dr. Michael Hayes and Dr. Leanne Rivera, he worried he was nowhere near ready.

In his many years attending international conferences and delivering keynote speeches, he knew there was always a list of unanticipated items that would confront him moments before a presentation. This morning his head ached from the lack of sleep and the pressure of having to be ready to present something so important overnight.

He downloaded everything onto his computer. The police station's briefing room was not modern like the conference rooms he was used to at five-star hotels, but he put all his effort into improvising. With relief he saw he had access to a large screen on which to project his proposal.

He wiped the sweat from his forehead with a napkin he had in his jacket pocket.

"Greg, it's okay," Lee said, "we're not before the Society."

She was referring to the American Society of Ichthyologists and Herpetologists, one of the national bodies of professionals specializing in reptiles. A short, stout, woman loaded with energy, she kept a cheery smile on her face whenever she mingled with her colleagues.

"I know, but this is the find of a lifetime! We've got to convince the state police to let us go in." He grinned at the widely-respected researcher, whom he first met a few years ago after the Gulf of Mexico oil spill.

Back then, he led a team rescuing sea turtle hatchlings on the affected western coast of Florida. While spearheading the initiative on the beaches and the wetlands, he met up with Lee, who was researching the effects of the spill on coastal wildlife. The project itself was arduous and the hours long, but after Greg recovered from his exhaustion back home, he valued the experience as one of the most profound of his working life. The two had continued to keep in touch when she consulted with him on a study she conducted at the Hartford Connecticut Research Center.

He pulled down the screen and turned on his laptop. He wanted to see what the picture would look like, but the image did not appear. *Damn it. Now what?* Frowning, he hit the keys and jiggled the mouse.

"Let me help you with that," Mike said. "Did you activate the external display?"

He sighed. "Nope—I forgot."

"You look nervous. Take some deep breaths."

He glanced up at his friend. "I will. Thanks."

A tall scientist, Mike's striking full head of silver, gray hair lent him a quiet dignity. Kind and soft- spoken, he remained one of Greg's oldest friends. They first met during a college internship at the Beardsley Zoo almost forty years ago, bonding over the difficult task of locating and safely returning the zoo's escaped king cobra. Together they organized a petition to the governors of New Mexico and Texas to ban inhumane "rattlesnake roundups," making the two of them academic and philosophical allies.

Sean poked his head through the door. "How's it going?"

"I think I'm just about ready," Greg said. "Thanks to Lee and Mike here."

Sean walked in, and Greg introduced his colleagues.

Sean shook their hands. "Glad you both could make it."

He gave off a heavy sigh. "We worked through the night on it."

"Oh, man," Sean said with a sympathetic tone. "Just know that I appreciate the hours."

Mike chuckled. "Let's just say I'm looking forward to a rest later."

"We have half an hour left. Do you need to do anything more?"

Greg hesitated, but admitted, "I think we're ready to go."

"Good. Do you mind if you practice with me? Quickly?"

Greg perked up. "You just made my day. I do need to go over this."

Relieved he had the opportunity to spot any mistakes now rather than in the glare of a full briefing led by the upper ranks of police in his state, he started the presentation.

The small group stepped back as a viewing a vibrant, realistic image of the giant reptile.

"Wow. You made an even more accurate drawing of it," Sean said.

Pleased Greg smiled. "Thanks. I knew it reminded me of a

Plesiosaur, like a Thalassomedon or Elasmosaurus."

"What did you say? Is that like a dinosaur?"

"It's from the same era. Dinosaurs and Plesiosaurs both thrived during the Jurassic Period from around two hundred and one to one hundred and forty-five million years ago. Plesiosaurs are marine reptiles. Dinosaurs lived on land. There's only one known exception, the Spinosaurus, which is a dinosaur, but it spent most of its time in water."

"This creature's really from that far back, millions of years ago?"

"I'm just saying there's a remarkable resemblance," Greg said. Used to pacing in front of an audience, he cast a dark shadow on the screen and walked up to point out key features of the creature. "You see the proportions of its neck and head are very similar to an Elasmosaurus, a genus of Plesiosaur." He spoke with mounting excitement. "And those flippers, right there and near the tail."

"Man! It's hard to believe it's real," Sean said.

"It's amazing. I never thought I'd ever be a witness to anything like this," Mike said, rubbing his eyes.

"How can it be alive now?"

"No idea," Greg said, still spellbound by the thought. "Either someone's invented a way to bring back prehistoric DNA and wants to spring this on the world through a dramatic debut, or it could be some kind of mutation."

The four of them stood, staring at the image that would eventually astound the whole world.

Lee pressed her colleague. "Greg, you still have to practice before the state police get here."

"She's right," Mike agreed.

Just then, administrator Charter came in. "Sean, Colonel Gunner is here with three of his men."

"They're early," Greg stammered.

Lee bit her lip.

"Tell him I'll be right there." Sean thanked Marcy for tipping him off, then excused himself from the group.

Greg heard some scurrying in the hall. A few minutes later, three of Sean's officers walked in, followed by three of Frank's, with Sean bringing up the rear. Amidst the procession, Officer Ann McKay entered, her limp nearly completely concealed by her determined stride.

Frank introduced himself and then gestured toward his entourage. "I've brought Lieutenant Colonel Eric Hoskins, Brenda Carswell, Assistant Director of Public Relations, and Jeff Ashworth,

Director of Public Safety." Hands on his hips, he glared at the others.

Everyone shifted glances without speaking as they took their seats. After all the introductions were complete, they turned to Sean.

He opened the meeting by introducing the three herpetologists once more. Greg started to stand when Public Relations Officer Carswell spoke. "Let me just start out by saying I'm pleased we have three distinguished scientists volunteering their valuable time today. Now, first you have to tell me—is this thing for real?"

"It's only circumstantial evidence at this point…" Greg began.

"I saw it myself," Sean said, looking directly at Officer Carswell.

"So did I," Ann said in a detached voice.

"I spoke to Detective Roberts this morning," Frank admitted. "He confirms this too."

"My phone's been ringing off the hook," Brenda said. "When I get back, they will have lots of questions waiting for me, so anything you can tell me will be much appreciated."

"Let me start with the first detailed diagram I have of the creature," Greg said, as one of Sean's officers dimmed the lights.

There were gasps and grunts all around as the professionally rendered drawing of the reptile appeared on screen. Greg darted a curious glance at Ann. Her mouth hung open. It must have shocked her to see the creature which had attacked her so accurately rendered on screen.

"So, what *is* it?" Frank asked, gesturing at the image.

He gulped. "This is a drawing of the reptile in the park. My colleagues and I have, for now, determined that the animal is of the class *Reptilia*, possibly from the order *Squamata*, which includes lizards and snakes."

The group sat in silence. He spoke for nearly fifteen minutes about the reptile's possible origin, gaining confidence as he went.

Frank then asked Greg to go over the details of the proposed capture.

He glanced at Lee and Mike, who both looked on. "Well, because it's a reptile, even if it's a large one, it will need to find heat to regulate its body temperature. Based on that requirement, we've come up with a way to contain it."

Frank said, "I know that. I took high school biology. But you haven't answered my question, *how do you plan to find it?*" He moved his arms up and down, showing his exasperation.

Lee moved in and rescued Greg. "Yes, Colonel. I know exactly what you're asking. The weather has been getting colder so this time of year works for us. We don't actually need to find it. Instead, it will come to us. Snakes, lizards, crocodiles—they all look for warmth in late fall or early winter. We can put a large metal cage on a trailer, warm it with heat lamps, make it noticeable with lights, and the creature will be drawn to it. Since it's obviously active now, we have a very good chance of being able to entice the animal into the container. Once it's locked in, it can be safely removed from the park."

Greg waited for Frank's reaction. However, the others in the room, including Brenda and Jeff, murmured in agreement, reassuring him.

Thankful for Lee's timely intervention, Greg reached for the topographic map of Quarry Head Park and spread it over the table. He pointed to a small clearing on the paper, prompting all the attendees to stand up and take a closer look. "We can do minimal clearing to get a trailer through to this point. It's near the last place where we saw the reptile. The area's openness to sunlight is likely attracting it there. In addition, we should set up a small mobile office at the main entrance of the park, where we can remotely control the equipment and film the entire operation. I don't know if the state police own or have access to a mobile office, but I've rented them for field studies on very tight budgets."

"Right," Sean said, jumping in. "Since it's remotely controlled, that means fewer officers are needed in the field."

"That's fine for during the capture. But what about the danger involved in setting up the cage and equipment."

Murmurs reverberated around the room.

"Even if I decided to approve this wild idea, and I haven't, where do you propose we move this thing to?" Frank asked, his expression impassive.

"To the Kent Wildlife Sanctuary," said Greg, once more finding his confidence. "It's about forty-five minutes north of here. The facility has an impeccable reputation, and the director promised me the reptile would be kept in an area with adequate land and a natural pond. This also means the creature stays in Connecticut."

Frank thrummed his fingers on his thigh frowning. "Okay, I acknowledge you have a workable plan. But I'm mostly concerned about public safety. It seems to me the safest outcome is just to kill it."

"I agree with Frank," Lieutenant Colonel Hoskins said. "There are just too many unknowns. It could get into town and confront our citizens."

Greg, succumbing to stress, blurted out, "Killing it is not an option! There's too much at stake here, too much that could be lost for science. This reptile is one of a kind. There's so much we could learn from observing it."

"Then dissect it," Frank said.

"You can't compare studying a living sample to dissecting a corpse." Greg's voice was an octave short of a shout.

Mike intervened. "It's like going to see taxidermy instead of going on a safari."

"I saw it," Sean almost whispered. Everyone in the room turned in his direction. "It was only feet away."

"It was the scariest, but also the most fascinating experience of my life. Just seeing it stand there, well…" Ann shook her head.

The colleagues whispered to one another.

"Greg, why don't you explain to us how we will benefit from studying it alive," Sean said.

"Certainly. There are things we can learn from a living organism we simply can't learn when they're dead. For example, how animals react to stimuli, and why. When we observe how a creature behaves, we not only gain knowledge about that particular species, but we can also gather information that benefits people." He held out his arms. "Take for example the studies done on how bats and dolphins use echolocation. These studies have given us valuable information to help the blind."

"True," Lieutenant Colonel Hoskins agreed.

"In addition, there may be something about this animal's physiology that could be beneficial to us. There are constantly new discoveries being made in uses for snake venom for example," Mike added.

Passion filled her voice as Lee said, "This will put Wilton on the map." She pointed to Brenda. "As you've said, your phone has been ringing off the hook. I bet some people want you to save the animal, don't they?"

Brenda sighed. "A lot of people are scared and calling for us to kill it immediately, but a surprisingly large number want a humane solution."

"Look," said Mike, showing a little bit of frustration in his voice, "There is no other animal like this on earth. Just for that reason alone, isn't it our duty to try to save it? If you accept this plan, the reptile can be captured and taken to a secure facility where they will provide a large outdoor habitat surrounded by an electric fence. The public will be protected."

Jeff held up his hand. "My department will approve a plan to capture the reptile if you can assure me it will not escape into the town.

How can you give me that assurance?"

"I can tell you this," Frank answered. "If you're giving the go ahead, I'll locate the equipment and organize the capture. If things go wrong or anyone is in danger my back-up plan will be to kill it before it causes any harm."

"I'd have to go along with that," Jeff said to Frank. Then he turned to Greg and asked for a copy of the proposal.

"I have it right here," Greg said and handed out hard copies to the ranking members of the group.

Eric, Brenda, and Jeff stood, traces of smiles on their faces.

"That's it for now. Thank you all for coming," Frank said.

Greg and everyone else in the room, respectfully waited thirty seconds after Frank and his colleagues' departure, and then they whooped with exultation.

Right now, it was a victory for science.

Eleven
Weekend

Vanessa usually took the day off on Sunday, but she couldn't resist the urge to do a little business for her beleaguered store. She parked at Otis Field and walked across the grounds to the senior living facility, *The Greens,* where she supplied cards and gifts to the small convenience shop in the lobby.

After taking inventory, she took a leisurely walk back through the park, glancing at its soccer and baseball fields as well as its dog-friendly area.

One of her fondest memories as a child was when her mother took her and her sister to the park with their dog, Pebbles, an adorable cocker spaniel with patches of ivory white and chocolate brown.

Vanessa thought about her time with Sean at the Norwalk Hospital a few days ago. The encounter intrigued her despite the frightening revelations that prompted her to reach out to him.

Now she hoped he would call her, but she pushed away the idea when she realized that she should be anticipating news on Jason, not merely hearing Sean's husky voice.

For the afternoon, she planned to meet a friend at a local craft fair. She enjoyed browsing through the handcrafted items, touching them one at a time so she could appreciate the physical connections to the town's local artistry.

Plus, they inspired new gift ideas for her store.

This show included one of her favorite venders, a glass artist. She brushed aside a fresh stab of worry over adding to the debt on her line of credit, reasoning the designer bowls and vases were some of her best-selling items.

With her car in sight, she noticed an attractive man about her age strolling into the park. She stared for a moment trying to remember if she knew him.

He was walking his dog, a golden colored mixed breed with lots of energy. The man wore jeans and a comfortable-looking black cotton sweatshirt that showed off his broad shoulders. She smiled.

Then, to her discomfort, though it set her heart racing in

anticipation, he started walking toward her. He flashed an easy smile that added light to his eyes.

That looks like Sean.

"Hello Vanessa. I'm glad to see you again."

"Chief? I mean Sean? I didn't expect to see you here."

Caught off guard, she hadn't recognized him without his uniform. He looked rugged and handsome and definitely not as serious as the other times they'd met.

Naturally. "I didn't know you had a dog."

"I didn't. I found him the day we searched Quarry Head Park. So far no one's claimed him, so I took him home with me."

"Aww, he's so cute," she said as she bent to pet him. "What's his name?"

"Scout. He's cute now, but I didn't find him that way," Sean said with a chuckle.

"Poor thing. He looks like a golden retriever."

"The vet told me he's a golden retriever and border collie mix. Those breeds are supposed to be smart, and they need lots of exercise. He's friendly, and he loves to play, so here we are."

Scout tugged on the leash. Vanessa didn't want to bother them, but she hadn't spoken to Sean in days.

"I was going to call. There's news about catching the reptile in Quarry Head Park all the time now," she said.

"I thought you were going to stop watching the news?" he said with a grin.

"That's right, I did say that." She returned the smirk.

"Would you like to walk with us?"

"Sure."

After they found a good spot for Scout to run freely, Sean unclipped the leash. Scout pranced in front of Sean waiting for him to let loose the tennis ball he'd been carrying.

"Go, get it!" He threw the ball near a cluster of trees. Scout ran after it, tail wagging. "Ethan's doing better. I told him I saw you that night and you wished him a speedy recovery. Believe me, he was flattered."

She tried to hold back an oncoming blush. "That's nice."

"So, what brings you to the park?"

She pointed in the direction of the senior home. "I just came from the The Greens. I help keep their store stocked. It's a nice place. There's always fresh cut flowers in the lobby, and the people are friendly."

"Yes, it's a great place. Adeline Hogan celebrated her

hundredth birthday there over the summer. Everyone at the station signed a card for her."

Nice...he seems to truly care about the people in the community. "Sounds like they made the day special for her."

Scout ran back with the tennis ball and dropped it at Sean's feet. He picked it up and asked her if she'd like to throw it. The last time she'd played with a dog at the park she lived at home with her parents. "Sure!" she said, tossing the ball.

The sight of Scout darting after the ball gave her a burst of energy.

Sean commented, "I want you to know we haven't found out anything new that would lead us to finding Jason, or I would've called."

"I thought so." She paused for a moment at the mention of her friend. "You must be very busy preparing to take away the reptile."

"That's true. There's a lot of work that goes into capturing it."

She found herself wanting to know more about Sean. "Can I ask you a personal question?"

"Sure."

"Can you tell me why you decided to join the police force?"

He didn't answer for a moment, glancing away leaving her concerned that she had crossed a line. "Oh, I didn't mean to pry. You don't have to tell me."

Scout brought the ball back to Sean who kept the game of fetch going with a good throw. "No, it's okay. It's because of something that happened to my aunt when I was growing up."

"Did it involve the police?"

"Sort of. When I was around seven, we got a phone call telling us she'd been mugged. I was too young to understand what that meant, but the next time I saw her, she didn't look the same. One of her eyes was permanently damaged. Her nose was broken, and she needed plastic surgery."

Vanessa gasped and covered her mouth. "Oh, my, that's terrible."

"Yes. It had a big effect on me. I became anxious and sensitive to things. Loud noises bothered me, and I was worried all the time. I was this frightened awkward kid, and the other kids picked up on this and bullied me."

She discreetly looked him over. *Six feet tall, muscular body...* "I'm sorry to hear that. It's hard to imagine you getting pushed around."

"I wasn't always built like this," he said, gesturing to his physique. "Things didn't get better for me until high school. The first week of classes, someone shoved me into my locker. By then, I'd had it with being bullied. I turned on him and punched him twice."

"Oh, wow." She didn't condone violence, but she liked that he stood up for himself.

"The pure physical exertion felt so good I began to work out. I joined the boxing team and the wrestling team. Lifting weights did me a lot of good, and I stopped being scared all the time."

"I've had my own anxiety issues, and I found yoga and exercise really helps me feel better," Vanessa said.

"Exactly. It's the physical activity that really does. I guess we have something in common."

"So, is that when you decided to join the police force?"

"Yes. I met Ethan on the wrestling team, and when he said he was applying to the police academy after college I realized that's what I wanted to do. I mean some asshole destroyed my aunt's life and messed up me and my family—maybe I could spare someone else from that kind of trauma."

"I can't think of a better reason." For a moment, the outside world disappeared, and she found herself gazing into his eyes until the sound of a text message on her phone distracted her.

With a start, she remembered her prior commitment. Reluctantly, she turned away. "I have to get going. I'm meeting a friend."

Scout came back to Sean, dropped the ball at his feet and then stood there staring at it.

"I think Scout and I are going to stay just a little longer," Sean said.

"I had fun. Thanks for letting me join you."

"Anytime. We're here a lot. Maybe we'll see you soon."

She glanced over her shoulder as she walked to her car and thought she caught him still looking her way. It was a good feeling.

~ * ~

Later that evening Sean visited Ethan at the hospital. Flowers and cards covered the window ledge. The monitor on the table next to the bed displayed his heart rate; and he still had an intravenous antibiotic fluid-filled bag on a stand near the wall behind him pumping the medication into his vein. Sean tried not to make too much noise as he pulled up a chair. Ethan's eyes started to open.

"Hey. How're you doing?" Sean asked.

Ethan gave a slight nod, slurring some of his words as he spoke. "They have me on a heavy dose of pain meds. I feel good but sleepy. How are you?"

Sean smiled, glad Ethan felt up to having a conversation. "I'm good. Did you hear? We're going to capture the creature. We just have to wait for some of the equipment to be brought in, and then we'll go in and set it up. They're putting a rush on everything, but it will still take a few days because the container has to be customized and there's some clearing needed in the park to get the equipment in place."

"Yes. I like the plan. My friends from the station are filling me in."

"Hey! Guess who I saw earlier today."

"Who?"

"Vanessa."

"What are you talking about? Are you guys dating?" Ethan leaned forward from his position propped up on pillows but groaned and made a face.

Sean grinned and gave him a very light push back onto his bed "You need to rest. We'll talk about it another time."

"Not so fast. What's going on?

"I saw her at the dog park in Otis Field. See, Scout's brought me luck. If I listened to you I wouldn't have a dog to take to the park."

"Let me get this straight. I'm dying in a hospital bed, and you're hanging out with her?" He raised his hands and swore in an amused voice, "Fuck."

"You're definitely not dying."

Ethan cursed again, continuing his "poor me" charade. "You obviously like her. Why don't you just ask her out?"

"I might."

"You should."

Shaking his head, Sean scanned the sterile hospital room, searching for a distraction. When his gaze rested on the blank television screen, he asked with concern, "Are you up to watching some football?"

"Yeah, I am," Ethan said, taking the bait. Clicking on the remote that rested on his bedside table, he lucked into a crowd-roaring touchdown by their favorite team, the Giants.

They both cheered and for a relaxing period of time, Ethan's injuries were forgotten amidst the thrilling play-by-play.

At half time, with their team still leading, Sean caught Ethan wincing. The pain medication was wearing off.

"Should I get someone to help?" Sean asked.

"No. It's time for my meds, so the nurse on duty will bring them. Let's call it an early night. If you go now, you'll be home for the end of the third quarter."

"Are you sure?"

"Yes. As soon as I get those pills I'll be conked out anyway."

"I'll come see you tomorrow and update you on the capture plan."

"Looking forward to it, and when you go to the park, watch yourself."

Twelve
Shock

Media reports and rumors about a gigantic, never-before-seen, creature spread all over the national news. The state police succumbed to pressure and released a crude drawing of the mysterious reptile rather than the expert's rendition of the animal which more closely resembled a plesiosaur. This caused Greg to gnash his teeth in frustration.

Today was the day for the rescue operation. He had trouble falling asleep the night before and had lain awake thinking about seeing the massive reptile. He woke early, anxious to do a final check on the equipment in the park. Friends and neighbors had been calling Greg's wife, Judy, reporting that they'd seen his picture on television.

Armed policemen confined the crowd of reporters and curious onlookers to the sides of the dirt road that led into the main entrance of Quarry Head Park. He lowered his car window to flash his identity card to the officers so he could drive through. After parking the vehicle, he wanted to check out the set up in the mobile office which was next to the forested area. On his way he passed the generator that would power the equipment.

In the distance, past the office trailer, he caught a glimpse of the rows of basking lamps and lights sitting high above the canopy of the trees. They reminded him of the nighttime spotlights used in football stadiums. Technical Specialists had worked to set up the equipment since sunrise, fortunately with no incident.

One of the workers not in a police uniform approached Greg and introduced himself. "I'm Aaron," he said, shaking Greg's hand. "I'll be coordinating the team of technicians today."

"Dr. Greg Mitchell," Greg replied. "I'm one of the herpetologists who originated the plan. Can you show me the video set up?"

"Of course. Come this way," Aaron said, leading Greg into the eight-by-ten-foot trailer.

"This looks perfect," Greg said, impressed with the size of the computer monitor.

"Yes, it's a good system. We have ten wireless security cameras. Two are attached to the top of the cage. They'll show the creature when it's caught. The other eight cameras are placed all over the park. Each of those cameras will capture a different broad range view of the forest. We've divided the park into eight sections, so we can identify where the creature is. The cage sits in the area labeled Q-4."

"It's a big park. Do you have enough cameras to cover it all?"

"Most of Quarry Head but not the neighboring Tribol Preserve. We pored over maps of the park, and this was the best outcome we could get. Do you want to see how it works?"

"Yes, please."

Aaron started clicking on the keypad. He gave Greg a demonstration, which proceeded without a hitch.

Pleased with it all, he asked to see the cage.

A heavily armed officer escorted him on the fifteen-minute walk into the forest and up to the heat lamps, perimeter lights, and giant crate. He marveled at the size of the structure—thirty feet long and twenty feet wide. A flat metal roof topped off its twelve-foot height.

Standing in front of the enormous pen, the wind kicked up blowing cold air at him. Greg felt a chill run through his body. He rubbed his hands together a couple of times and took brisk steps while he looked around the cage. Mindful of the time, he glanced at his smartphone. The screen showed 8:25 a.m. which meant he had plenty of time to get to the nine o'clock meeting at the police station.

"Can you escort me back to my car?" Greg asked the machine-gun toting officer.

Just before he left, he gathered handfuls of fallen leaves and branches and tossed them into the container in a vague attempt to make it look and feel more natural for the creature.

Reaching for his keys, he could see his hands had turned red from the cold. *Ahh, that's good. The cool weather will drive the reptile toward the heat lamps.*

After he arrived at the police station, Greg parked and spotted his colleagues, Mike and Lee, chatting to each other by the steps of the building. With renewed vigor, he and the others entered and made their way to the conference room where Frank conducted the meeting.

He went over the details of the plan. After answering questions, he introduced his weapons specialist.

"Everyone," he announced, extending his arm toward a bald man in a Connecticut State Police uniform sitting by the wall. His crossed arms and straight posture demonstrated confidence. "I want you to meet Sergeant Gordon Taylor. He runs a division of the Connecticut State PD that specializes in the use of firearms and explosives. We call him Sergeant *Tent*, as in T-N-T, because of his expertise with dynamite. He will be providing armed support during the capture in case of emergency."

Sergeant Taylor nodded in acknowledgement.

"How will we signal for help?" Lee asked.

"We will be using dedicated channel police radios. You will be working inside the mobile office the entire time with Greg and Mike. There will be a technology officer with you equipped with this device." Frank held up his radio to show them.

The meeting ended, and he dismissed the group. They all car-pooled in various vehicles and gathered once more at the main entrance of Quarry Head Park.

"Sean, are your officers ready? Greg, how about your team?" Frank asked, squinting in the bright morning sunlight. He looked much shorter here in the outdoors.

"Yes, Colonel," Sean said.

"We're ready too," Greg replied, glancing at Mike and Lee who both nodded eagerly.

"Then let's get started."

"Officers take your positions," Frank commanded. Several of them took off on dirt bikes, and a few climbed onto rock ledges around the perimeter with their machine guns.

"Come, we'll see if we want to adjust the camera angles," Greg said, and the group headed to the trailer.

"Frank gave me the go ahead. I'm going to start now. Are you ready?" Aaron asked.

"Yes, we are," Lee replied taking her seat.

As Aaron typed in commands, the generator grumbled angrily to life. He turned on the lamps and lights, causing several bright beams to converge over the cage. Not done yet, he then opened the program for the video transmission, ensuring that all "eyes" were on the park so they could spot the elusive creature and receive visual information on any officer who might be in danger. There was a live feed from eight cameras around the park and two more inside the cage. The monitor could show six views; the onlookers decided which of the ten video feeds to open at any given time.

Greg and the other scientists grabbed beige metal chairs and set up their positions, watching the technician work.

At first, he couldn't contain their excitement, but once the novelty wore off, he settled down to the realization that this would likely be the same as any of his scientific experiments; mostly waiting with an elusive chance of a breakthrough discovery.

He focused on tracking the six images on the screen. Different angles showing natural forested land filled the monitor. Greg stared until his eyes burned, then he'd blink and continue watching. A police officer passing through on a motorcycle would break the monotony for a moment of excitement.

Morning hours passed, and several times someone would radio Aaron and say, "See anything?" but his response was always, "Nothing yet."

At noon, Greg took out the food and beverages he'd packed. He ate a homemade turkey sandwich and potato chips while watching the screen. As he'd been resigned to sitting for hours, he, Mike and Lee took turns stepping just outside the office to stretch and enjoy the fresh air.

For their part, the police officers on motorcycles took short runs through the woods, back and forth, searching for any sign of the gigantic creature. Officers stationed on rock ledges had expansive views, but still, no reptile.

Greg studied the monitor. Aaron showed him how to adjust the cameras so they could zoom in on the ground from different angles. Nothing… then a squirrel flitting up a tree… then nothing again. He straightened. A twinge in his lower back from slumping in his chair shot through him.

The wait to catch sight of the reptile gave him time to familiarize himself with the land. He had strolled down the paths through Quarry Head Park before, but not recently. He adjusted one of the cameras so that it zoomed out and tilted up. Lee and Mike commented on the breathtaking view of cliffs that appeared on the monitor, giving way to orange, red, and yellow treetops, then mountains that faded out toward the horizon.

The few seconds of toying with the angles of the camera wouldn't gain him any sighting of the giant creature, but Greg knew very little opportunity was lost. As he joined them in admiring the beauty of the view, a speck of Long Island Sound in the distance stared back at him. Windswept leaves scattered about in front of the camera lens, delighting him. Sighing, he reluctantly zoomed the camera back to its target zone in the forest.

His right leg tingled from keeping it in the same position too long. He needed another good stretch so he stood for a moment and kicked it out. Mike commented, "Me, too," and rose from his seat to pace back and forth in the small office.

The day dragged. Soon it would be dark, and they'd have to reconvene tomorrow. From Greg's experience teaching college, a good glass of chilled water would help him stay alert. He grabbed his ice-cold beverage and took a swig before sitting again.

Then, more nothing... a slight sway of a tree branch in the wind... still no creature, and then...

Something happened. He could sense it and peered closer at the image of interest on the crowded screen.

At the bottom of the monitor, the second camera feed from the left portrayed the forest in the northwest quadrant. He detected a sudden motion in the foliage, his nerves on edge. He saw nothing disturbing, yet the rustle of the bushes and tree branches indicated an animal of massive size was on its way.

This was it!

"Follow it," Greg urged Aaron. He pointed to the exact image on the monitor.

"Got it!" Aaron said, typing a command that caused the relatively tiny video to jump six times the size to full screen.

"Everybody look at this," Greg cried out.

Lee and Mike rushed over from their seats to stand behind Greg, clutching the back of his chair.

"I see it too," exclaimed Lee. "It's camera 4!"

Aaron picked up his transmitter and radioed Frank. "Colonel, we got it. The reptile's been spotted in zone Q-3."

"Q-3?" Frank's astonished voice came though. "That's the area right next to the cage. Keep the cameras on it."

As a force lifted up a tree branch, the giant creature appeared on the monitor, the first time it had ever been captured on film in the history of the world.

"There it is!" Greg pointed at the image. Its head turned in the direction of the camera for a moment, then its body shifted out of the recorder's line of vision.

"Oh, my God," Lee said, transfixed, staring at the creature's steady side-to-side gliding motion now in view as it tackled the rough terrain.

"Frank, it's heading for the cage," Aaron said. "The heat lamps are working!"

"Got it. Keep this channel open," said Frank, his voice rasping through the radio.

Greg nodded. "I can make out its long thick neck, here, and this is its head. There's a fin, no, two on each side of its large body. Its earthy brown, muted green, and rust orange colored scales blend with the foliage; I can just barely see it through the bushes." He announced his observations much like a sports caster announcing a play-by-play of a series finale.

"It's an amazing creature," Lee said, breathless. "Unlike anything I've ever seen living before. Look at the size of its neck relative to its body!"

Mike's eyes were wide. "See the fin? It's like that of an ancient reptile from the sea."

Greg and the others huddled in front of the incredible video clamoring over one another as they spotted more details on the giant creature and observed its behavior. Instantaneously, they were able to pool together many years' experience of lectures, research, lab work, and textbooks.

"How long do you think it is?" he heard Lee ask.

"Oh, fifteen feet, easily," Mike answered.

Greg spun toward him. Heartrate quickened.

"What's wrong, Greg?"

"What did you say?"

"I just said it was fifteen feet. Why?"

Greg swiveled the chair back to face the monitor. "Fifteen feet…" he mumbled, trying to figure out why this thought bothered him so much.

"Do you think it's bigger?" queried Lee.

That was it! Greg leaped from the chair. He looked at Aaron. "Get me Sean!"

Aaron frowned. "This is an open mike. Everyone can hear you."

"What's going on?" Frank's voice reverberated. "Tell me now!"

"I'm here," Sean said, adding his presence.

Greg spoke urgently on his transmitter. "Sean, how big did you say the creature was?"

There was a pause, then he responded. "About twenty-five feet. So the cage is big enough, isn't it?"

"We have to turn the lamps off and get everyone out of the park. Now!"

"Why?"

"What?" Frank's raised voice echoed through the room.

"It's not the same one!"

Thirteen
Rage

"What's going on, Greg?" Sean asked by way of radio from his position within the forest.

"I see two more!" He heard Mike yell. His voice added to the chaotic atmosphere.

"Tell me what you see on the monitor," Sean said.

"The creatures are charging the cage. They're after the heat," Greg said.

"How many?" Sean asked.

"There's two braced on their four flippered appendages, pressed against the wall of the metal container; a different one's slithered halfway into the crate. Looks like zone Q-5 has one too. It's hard to see on the split screen because the area is dense with evergreens.

Aaron spoke. "Wait. There are at least four now. Three near the cage, and I can confirm there's one in zone Q-5."

"Withdraw! Withdraw!" Frank sounded the alarm.

"Turn off the equipment!" Greg yelled to someone, probably Aaron, on the open channel.

The lights went off one at a time. Deprived of the warmth from the heater, Sean hoped that would send the reptiles back into hiding.

He followed Frank's command and ordered all his officers to return to the edge of the park near the mobile office.

Shit, thought Sean, as ice-cold dread gripped his stomach. His naïve, quixotic plan to capture "one" creature alive evaporated with this dash of cruel reality. As he made his escape out of the park, he listened and scanned the area for any indication a creature lurked nearby.

A swooshing noise caught his attention. He turned and looked up. On the ledge, only yards away, branches on trees bent and whipped back.

Adrenalin coursed through him. *It's one of them.*

Uncertain if he should run or be still, he didn't move. In that moment he witnessed the scaled head of the reptile drop over the side of the ledge. Long rows of sharp, pointed teeth protruded from its immense open jaw.

The instant the creature's deep red, forked tongue flickered out, Sean raced toward the forested area in front of him, terrified by the image and the protracted hissing sound.

A crash of the cage and lamps, just yards away, toppling over reverberated through t forest. *That noise could scare it away!*

By the time the crackle and snap of falling metal ceased, he had made it to the stone benches on the grassy area near the entrance. He could see the other officers in the distance near the mobile office. He stopped running and turned around. No creature in site. Sweat dripped from his forehead. He wiped it away with the back of his jacket and swiftly met up with his team to be certain everyone got out.

The forest rustled as the reptiles slithered away from the destroyed cage. Thick foliage in the vicinity quivered in reaction to the pandemonium. Young trees snapped under their weight; bushes were compressed to the earthy floor.

In this state of emergency, officers waited for their new orders. Sean sent some of his team to block off additional roads leading up to the park and the rest to join state officers who had to usher away reporters, news teams, and bystanders that had been allowed to come closer to the area before the situation got out of control.

Then he opened the door to the mobile trailer to meet up with Greg and the team, who had formed a huddle, talking in urgent voices to one another.

"Have the reptiles knocked over all the cameras?" Sean asked.

"We can't see anything in the area where the cage was. All those are destroyed," Greg said.

"We have to leave. Frank's orders," Aaron said, his tone insistent.

A distraught voice broke out over the transmitters. "Sergeant Tent, I need you now!"

"Tent here."

"There's one after me! I'm just south of the cage."

"Go get 'em, Tent!" Frank yelled.

"On my way!" came Tent's rapid-fire, tense response.

Sean hurried outside. He stayed on guard close to the mobile office where he stationed a motorbike for emergency use. The noise in the park quieted enough for Sean to listen to the sound of Tent's motorcycle. Then he heard the staccato-like blasts of gunfire ring out. If there was a call to assist he would be ready to go in. Now he waited, concerned someone could be hurt. He pushed for this plan.

This is my fault.

There was more machine-gun fire. Sean's stomach twisted. "What's going on, Frank?" he shouted into his radio.

There was no immediate answer.

Finally, the roar of motorcycles reverberated louder. Sean glanced in the direction of the sound hoping it meant Tent saved the officer. Holding his breath, he stared into the forest, silently pleading for their safety. Seconds later the man came into view, followed by Sergeant Tent. A wave of relief swept over Sean. He rushed over to see them.

"Is everyone all right?" he called.

Sergeant Tent maintained his stoic expression and jerked his head sideways indicating to him someone else would be answering. Close behind, Frank stomped up to the parking lot.

Seething, he pointed an accusing finger at Sean. "We missed them! The bastards've taken off!" He shouted so loud everyone snapped to attention.

Sean responded as calmly as he could. "Is anyone hurt?"

"I don't know! And no thanks to you! *You* wanted to save them!"

"I didn't know, Frank..."

The colonel pulled off his brimmed police hat and slapped it against his thigh. "You didn't know? Do you realize your mistake nearly killed us all?"

Tent walked over, stepping between them. "Frank, I got a message. Darren's been attacked."

Frank's eyes bulged. "Where is he?"

"Todd rescued him. They're on the edge of the forest in Q-1. Want me to go or direct the paramedics?"

"Send an officer to the area with a machine gun. I'm going in." He darted the short distance to his motorcycle then straddled the bike and jabbed at finger at Sean. "We need you! Now!"

He scrambled to his own bike, jumped on then pulled up beside Frank.

"Okay," Frank shouted above the din of the engines. "Let's go help them."

They swerved off in the correct direction through the woods, navigating clear of the dense undergrowth. Sean spotted two uniformed figures up ahead. The kneeling officer was Todd, and the other state trooper who was lying amidst the leaf-strewn forest floor had to be Darren. Sean's heart skipped a beat. He could not tell if Darren was moving.

As he neared, he saw Darren gasping, his body writhing. Todd tried to calm him while he attended to his many wounds. He had taken off his police jacket and wrapped it tightly around Darren's injured right arm. Blood soaked through the fabric.

"Damn it," Frank muttered, his face softening at the sight of his wounded officer. He squatted beside him and checked Darren's pulse.

"What happened?" Sean asked Todd.

Sweat poured down Todd's face, and his eyes were glassy. Breathing heavily, he answered, "I saw the creatures by the cage. Then I heard the order to evacuate. I started running for the exit, but then saw Darren racing across the forest toward me. He called out something, but I couldn't hear him. He must have known something was after him." He stopped and sucked in a shaky breath.

"Try to relax. Take your time," Sean said.

"I'm all right," he continued. "Darren was shouting at me to keep going. I kept running but had him in my line of vision. He had almost caught up to me. I turned my head so I could see where I was going, and that's when I heard him scream. When I looked back, he was gone. I heard muffled noises like something dragging through the forest. That's when I saw the reptile. I drew my gun and started firing." He stared at Darren. "The reptile swung its neck around. It was dragging Darren by his shoulder."

"Goddammit," Frank said, shaking his head.

"It's okay, Todd—" Sean said, but Todd cut him off.

"I don't know for certain if I got it but for a second the reptile turned in my direction and dropped Darren to the ground. His arm was ripped open. I could see the bone." He tilted his head up to Frank. "I did the best I could."

"You did a good job," Frank said and placed a hand on his shoulder. "Jesus." He barked into the radio, "When is that goddamn ambulance coming?"

"It just pulled in," Tent replied. "We're on our way."

"Sean will come meet the ambulance so you can stay and guard the perimeter." Frank turned to Sean. "You know the area. Go!"

Sean jumped onto his motorcycle then sped back toward the parking lot. He pulled up to the ambulance and directed the driver into the forest. They moved quickly on the open parts of the trail, while the man at the wheel had to take it slower on the sharp bends or uneven terrain, until he had to stop when the foliage got too thick. Fortunately, they were close to Darren. Two paramedics dismounted and removed the stretcher from the back. Sean jumped off his bike and led the way, crossing twenty yards of brush to reach the injured officer.

The emergency crew were quick to attend to Darren's severest wounds, wrapping a tourniquet on his arm and securing it with a splint. Moments later, with care, they rolled him onto his side and placed the backboard under his body before laying him back onto it.

Sean's throat tightened as he watched the gut-wrenching scene, his mind replaying the vivid images over and over again.

With a glaze that blazed on his face, Frank approached. "I'm going to get you for this, Sean. From now on, this park is mine."

He glanced at Frank, but stayed silent. Frank yelled to the officer, "Time to go! Help Todd out."

They all mounted their motorcycles then followed the ambulance. After nearly choking on a forced deep breath, Sean commanded himself to go too.

As the four officers reached the parking lot, the ambulance finally pulled away and screeched out the exit to deliver Darren to the emergency ward.

Once Frank ensured everyone was accounted for, he stormed out into the parking lot to face off against Sean once again. "You lead us into an ambush," he roared. Officers in earshot started watching. "We could've all been killed!"

"Just how the hell was I supposed to know there was more than one?"

"We should have been better fucking prepared! There's no excuse for this."

Sean's jaw tensed, but he held back

"Jesus, how did you become chief?" Frank jabbed a finger into Sean's chest and growled, "You're done here. I guarantee it."

Sean looked up in time to see several of his staff walk to their cruisers with their heads down and drive off. They were no longer permitted to stay.

Chests heaving, Greg, Lee, and Mike rushed into the parking lot. "Let me try to—" Greg's outburst was halted by Frank's withering stare.

"It's time for you to leave. I want everyone except my officers out of the area. Now!"

"But, Frank, we think we can still fix this," Greg pleaded.

"Too late for that. Your help's no longer needed."

Frank commanded several more officers to guard the perimeter of the park with machine guns and strode to his police car murmuring a string of expletives. His vehicle's engine roared as he drove off.

"What about the creatures?" Sean asked a state trooper, who averted his gaze. "What's going to happen to them?"

"Frank has given everyone orders to shoot them," the officer replied, looking down. Passing by Sean, he got back on his radio.

"What are we going to do? We can't let them hunt them down," Greg said to Sean.

"Why not? Didn't you see what happened?"

Dr. Mitchell persisted. "You don't understand. What Frank's doing could be more dangerous."

"There's nothing we can do."

"If he sends officers to hunt the reptiles he could end up driving them into town."

This revelation gave Sean new cause for alarm. "Just give me a minute."

The three scientists stood together, shifting position as they stood. Sean paced back and forth, rubbing his temples. "All right," he said, "You need to explain to me what's going on. How could there be so many? Where are they coming from?"

"We do have an idea about that," Greg said. He glanced back at his colleagues. "It's just that we need to look at a map that includes the surrounding areas to explain it all, and I don't think we're exactly welcome here right now. Can we go back to your office and go over everything?"

"Yes. I'll meet you there now."

Nodding, Greg, Lee, and Mike went to Greg's car. Sensing a massive headache coming on, Sean headed for his cruiser plagued with feelings of guilt and anger. His emotions consumed him. Worst of all he felt powerless, a throwback to his childhood.

Once inside the vehicle, he slammed the door so hard the car shook. "Goddammit!" he roared. Clenching his right hand, he banged his fist into the dashboard. His rage so powerful he bruised himself upon impact.

A state officer standing near his cruiser looked on, offering no sympathy.

Fourteen
Origin

On the way to the Wilton Police Station, Greg, Lee, and Mike discussed the giant creatures and the shock of discovering that more than one existed. Mike strained against his seatbelt from the back row to better hear and talk with the others.

"I feel terrible," Greg said.

"Don't do that to yourself. We all agreed on the plan. None of us imagined there were so many of them," Lee said in a somber tone.

"You know there's no way we could've known this would happen. We did our best. There's nothing we can do to change the past, so let's focus on what we can do now," Mike said.

"What do you think they are?"

"I believe they're an entire species of marine reptiles that may have survived unseen for millions of years," Greg said.

"Based on the flippers?"

"Let's go over it again. Their necks are a good two thirds of their size, and their heads are considerably small for their proportions. They had a tapering tail and four flippers. I would say they ranged in size from fifteen to thirty feet long and I think they're related to a Plesiosaur."

Lee nodded. "Plesiosaurs lived in water. Some theorized that they came onto land for short periods of time, but what we saw just tucked its fins up and moved like a snake."

"Oh boy," Mike said, as he leaned into the space between Greg and Lee's seats. "There's so much we don't know. There's the Spinosaurus dinosaur that spent much of its time in water and now, possibly, a Plesiosaur that can live on land."

At that moment a van heading in the opposite direction with *Channel 14 News, 24 Hour Delivery at Your Service* painted on the side rocketed past them, obviously pressing the speed limit.

"Damn it! I can imagine they're going to scare everyone now," Greg said, rubbing the back of his neck. "They'll dramatize the crisis, causing panic, and that's never a good thing."

"You just said so yourself. This was a *crisis*," Lee said.

"Do you know the channel number for the local radio station?" Mike asked. "Maybe the news is out already."

Greg turned on the radio and pushed the second button on the control panel. Just as he feared, a reporter was heard announcing the events unfolding in Quarry Head. In a rapid-fire voice, she said, "The park has been closed indefinitely. The dirt road leading to the parking lot and the section of Ridgefield Road right before it are now declared dangerous and off limits. We can see state police with guns moving in to cordon the boundaries of the area. The police have no comment as to casualties at this time, but an ambulance was seen leaving the front entrance. Now, we have here…"

"Turn it off. Our time is better spent focusing on what to do next," Mike said.

Greg pushed the button, causing silence to fall. "Did you see how angry Frank was? We all heard that he plans to kill them."

"You don't seriously think he would go ahead and hunt them?" Lee asked.

"Of course, he would," Mike said. "My neighbor told me she once called Animal Control because she was concerned when she saw a fox in her backyard. The officer told her that a fox was considered a nuisance animal, and he would kill it. How many news reports have we all heard where some exotic animal got loose from a zoo or preserve and the *solution* was to hunt it down." He groaned. "I can go on and on."

"We're not going to let that happen. Sean's on our side."

"But Sean's only the chief of police in this town; Frank's the head of law enforcement for the entire state. He has much more power," Mike argued.

"This isn't helping. Let's come up with a new plan to save these reptiles that also ensures everyone's safety," Greg said as he parked his car in a spot next to the Wilton Police Station.

"You're right," Lee agreed, before she exited the vehicle.

As the scientists headed in the front door, Marcy was gathering her belongings to leave for the day. She recognized them right away and stayed to help.

"I heard," she said with a sad glance. "You'll be wanting to see Sean, right? He's not back yet."

"Yes, and we know that he might be a while," Greg said.

"Follow me. I'll let you all wait in the briefing room." On the way down the hall she showed them where they could help themselves to water, coffee, or tea. "Can I get you anything else?"

"I do have a favor to ask," he said. "Is there a topographical map we can look at of the Tribol Preserve?"

"I think I can find you one, but it will have Quarry Head on it too."

"That would be perfect."

A few minutes later, she brought them the detailed drawing. He and his colleagues poured over the topographical information and strategized for the next few minutes as they waited for Sean to arrive.

When Sean walked in, his jaw clenched, and eyes narrowed, Greg stopped talking.

"Is there any news on the officer that was taken to hospital?" Lee asked Sean.

"No, but the reptile tore his shoulder all the way to the bone."

"Oh no," she exclaimed.

"Awful. Just awful," Greg said, his head bowed.

"Anyone else injured?" Mike was quick to ask. "Is everyone out now?"

"Nothing life threatening," Sean said. "The park's been evacuated. All officers are accounted for, and now they're guarding the perimeter. When I left, Frank was adamant about having the reptiles destroyed."

"I didn't imagine there were more..."

Sean put up his hand and stopped Greg. "I know you didn't expect this to happen, none of us did, but now we have dangerous animals in the park, and I need to understand what's going on. What are these creatures and where did they come from?"

Through glances, Greg shared his relief with Mike and Lee at Sean's willingness to hear them out.

Greg said, "We believe the reptiles in Quarry Head are a species of marine reptile that has somehow survived for over millions of years. The fins on their sides clearly indicate that they are at least semi-aquatic. It appears to be a relative of the Plesiosaur, which is believed to have died out during the late Cretaceous period. More specifically, their proportions and features resemble a genus of Plesiosaur known as an Elasmosaurus."

"I don't understand. How can some kind of...?" Sean waved a hand.

"Plesiosaur," Lee said.

"Right. How could that be in our park? It makes no sense. Where did they come from?"

"We've been going over it, and we think we have the answer."

"You do?" Sean lifted his brow.

"Yes," Greg said with vigor as he gestured to the spread-out drawing. "We're convinced the reptiles are coming from Echo Lake, which is located in the middle of the Tribol Preserve."

Sean grimaced. "What makes you think this is where they're from?"

"There's no other realistic possibility," Mike said. "You see, we believe the creatures need water to survive, and the largest source of water is Echo Lake."

"Ah."

"It would also explain why the creatures were never seen before. This lake is in a remote area far from trails," Lee said.

"It's true. Very few people ever go into the Tribol Preserve, so it's been left natural and untouched. It borders Quarry Head over here," Sean explained as he pointed to the thick black line in the southwest corner that marked the border. "If someone wants to go for a walk or ride a bike, they go to Quarry Head. So that may explain why no person has come in contact with them before, but why are these creatures showing up in the park now? And how the hell do they still exist, millions of years later?"

"This is our theory," Greg said. "During the Cretaceous-Tertiary extinction, roughly sixty-five million years ago, most of the huge marine reptiles became extinct. However, Echo Lake may have many underwater connections. Some may go to the Long Island Sound and then lead to the Atlantic Ocean. If the underwater system is extensive, it may have provided enough of a safe haven for a species with an extraordinary ability to adapt, like this one."

Lee jumped in. "If this creature lived through the Cretaceous Period, it might have become isolated in the lake when the ocean receded or it may be using underground channels to go back and forth while staying hidden."

"But how can something that lived in the ocean survive in a fresh water lake?" Sean asked.

"You're right that the ocean is saltwater, and the Long Island Sound is an estuary where saltwater from the ocean mixes with fresh water, but remember, we're not talking about fish or animals with gills. These ancient reptiles breathed air, so it could live in saltwater, fresh water, or both."

"How did it adapt to live on land?"

"If this water reptile's home has been changing for millions of years, it could have evolved over time to survive, but it most likely still needs water to live," Greg said.

Sean scratched his head. "Okay, now we're getting close. Why now? Why are they leaving Echo Lake?"

Mike answered, "Well that's another mystery. If we're right and that's where they're from, something must have happened that forced them to leave the water. Like a recent threat to their environment could have initiated their migration to the land."

"And we believe these creatures may be looking for another suitable body of water," added Lee. "We'll have to check what's happening with Echo Lake that's making them abandon it. However, they're very aggressive, possibly because they're stuck on land. They're showing signs of stress and agitation."

Sean scoffed. "Yeah, they sure are. So, what do you suggest we do?"

"We must first verify that Echo Lake is their home, and then find out what happened to their environment and figure out if they can go back to it," Greg said.

Mike agreed. "I don't think they can survive for very long without access to water. They wouldn't have retained their flippers if they no longer needed an aquatic environment."

"You're suggesting we go into the Tribol Preserve to check out the lake?" Sean asked.

Greg nodded. "We have to. We must see if the reptiles are coming from there and if the area could sustain them again."

"And then what?"

"Then we reverse their migration."

"Brilliant," Lee said. "A reverse migration's certainly possible. You know, I could ask Dr. Irene Stone to help us assess Echo Lake."

Greg turned to her, smiling with approval. Dr. Stone was a well-respected Aquatic Ecologist at the New England Aquatic Institute in Boston.

"But what if they're *not* from there?" Sean asked.

"I don't want to admit it, but if we can't figure out where they're coming from we might have to support Frank," Mike said.

Lee glanced at Mike, her mouth in the shape of an O. Greg frowned.

Mike held up his hands in defense. "I know, I'm just being realistic. If Echo Lake is out, then they would no longer have a natural environment close by. As we've seen, it's too risky to attempt to capture them all alive."

"Mike!" Greg couldn't believe what he heard.

Mike pressed on. "Like you saw, the creatures are out of their natural habitat. They're not going to survive much longer in the cold anyway. If we can't help them, we would be doing something humane if we put them to a quick and painless death."

"No, no, no..." Greg muttered, shaking his head and waving one hand in dismissal.

"Okay, but that is a last-ditch solution. First, we have to try to find out where they came from," Lee snapped.

"Exactly," Mike said. "I'm not saying that we give up, but that shows how hard we have to work. We'll need additional expertise: a geologist and a paleontologist."

"That's more like it!"

"What king of specialists?" Sean asked.

"Oh, sorry," Mike said as he turned to Sean. "Basically, we need a geologist to help us understand how the land in both parks has changed over time and we also need a paleontologist to confirm that these really are descendants of the Plesiosaur."

"Thanks. What's paleontology?"

"It's the study of fossils, so these people tend to specialize in dinosaurs and other related prehistoric reptiles."

"We won't have any trouble finding scientists to work on this, but Sean, will the state allow us to go to Echo Lake and explore it?" Greg asked.

"I'm not a fan of these creatures after what they did to my friend and my colleagues, but I can support the idea of sending them back to their natural habitat. Right now there is no chance Frank will change his mind."

"But reverse migration is the *only* safe solution. We have no idea how many reptiles there are. If the police try to hunt them, some could escape and be driven into the population," Lee said.

"And I want to point out, that even though these reptiles are huge, they blend really well with their surroundings. There're a lot of woodlands in this town," Mike said.

"That's right. Despite their size they're not easy to see in the forest. Sean, you saw the experiment I'm running now with corn snakes and how tricky it is to see a reptile that blends in with its environment," Greg said.

"I understand the dangers but every day they are alive and living in Quarry Head Park, the town is at risk. How can I keep the community safe?"

"If they *do* come from Echo Lake and we get them back there, that part of the preserve can be sectioned to contain them. We can construct electric fencing and concrete walls. They've lived in Echo Lake for millions of years, and they were never a danger before. We'd be able to monitor them and make sure they stay there."

Greg and the others had said their piece. He gazed at Sean as he rubbed his chin, waiting for his response.

"The Tribol Preserve is not state owned or funded. It's Wilton's preserve, and while I still have my job, I'll see that your team can explore it." Sean's face now conveyed a new resoluteness. "But how can we get in there without being attacked?"

"Reptiles in their natural environment should not be as aggressive, and we have tranquilizer guns. I'll load the darts with etorphine, which works on elephants," Mike said.

"Better make it a double," Sean quipped. "If we can't find any proof the reptiles lived in the lake, there's nothing more I can do, but, I'm willing to try."

"Give me one day to get everyone together. Some of the specialists I want to get are from out of state."

Sean started closing up the map on the table. "Have everyone ready tomorrow. If Frank knows what we're planning, he'll find a way to stop us."

Fifteen
Injunction

Sean arrived early to work the next morning to go over the plans he mapped out for the exploration of Echo Lake. The lack of emergency messages reassured him that things were under control.

He opened the file labeled Quarry Head Reptile. His notes about the attack on Officer Smith caught his attention.

Earlier in his career Sean overpowered a petty criminal who was robbing a convenience store. The thief had shot two bullets at close range into the shop's owner when he refused to open his cash register.

Sean vividly recollected the crimson pool the victim had been lying in. God. The amount of blood that had gushed out of the gunshot wounds in his left arm and upper left torso. Thankfully, the shop owner had survived and, as far as he knew, made a full recovery. Not until this past week had he seen so much gore again.

Flashes of Ethan lying on the ground motionless, with both legs savagely crushed, invaded his mind. And just yesterday, Sean had witnessed the same damage to Officer Smith's shoulder as he lay on the forest floor. The memories sickened him just like all those years ago when he saw his injured aunt. Instead of reacting like a scared child, the violence made him angry and frustrated because he could not do anything to prevent it.

Now, he had to decide his next step. It did not fall neatly in the jurisdiction of any police protocol. Rather, the situation in Quarry Head Park was very complex and far removed from the type of crises police chiefs were authorized to manage. *Besides, Frank made it clear that he was now in charge, didn't he?*

I could just ignore this. He could handle it. If anything went wrong from this moment on, he would face the consequences. All I need to do is continue my supervision of my officers' duties and my administration of this station.

And yet…

Sean couldn't just let it go. He passionately wanted to resolve the dangers now threatening the safety of the citizens he'd sworn to protect. Believing the scientists had the most educated response he knew he had to listen to them. The media, rife with various calls to action and vehement opinions from both sides of the divide, stirred the debate.

He got up and paced the room. *I need to buy them some time. I have to figure out how to handle this new species... this rare species... That's it! We could be dealing with some kind of endangered species, and there are laws to protect those.*

Unable to contain himself any more, he paged his two most trusted officers, who had just arrived at work: Doug and Ronald. Next, he radioed Ann. She had seen the creatures first hand and had already shown that she did not share the fears the public had exhibited toward them.

Doug and Ron entered Sean's office a few minutes later.

"What's going on?" Doug asked as he and Ron sat in the two chairs in front of Sean's desk.

Sean walked over to get a spare chair from the corner of the room. "Ann's coming," he said. "We'll just wait a minute."

"Sure," said Ron.

Ann walked in with a brisk stride. She greeted everyone. "So," she said, as she sat in the empty chair. "What's going on?"

Sean exhaled as he clasped his hands and leaned on his desk, "It's about Quarry Head."

All three police officers straightened.

"We all now know there's more than one giant reptile in the park. In fact, it looks like a new species has been discovered. I'm going to be working with Greg and his team of scientists to see where the reptiles came from and if they can be corralled back there."

"Do they have any idea where that could be?" Doug asked as he leaned forward.

"The Tribol Preserve."

"The land that borders Quarry Head?" Doug asked.

"That's right," Sean said, rising to open the map he and the scientists had studied the evening before. The three officers stood as he showed them a particular spot in the preserve. "They think the reptiles came from right there, Echo Lake," he said, the tip of his finger firmly on the irregularly rounded shape, indicating the water.

"That's very interesting," Ann said, her eyes widening.

Sean's intuition told him she was thinking of the giant creature that had attacked her.

"But, Sean," she continued with a frown. "I heard Frank on the radio. He said all the creatures were to be killed."

"Yes," he acknowledged. "He's assembling an elite team to

hunt them down, but while he's doing that, I am trying to find a way to save them."

The officers gazed at him with astonished expressions.

"Wow," Ron said.

Sean couldn't tell if Ron's reaction conveyed admiration or incredulity.

"You've got guts, Chief," said Doug, smiling.

"So exactly what are you planning to do?" asked Ann.

"I will be going with Greg, Mike, Lee, and some other specialists, to explore Echo Lake in the Tribol Preserve tomorrow. You three are my first choice to come with us. But I'm asking if you *want* to go. This is not an order."

"Well," Doug began and then paused.

Sean could tell he was hesitant. *Could just be that he has a wife and two young kids at home, and he thinks the exploration is too dangerous. Or it could be that he didn't want to risk upsetting his colleagues, especially Colonel Gunner, and derailing his career.*

Sean turned his attention to Ron, who was looking down and tapping his leg.

Ann interlocked her fingers on her lap. "I'm still somewhat in shock after being attacked by that creature," she said. She appeared as calm as if she were talking about nothing more serious than awarding a traffic ticket, yet Sean could only assume how conflicted she must be. "I don't know if I can face it…them…again."

He nodded, dreading she'd be the first to decline. *It's okay, Ann, go ahead and say you've gone above the call of duty. I can't say I disagree.*

To his surprise though, she continued, "But… I admit it has my attention. I've seen it, so I know it's unique. It deserves a chance at survival."

Yes! He exulted silently. "Good, I'll count you in."

"I'm in," Ron said. "Even though you've said it's not an order, I still consider it my duty."

"Thanks," Sean said, beginning to feel fired up now that he had a team to work with.

"I trust Sean. I'm in," Doug added.

He dared not show his relief in front of his three officers. "Excellent," he said, striving to keep his voice even. "I know I'm asking for a lot of faith, but something tells me it's the right thing to do."

"There's one other thing, though." Ann had lowered her voice to a whisper, even though Sean's office door was closed. "I'm sure I don't have to tell you, but I've heard some officers here saying that you blew it."

He gritted his teeth but said nothing.

"In fact, I've heard second hand that there's some talk…well, let's say, they've been saying we need a new police chief."

Before Sean responded, Doug spoke. "Let them gossip," he said. "They have nothing better to do."

"Agreed," said Ron, leaning back in his chair.

"Okay," said Doug, puffing up his cheeks and then expelling the air in one long exhale. He glanced at everyone. "Sounds like we have a plan."

"Good," Sean said. "We'll all meet at the station tomorrow morning at 8:00 a.m."

"I'll be here," Ron said, he walked with Doug and Ann out the door.

Next, Sean paged Officer David Haig.

"Please, take a seat," Sean asked the rookie officer, who had a background in environmental regulations prior to joining the force.

Shifting with nervousness David sat, but Sean reassured him that he just wanted some information. "Do you know anyone at either the United States Fish and Wildlife Service or the National Oceanic and Atmospheric Administration.

"No, I can't say I do, but if you're looking for a way to stall Colonel Gunner…"

Sean grinned. Dave was sharp.

"…I used to work with the head of the EPA. You could appeal to that department on the grounds that the ecology of the area could be destroyed if there's a massive hunt within the park."

Aha. Dave's quick assessment of the situation impressed Sean. Even though he was the youngest on the force, Dave's intelligence and willingness to put forth suggestions made him one of his finest officers.

"That's a good idea, but it won't work. Frank will claim there's an impending threat to personal safety. Instead of using the Environmental Protection Act, I want to try to use the Endangered Species Act."

"Right," said Dave with a gleam in his eyes. "And both of those agencies would deal directly with protecting the animal."

"That's what I was thinking."

"What do you want me to do?"

"I'm going to send the information on the creatures to the heads of the FWS and NOAA. The FWS deals with fresh water animals and NOAA deals with ocean animals, but we just don't have enough scientific information as to whose jurisdiction the reptiles fall into so I want to appeal to both agencies. I'll call ahead so they are aware this is an emergency situation that needs immediate attention."

"You want me to follow up with them?"

"Yes. I won't be in the office tomorrow morning, and I don't think they'll do anything about it today, so you'll have to act on my behalf. I want you to stay on top of this and try to get an injunction."

"An order to stop Colonel Gunner?" Dave asked.

"What I'm looking for is a mandate that will prohibit the killing of the giant reptiles by the Connecticut State Police or anyone else until the Tribol Preserve and Echo Lake have been adequately explored. You may have to file some additional paperwork with the U.S. Department of the Interior. I'll give you a copy of the documents so you can send them the information as well. And make sure they know we're asking that the case be treated as an emergency."

"I believe at least one of them will pick up the matter," Dave said.

"Let's hope so," Sean replied and dismissed the officer.

Alone in his office once more, he took a moment to ponder his motives in trying to save the prehistoric reptiles. Confronting Frank meant putting his job on the line. What this the right action?

Sixteen
Experts

Greg dimmed the lights in his snake observation tank as he eagerly set up his laboratory to convert it into a decent meeting room for the three new scientists arriving tonight. Lee and Mike oohed and aahed over the giant reptile habitat, remarking on the importance of the study especially since they were aware of the decline in the corn snake population in certain areas. Secretly content with the opportunity to be alone, Greg spent the time clearing off the piles of papers on the lab tables without appearing too conspicuous. Soon Dr. Irene Stone of the New England Aquatic Institute in Boston, Dr. Manny Laurence, a geologist of the American Museum of Natural History, and Dr. Tova Banet, a paleontologist who occupied a senior lecturer position at the New York University would be arriving.

The University of Connecticut seemed the best place to have this hastily called meeting, which he set into motion mere minutes after saying goodbye to Sean at the police station last night. Here, at least, the six scientists would have access to Greg's world-class database, textbooks, and tailor-made research intranet. The McManus Center for Biological Sciences building, where he had his lab on the second floor, had to be kept open especially for the conference. He hoped the security staff had remembered to leave the front doors unlocked, as instructed.

The other specialists were running late, understandable on such short notice. He finished clearing the table and used the additional few minutes to come up with a name for the reptile.

He sat behind his desk and took out a notebook from the top drawer. He started to scribble—

Naming the creature—

Honor the animal's greatness and show respect for the land it came from. Possibly Quarry Head but more likely the Tribol Preserve.

Combine Tribol, with common Greek roots like "hadro"—from the Greek word "hadros" meaning large, or "mega" from megas meaning great—I might take, "bronto" from bronte meaning thunder—

Comment on its shape using "morph." Put together with

"saur" for reptile… Tribolhadro… Tribolbront… Tribolmega…
Tribolmegasaur!

Tribolmegasaur—the Tribol Preserve's great reptile.
That's it! I'll share this one with the group.

There was a sharp knock on the door, and before he could respond, in walked Dr. Irene Stone, a tall woman in her fifties with black-rimmed glasses and short curly brown hair. She wore a turtleneck under a fashionable leather coat, which she took off upon entry. The two-and-a-half-hour drive from Boston did not appear to have tired her. Greg put his notebook away as she extended her hand and introduced herself to him and Mike.

Then she turned to Lee and said, "I remember you from my lecture in Boston."

"That's right," Lee said, a grin tipping up the corners of her lips.

"I read the news about what happened in the park," Irene said. "I'll do anything to help preserve this incredible find."

Lee glanced about the room. "I know. We're just waiting for two more people, then we can begin."

"They phoned half an hour ago. They were stuck in some traffic and said they'll be at least ten minutes late," Mike said.

"Actually, make that on time," an exuberant female voice interjected from the front hallway of Greg's lab.

"You made it," he said, walking over to shake hands with Dr. Manny Laurence and Dr. Tova Banet. "We spoke earlier, I'm Greg Mitchell, and this is Lee Rivera, Mike Hayes, and Irene Stone."

"Pleased to meet all of you," Tova said. Everyone took turns introducing themselves and shaking hands.

"Did you two come together?" Irene asked.

"Yes. Greg put us in touch with each other because we were both working in New York," Tova said.

Manny was the oldest, perhaps mid-sixties. His silver white hair gave him a distinguished gentlemanly look above his plaid buttoned-down shirt. Slim, he wore a perpetual look of curiosity behind his modern-looking glasses. The youngest of the scientists, Tova was short and slender, with comfortable clothing: a cotton long-sleeved shirt, beige khaki pants, and sneakers.

Standing in front of his colleagues, Greg laid out a map on the discussion table and gestured to the six chairs which encircled it. When he was ready he looked up, uniting them with his introduction.

"I appreciate all of you coming on such short notice. Now that you're aware of what we discovered in Quarry Head Park you can see how invaluable your expertise will be," Greg said.

Irene responded first. "This is so hard to believe! I wouldn't miss being part of it."

"Same here," Manny said.

Irene nodded. "I can't wait to see Echo Lake. I've studied maps of the area, but I have to see it for myself—"

"Yes, that's our plan—" Greg said.

"Right, right," Irene said. "We have to get proof that they lived there, and then we have to find out if anything changed significantly that might have caused the creatures to leave the area."

"Are we sure this reptile is from the lake? I mean, I'm convinced it is, but does everyone agree?" he asked.

"Let me give you all some background on the inland waters here," she began. "I think it will clarify why I'm certain we have a marine reptile. You know that Pangaea sat within Panthalassa, the mother ocean, you might say."

"Yes," he said. He knew the facts by heart. Pangea was the precursor continent before the tectonic drifts that had split up the giant land mass into the continents of today around a hundred and twenty million years ago.

"With the separation of the mother ocean into distinct bodies of water, the animals that lived in them had to adapt," Irene continued. "Your town is not far from Long Island Sound. The animals in your waters survived due to their adaptations to their environments, specifically those that allowed them to live away from the great sea."

"Do you all agree then that it's from the water and possibly related to a Plesiosaur?" Greg asked.

"Yes. Let me show you something," Tova said. From her briefcase she extracted the printed copies of the giant reptiles he sent by email.

The reproductions appeared detailed and of professional quality. She then picked up a thick textbook, opened it to the spot she had bookmarked, and laid it flat down on the table for all to see.

She pointed at the sketches, then to the scientific drawing within the book. Greg spotted the striking similarities between the sketches and the textbook illustrations and glanced around to see everyone else nodding.

"This reptile has fins and a relatively short tapering tail compared to the length of the rest of its body," she continued. "Archeologists discovered prehistoric marine reptile skeletons with these exact characteristics. Its size and features, such as its long neck and flippers, resemble a Plesiosaur. Its similarities are so striking I am convinced while it originated from the sea, it has adapted to the lake and the land. It can breathe air, but my guess is it still needs to spend time in water to survive."

"Their adjustment to land is remarkable," Mike said. "Particularly how their snake-like motions allow them to move easily on the ground."

"Yes, but their flippers tell me that they could move effortlessly in the water too. We can also learn from its fins. A boned fin would indicate a terrestrial animal, whereas a non-boned fin indicates aquatic beginnings."

"We can't make too many assumptions right now, but if this reptile is as old as we're saying, it could give us new insight into evolutionary biology," Lee said.

"So why are we seeing these reptiles now?" Greg asked.

"I hope I can help answer that for you," Manny said. "While I'm not an expert on reptiles, especially those from prehistoric times, I can tell you about the land in the Tribol Preserve. Before I came here, I studied maps of the area. Because Quarry Head was an active quarry, the area was blasted for excavation purposes. The movement of rocks can change the course of ground and surface water systems that run into waterbodies miles away. It may have set some disturbance in motion that took all these years to have a significant impact on Echo Lake."

Just then, a clanking was heard at the door, and the janitor shuffled into the room pulling supplies and a mop. Greg, caught up in the discussion, gasped at the sight of the man in gray overalls near their table.

"Sorry, Dr. Mitchell. Should I come back?" the janitor asked, chuckling.

"Can you skip this room tonight? And please call me Greg."

"Righto. Good evening, Greg," he said with a nod and glanced around the room. The attendees nodded and returned the smile as he departed, pulling the large bucket and trolley with cleaning supplies.

The brief interruption gave everyone a minute to stretch their arms and look around.

"Where were we? Oh yes," Greg said eager to continue. "That's what I was thinking too. That something happened to change their environment. If the reptiles sensed that their habitat could not support them, they may have felt forced to migrate."

"Tomorrow I'll try to determine if something happened to the land that could have disrupted the flow of water to and from Echo Lake," Manny said.

"And I will evaluate if the lake has undergone any changes. The flow of water is key to *how* it happened, and I will figure out if a change *actually* took place," said Irene.

"I would need to study them to see if we truly have a living genus of Plesiosaur. With the information I have now I may be able to tell if Echo Lake is their home. The thought of seeing this prehistoric species alive today is overwhelming. We could watch it feed, learn how it reproduces, the information we could gather is invaluable," Tova said.

"I have something I wanted to bring up," Greg said placing a hand on his journal. "I'd like to take a moment to discuss a possible name for the creature. I'm jumping ahead, but if we find evidence they are from the Tribol Preserve I'm suggesting the name Tribolmegasaur."

"The Tribol Preserve's great reptile! I think that's perfect. You must be feeling confident they're from Echo Lake," Tova said.

"Calling it 'the creature' allows people to distance themselves from it. Giving the reptile a name will help the world begin to feel more familiar with it and less afraid," Lee said with support.

"That's what I was thinking. Without a proper name the reporters are using words like 'monster'. But of course we first have to be certain they're from the Preserve. I just want to be ready."

"I'm in favor of it. We can call it the Tri-meg or T-meg for ease of reference," Irene said.

Greg liked the sound of the shortened name too. He concluded the discussion with, "Then if we all agree, tomorrow we may be christening the most remarkable new creature in modern times with an identity that would resonate for generations to come."

Seventeen
Confession

Vanessa squirmed as she watched the latest episode of the crime drama, *The Precinct*, on her large screen television. She always loved that show, but ever since she met Sean, the drama made her uncomfortable. She no longer enjoyed it as she used to but kept telling herself that this season had one or two bad shows, and she would get right back into liking it. But she bit her lower lip as she tried to pinpoint exactly what caused the recent shows to disappoint her.

"I need backup now," her favorite character, Armstrong, hollered into his radio. In the next second, a shot rang out, and he collapsed to the asphalt. His gun rested a foot away from his outstretched hand, then his dropped radio transmitter blared, "Where are you? What's going on?"

"Ugh," she said, clicking off the set with her remote.

Earlier that evening on the news, they showed footage of reporters talking anxiously from the side of Ridgefield Road, the one leading to Quarry Head Park. She had driven it many times, but now she wondered if anyone would ever venture into the park for a walk or a jog ever again. The images of another injured officer being rushed to the hospital by ambulance upset her the most.

Where is Sean? As far as she knew, he was safe. The reporter had identified the fallen officer as a man from the state police, but she couldn't help fretting. She thought about calling the station to speak with him, but decided not to. *He'd be too busy to take my call.*

It also crossed her mind that any minute she would hear on the news that they'd discovered Jason mutilated by one of the creatures. If nothing else she wished Sean would call and tell her they had found Jason out of state, alive and running away from his debts.

I need to relax. Anything to push Jason and Sean out of my mind.

She looked over at the folder on the end table. In it sat the paperwork she'd started for an equity line of credit on her home. Looked like she would need the financing to cover the balloon payment coming due on the loan she took out to renovate the store. *Then again, why bother? In another month I may have to sell the store anyway.* Only a slim chance existed that the upcoming holiday season would bring in enough money, and time was running out.

Soothing music always helped her to relax. She searched the playlist on her phone for an old rock ballad by a band she'd faithfully followed since high school. It had a calming beat and somber minor chords; exactly what she needed.

Tilting her head back to rest on the big throw pillow, she took in a deep breath. A low-key scratching sound caused her to sit right back up. She looked out the front window. The branches from the weeping cherry tree brushed against the glass.

What a windy evening.

Deciding she wanted a snack, she left the couch. In the kitchen, she sliced up some apples to eat with her favorite Brie cheese. This time of year, she enjoyed apple picking and thought about calling her sister to see if she'd like to join her on Sunday.

And yet…

Vanessa was lonely.

It didn't help that people she knew tried to fix her up. Last week, an old friend she hadn't seen in almost a year, Michelle, came into her shop. Feeling obliged, Vanessa told her about her breakup with Richard. Michelle immediately offered to give her number to a friend twice Vanessa's age.

She'd forced a smile and said, "No thank you, I'm still getting over my last relationship. I need more time."

Michelle replied cheerfully, "Well, don't wait too long," making her feel even worse.

When Vanessa first started dating, she worried about bringing boyfriends home, concerned her father would be in one of his drunken states. This caused her to wait until college before dating anyone seriously. After all, her dad used to sprawl himself out on the couch, or stumble around the house with bloodshot eyes and slurred speech. When she turned seventeen she asked her mom, "How can you still love Dad after all he's put you through?"

Vanessa'd lost count of all the times her father didn't come home or missed accompanying the family to a social gathering because he was too inebriated to attend, or worse, embarrassing them at holiday gatherings with the extended family by voicing rude comments.

Her mother hadn't answered right away. But then she looked at her with tears in her eyes and said, "Your dad wasn't always like this. I can't leave him just because he needs help. But Vanessa, my life is hard. I want better for you."

Her mom's words stayed with her, and Vanessa vowed to find a man she could depend on. Her attraction for independent, successful men led her into relationships with partners who had money or status but were also indifferent and self-centered. The relationships ultimately ended badly, leaving her feeling inadequate and disrespected.

And lately, every time she thought about being with someone special, the image of Sean Dermott popped up in her mind. This thought came more often after seeing the handsome police chief in the park with his dog.

She was too practical. *No way I'm going to date the police chief. That line of work's much too dangerous. Even in this quiet town, the chief of police is on a bizarre case involving huge prehistoric reptiles.*

Still, I should call him, at least to see how he is. She grinned. She just wanted the excuse to hear his strong voice one more time.

Sean's rugged visage drifted into her mind. She daydreamed of being able to gaze into his eyes, like that moment in the park, without being noticed. When he told her about beating up those bullies it impressed her how he transformed himself. *No one would mess with him now with those muscular arms and broad shoulders...*

Sighing, she turned on the faucet and started filling her electric tea kettle. The clear, pure tone of the doorbell rang out, nearly causing her to spill the water. Who *could that be?* At first, she hoped Sean had come to see her. *Nah. Stop daydreaming and focus on something practical.*

Just ignore it. It's probably someone who's selling something, although it's late for that.

The bell rang again. *Huh? Usually canvassers quit after one ring. Maybe he's persistent.*

Vanessa went to the window and moved the corner of the drape to the side. *Sean! What's he doing here?*

She glanced at the front hall mirror, running her fingers through her hair to style it, and then opened the door. The brisk wind promptly undid her hasty efforts.

He was not wearing his uniform, but instead was dressed in regular clothes: jeans, sweatshirt, and a jacket. All showcased his raw appeal. She looked closer and realized something different about him. He appeared less formal, his expression softer. The same easy-going look she recognized from the park.

"Hi Sean. Is everything all right?"

"Yes. I just wanted to talk with you in person. You must have heard some of the news reports about the park,"

"I have. I've been so worried. Please, come in."

"Thanks," he said, captivating her with a smile. "Do you mind if we sit for a minute?"

"No. Not at all."

She led the way to her living room where they sat next to each other on the couch.

"I didn't mean to alarm you by coming by unannounced. There are news reports about another officer being attacked."

"I know. I've seen them." Her heart beat a little faster. She worried he'd come to tell her something bad about Jason.

"I came to let you know that we have no new evidence to suggest Jason was hurt in the park."

"Have you found out anything new about how he disappeared?"

"Not really. It looks like he's had financial problems for many years so we're focusing on that and trying to talk with anyone who may have information."

Vanessa tried to remember if she'd forgotten to tell Sean anything else about her friend that could help find him. Nothing came to mind. They spoke more about Jason's success as a coach. She appreciating being able to talk about his good qualities with Sean.

During a moment of awkward silence, Sean glanced around the room. "I probably should be going."

She sensed hesitation in his voice. Her heart skipping a beat, she replied, "If you're not in a hurry, I was just about to make tea when you arrived. I could make you a cup before you go back into the cold."

The gusty wind whipped the tree against her front window again. "Well, it is pretty cold out tonight," he said with a playful grin. "If it's not any trouble, I'd like that. Can I help?"

"No. I'll be right back."

Vanessa went to the kitchen. She appreciated his gesture to assist but wanted a moment to compose herself.

She returned with the warm beverages and shared the snack she'd prepared for herself earlier. Sean complimented her on her beautifully decorated home. Owning the shop gave her a good reason to discover new home décor items and select from a wide variety of goods to sell.

Behind her couch she had a relatively thin glass table with a collection of different colored glass vases and two painted ceramic doves. She placed her favorite decorative candles in every room. The living room wall opposite the television had a set of three paintings of landscapes in matching frames. Her spirits lifted because he'd noticed.

They spoke for over an hour getting to know each other better. Before he left, Sean confessed that he could've have called with the update, but that he came by because he wanted to see her. She was flattered. The more they spoke, the more attractive she found him.

Before he stepped into the cold windy air, he asked if he could call her for a proper date.

She took a moment, just to tease him because she knew immediately what she'd say. Then she smiled and whispered, "Yes."

Eighteen
Underground

When Greg woke, he sighed, finding himself alone in bed. His wife probably hadn't slept last night, and he could picture her downstairs, dressed in her robe, on her stool in the kitchen right next to the island counter. This seat became her favorite waiting spot when their two teenage sons stayed out late with their friends.

Perched on the landing, he spotted the light down below. Ready to explore Echo Lake, he rushed to get dressed and threw on the first items of clothing he could find: a worn out blue sweatshirt, plus his favorite jeans. He hurried downstairs where the smell of coffee greeted him.

Judy looked up from her laptop. She had dark circles under her eyes.

"Are you okay?" he asked.

"No. I was up nearly all night. I woke up at two, then three-thirty. At five, I gave up, so I decided to come downstairs and do some work."

Her job as an account manager for an international clothing company allowed her to handle her work from home or the office. "I made some coffee."

He poured himself a cup and offered to make breakfast. While he cooked the eggs, she asked, "Are you sure you should go?"

"The only chance I have of saving the reptiles is finding their original home. We have to at least try."

"What about your safety? Can't somebody else do it?"

"You don't have to worry about my safety. There'll be armed policemen and the police chief himself. Plus, Sean's insisting that we all wear bulletproof vests."

"I still worry."

As he glanced at his wife, he vividly recalled several incidents during their marriage where he had gotten injured on a project. He'd twisted his ankle during a reptile field study in upstate New York when he accidentally stepped into a groundhog hole. He'd also earned fifteen stitches in his left arm when he attempted to extract a five-foot red racer snake from barbed wire during an expedition in the Mojave Desert.

"I know," he responded.

She took in a deep breath as he served up the scrambled eggs and toast. "When you're done with your expedition, give me a call right away."

"I promise. You're okay with me going? You're not mad?"

"No. I'm not mad. I've seen you do some pretty dangerous things, but this time you've outdone yourself."

Greg laughed. He admired her for supporting him. When they first met, he did not hide that he liked to work outdoors. He told her he wanted to do hands-on research in the natural environment of whatever reptile or amphibian he studied, not just lecture in front of a classroom.

One night they went camping and got caught in a pop-up rain storm. Instead of packing and going home they huddled together inside the tent for warmth. He could feel how cold Judy's hands and feet were, but she told him the best part of her life was having these adventures with him. In the morning, even without a ring, he asked her to marry him. She said yes.

After breakfast he hurried down to the basement. There he filled a backpack with a lightweight floodlight style flashlight, a smaller pen flashlight, binoculars, a brush to lightly sweep debris off rocks, a first aid kit, plastic bags, water proof gloves, a small trowel, and some paper towels. He slipped a water bottle into the holder on the outside of the sack and a granola bar in the small front zipper pouch.

Next, he took his favorite Swiss Army knife, one that a colleague gave him on his fiftieth birthday, and put it into his back pocket. He also planned to carry his high-quality zoom lens camera in a special carry case with a long strap for over his shoulder.

Judy waited for him at the front door holding his warm jacket. They hugged and kissed goodbye. Since he could still see the look of worry in her eyes, he wanted to lighten the mood. "Tonight, we'll heat up the leftover chicken casserole. Hopefully I'll have some good news."

"I can't believe you're thinking about food at a time like this. Get going," she said with a smile, pushing him gently out the door. "I love you."

He arrived at the station, and the officer at the desk escorted him to where Irene, Sean, and three Wilton police officers, Ann, Doug, and Ron, waited. Sean had a dreamy look on his face, one that wouldn't go away. Pleased to see him in good spirits, Greg grinned.

Within minutes, Tova and Manny arrived and introduced

themselves to the officers. Mike was the last to show, carrying two long black cases that commanded everyone's attention.

"Good morning, Mike. Are those the guns you mentioned?" Sean asked.

"Yes. Two tranquilizer guns. I've loaded the darts with the etorphine. When used properly, the drug should subdue the reptiles."

"Let me take a look," Sean said.

Mike opened the latches and withdrew a weapon that resembled an air rifle. Three filled projectile syringes lay fastened into the case.

Greg watched Sean and his officers pass the guns around. They looked fascinated, like kids showing off an autographed baseball. Mike explained how the tranquilizer guns worked.

Everyone then looked at Sean for instructions. He began to talk through his plans, spreading out the map of the Tribol Preserve on the large table. Greg and the others stood around it and examined the pencil drawing of the path they would take up to Echo Lake.

"I'll run tests on the earth and rocks from around the water," Irene said. "I'll also try to gauge whether the lake has been receding or has gone through some other major change. I could do much more testing if I took a boat out onto the water, but for now this will have to do."

Lee held up a pair of binoculars as she spoke. "We all have these. We'll have to keep looking for any signs that the reptiles live there, like long rows of flattened undergrowth and sloughed off reptile skin."

Everyone fell quiet.

"Time to go," he said. "You all can follow me to Whitmere Road."

One by one the vehicles left the station with Sean in the lead. On the way they drove past Wilton's town center, then down a road with stately colonial homes on both sides of the street. The last few miles of the twenty-minute car ride, only forest could be seen outside their car windows.

Although the Tribol Preserve shared a border with Quarry Head Park, the properties had very distinct features and served different purposes. For a leisurely stroll or jog in spacious conditions, the park was ideally suited, whereas the Tribol Preserve functioned as a natural conservation zone with little human interference. No foot-trodden paths or routinely cleared trails existed there. A small wooden sign with the words, "Tribol Preserve" stood amongst the weeds—barely visible. Having led the procession, Sean parked his cruiser on the side of the road and the others followed suit.

Echo Lake sat roughly in the middle of the two-hundred-acre plot of land, requiring a lengthy walk through the bushy forest floor. Compared to the vibrant colors Quarry Head Park displayed in the peak of autumn, the Tribol Preserve appeared to double the breathtaking chromaticity. The hillier land weaved together a canvas of red, yellow, orange, and golden-brown hues.

Meeting up with the team, Sean arranged for Officers Hendricks and Ravos to remain on standby near the entrance in case of emergency. The exploration commenced with Sean and Ann leading the group into the woods with the two Wilton Police officers, Doug and Ron, bringing up the rear. In the middle of the pack, Greg and the other scientists stayed together along with two videographers Sean requested, who frequently worked for the police: Matt and Ian.

Manny breathed heavily after about twenty minutes of hiking.

"You okay, Manny?" Greg whispered when he observed him taking a handkerchief from his jacket pocket to wipe the sweat from his forehead.

"I'm fine. I still jog three miles every day."

"Sounds like a dedicated regimen to me."

Along the way, Matt and Ian captured vivid images of the excursion. Greg continued to scan all around them, searching for any clues, with the four police officers close by. The wind shook the branches, sounding just close enough to the hissing of a reptile to turn heads.

"Just the wind," he said.

Eventually, the trees parted to reveal the soothing mirror-like surface of Echo Lake. The group rested near the shoreline, gazes firmly fixed on the welcoming spectacle of dark blue water starkly contrasting with the rows of evergreens and deciduous trees. Thankfully it was autumn, Greg was spared the torture of buzzing insects and enjoyed the invigorating cool breeze. In some areas, rock ledges soared above the ground, covered by scraggly vegetation such as lichen and moss. Patches of cranberry bushes studded with deep red fruit dotted the area.

Irene walked near the edge of the lake in her waterproof hiking boots. "From what I can see, it doesn't look like the shoreline is receding. If it was, we would see more exposed rocks and dead plants where the shoreline regressed. If there was a change to the flow of water, I don't see it yet."

Manny carefully bent to fill a large vial with sand from the lake shore. He told Irene, "I'll continue looking for surface runoff and significant changes to the topography."

As the scientists compared notes, Greg overheard snatches of the conversations between Sean and the police officers. After a little time passed, Sean waved his hands above his head and announced, "We haven't found any evidence of the reptiles yet, so let's divide into groups and spread out."

Greg tilted his head toward Sean.

"Now..." he called, "we should have two groups. Tova, Manny, and Lee, go with Doug and Ron. I'll have Ian go with you to film. The rest of you will be with Ann and me."

Everyone shuffled into position.

"Doug," Sean continued, "You lead this group, and meet us back here in an hour. Check in periodically, anything important, you radio me right away."

"Yes, Chief."

"Let's go!" Sean called out as the two groups parted.

Greg joined Sean's team, and they took the counter-clockwise direction. After walking for about ten minutes, Greg spotted a few cliffs overlooking the edge of the water. Along the shoreline these rock ledges, composed of flat shelves, interspersed among huge boulders.

"Sean, is it okay if we stop for a moment in this area?" he asked.

After Sean nodded his agreement, Greg stood at the edge of the lake, the water lapping at his boots. Comfortable in this natural environment, he checked out one particularly flat shelf of rock, imagining the creatures lying on the sun-kissed shore or basking on the warmed granite.

Climbing the short cliffs, he searched for any sign of them, hoping to see just a shred of sloughed-off scaly skin. The rough surfaces of the boulders were perfect for that very purpose. He reached into his bag for his larger flashlight and illuminated the dark crevasses between the ledges.

"You okay?" Mike shouted up at him, only six feet down below.

"Yeah, just looking," Greg called down.

He squinted into one of the openings, astonished to see no reflection of light at the other end yet no end to the bright beam—it kept going. The passage into the area between the rocks looked large enough for him to clamber into, so why not?

"You going in?" Mike yelled.

"Just a bit. There may be some reptile skin down there."

"Careful."

Hearing Mike call out to the others to converge upon this spot,

Greg held his breath as he crouched inside the opening. The dirt floor descended to water level. With the aid of his flashlight his vision slowly adjusted to the increasing darkness. A chill ran down his spine as he navigated the irregular assortment of rocks in his path, walking hunched over as he entered further in.

Surrounded by pitch black, he held the flashlight in front of him and discovered that the passage continued even further, possibly below ground level.

Wow! Greg was excited by the depth of the space but at the same time overcome by apprehension and a strong sense of danger. What if this tunnel collapsed? What if it widened and one of these creatures was lurking around the corner, waiting with its jaws open? He wanted to return to the surface and alert everyone, yet… his curiosity was stronger than his fear, and he refused to turn back.

With only the narrow flashlight beam he could only get certain glimpses of the area. The floor flattened, with jagged rocks scattered about. The ample room within allowed him to stand straight. He arced his flashlight above his head and realized he stood in an underground chamber about ten feet high and ten feet wide. The air inside smelled musty and damp, but he could breathe easily enough.

The reptiles could not use this passage. It narrowed to only a few feet along the way—the creatures could never fit. Despite this, the discovery thrilled him, and he wondered if any geologists who had previously mapped out the lake knew about these caves in the layers of sediment. He felt an urge to radio Manny, to inform him of this discovery.

Cut off from the outside world, he started to feel foolish that he he'd so easily allowed himself to be separated from his group, even for a few minutes. His heart rate quickened. *Time to get out!*

The ledge underneath his feet crumbled. "Hey!" he shrieked. In a panic, he clutched at the walls of rock in a mad scramble.

Fear throttled him as he fell into a sickening descent. His flashlight dropped out of his right hand, smashed against the rocky surface then disappeared with a splash.

His feet protested as he landed on some irregular surface, leaving him dizzy and shaken. The backpack helped cushion his fall. The camera, still in its bag, slammed so hard to the ground it bounced.

He could barely see in the dim light, but he could feel the scratches and bruises on his face, chest, knees, and hands. The tips of his fingers were raw from scraping against the rock at breakneck speed. He wiggled them to make sure nothing was broken, but they hurt like hell.

Not yet ready to stand, he took off his backpack and camera. On all fours he looked down and gasped. A few feet away was a large drop. Beyond that, a luminescent surface of what appeared to be water. Trembling all over, he forced himself to pull out a loose rock from the wall and to throw it into the opening. A splash. *Definitely water.*

Somehow the air felt fresher, as if he were standing outside again.

How? Where am I?

"Greg!" Mike's voice echoed through the passageway above. It sounded distant, but Greg embraced it as a way out from danger.

"Here!"

"Are you all right? I can hardly hear you."

"I'm okay, but I can't climb out by myself. The wall's collapsed."

"Stay there, Greg! Sean's coming to help you."

Greg took in a deep, relieved breath. He stayed still but kept listening for any further sounds that might offer him clues as to where he'd ended up. As he focused, he became aware of the sound of rushing water. Off in the distance, a faint glow of light near a rocky ledge enabled him to see a waterfall.

His jaw dropped with the realization: *This is an underground lake.*

"I'm coming," Sean shouted.

"Careful! The ground isn't stable. It crumbled beneath me."

"Got it!"

Cringing from the pain of his many scrapes and bruises, Greg slowly stood. With caution, he put on his pack and slung the camera bag over his shoulder. A great swath of brightness circled him before settling above his head.

A closer scrabble of rock made Greg react. "I'm down here!"

The flashing radiance created by Sean's high-powered flashlight, enabled Greg to see more of his surroundings. Creamy white stalactites hung from the ceiling of the cave, approximately twenty feet above. He marveled at the natural world that had for so long been hidden from man.

With help on the way, he felt brave enough to gaze at the lake several feet below him. Bursts of color just beneath the water's surface surprised and delighted him. Glowing pink fish streaming together in a wave-like pattern flashed before his eyes. Seconds later, he delighted in viewing a school of bioluminescent minnow-size fish, lit in blue.

The sound of shuffling feet neared. Greg wanted to take pictures, but he could hear the tinkling of broken glass shards. Sean's floodlight swung around, flashing on the water.

"Hold the light there," he whispered. What Greg saw took his breath away.

Sean had reached the point where the ground crumbled and stopped. "Are you all right?"

"Yes. Yes. Shine the light down here but to your left if you can."

He swerved his flashlight, projecting a beam past Greg. Light penetrated the water. Greg's heart pounded at what he saw.

"Is that one of them?" Sean asked.

"Yes. They must be down here." Somehow it made sense to Greg that these exotic creatures had an equally exotic home.

For a moment he stared at Sean, both frozen in time.

"Grab this rope. I have to get you out of there. Are you hurt?"

"I fell, but I can use the rope if you help pull me up." Greg grabbed the end of the cord, exerting his feet onto any foothold surrendered by the rock walls.

With some effort Sean pulled him quickly to safety on the higher ledge. He carried Greg's camera bag and supplies while they made their way back to the opening in the jagged hill alongside Echo Lake.

The second they appeared outside the tunnel, the rest of their group ran over.

"What happened? Are you hurt?" Ann asked Greg as Mike and Irene voiced their concerns too.

Dirt covered Greg, and he had fresh scratches. Some of the wounds bled but nothing deep enough to require stitches. Sean had blood trickling down his temple from a minor cut where he'd misjudged the height of the tunnel roof.

"Nothing serious. I can't believe what's in there. We have an underground lake." Greg clasped his hands together. "And best of all—it's the reptiles' home."

"Yeah," Sean said. "I saw it, too."

Greg detailed his story as everyone listened.

"How big is this underground lake? What did you see?" Irene asked.

"At least as big as Echo Lake, but I can't be sure. It may be much bigger."

"You actually saw one?"

"Wow," Ann whispered.

"That's amazing," Mike said. "Now we know the name you proposed, Tribolmegasaur, is appropriate."

"Tribolmegasaur? You know, I'd been thinking we should give it a name. I like it," Sean said.

"Thanks," Greg said. "Hey! We have to tell the others."

"I messaged them. They're on their way back. Greg, you're scratched up pretty good. Would you like me to have an officer drive you to the hospital?"

"No. No. It's nothing, really. But it looks like you banged your head. Are you all right?" Greg also noticed Sean's left eye looked red.

"Yes," he said touching his head. "It happened in the tunnel. Nothing serious."

He instructed Matt to obtain valuable footage of the hidden environment.

Meanwhile Irene offered her assessment of the situation. "It's possible that the reptiles we've seen in the park have somehow lost access to this underground lake and are looking for a new home."

"I think you're right," Greg said. "An underground lake is such a unique environment—perfect for a creature their size. It would provide protection from the town's development in addition to keeping them hidden. Plus, an underground lake would not freeze, so in winter they would be safe."

"Perhaps the Tri-megs were using underground passages to swim back and forth between Echo Lake and their underground habitat. If the main passage collapsed, some of the Tri-megs may have been in Echo Lake at the time, and they can't get back to their home," Irene said.

Greg retold the story of his discovery when the others joined them.

Irene's fervor mounted as she said, "We need to go out on a boat and explore Echo Lake."

With eyes sparkling, Tova added, "This could be the discovery of a major network of underground channels. This could explain how millions of years ago, these reptiles arrived here from the ocean. Maybe we will even find passages to the Long Island Sound."

"Yes, we can look into that much later," Irene said, her forehead wrinkled. "First we have to figure out why the Tri-megs are leaving this area."

"That's right. I still don't understand why they wouldn't stay here, close to the lake," Sean said.

"I'm not sure. Some animals just need very unique environments to survive. This situation reminds me of the Bracken Bat Cave in Texas. The cave is so specific to the bats' needs that the area is now protected by a conservation group and the city of San Antonio.

Similarly, these Tri-megs may be so desperate to find their way back to the underground lake they may be looking for another passageway or even another underground lake altogether," Mike said.

"They won't find any lake like that in Quarry Head. The area is mostly ledge," said Manny.

"We have to find a way to get them home, but will we be able to safely explore Echo Lake?" Lee asked.

Everyone looked at Sean who said, "I'm going to have to speak with Frank. I was told he's starting the hunt in Quarry Head Park today. We may be too late."

Nineteen
Protesting

With everyone safely out of the Tribol Preserve, Sean hurried to his cruiser to call Frank. His eyes stung. Wearing the contacts affected his depth perception in the dark tunnel causing him to bang his head. He removed the lenses knowing he'd have to wait a while for his eyes to clear up.

Dried blood caked on his forehead. Shooting pain emanated from the cut on his head. Using an antiseptic wipe from the first aid kit he hurried to clean the wound. On the drive back to the station he dialed Frank's number.

The colonel answered with an icy tone, "What is it?"

"Colonel, this morning we went into the Tribol Preserve to find proof that…"

"What the hell were you doing in the Tribol Preserve?"

"We found their home. Now we can…"

"I don't have time for this. I told you to stay out of there!" Frank's angry voice reached a crescendo that made Sean cringe.

"The reptiles are from an underground lake. If we return them there, this crisis can be over."

"I don't know anything about an underground lake."

"Listen. We have to discuss this. I need to see you now."

"I'm heading to the park. You had your chance, and you failed. I won't make the same mistake." The line disconnected.

"Damn!" Sean slammed his fist on top of the dashboard. He pulled into the station and stormed past the front desk officer with an order. "Send Dave to my office."

Before he had his coat off, Dave walked in. "I need a quick update," Sean said. "We now have proof the creatures are from Echo Lake in the Tribol Preserve. What's the status of the injunction?"

"The information you sent yesterday is in the hands of the Secretary of the Interior, Brandon Cross. I followed up, and he said the case was a top priority, and he'd review it today."

"Good," Sean said, pleased at this news. "The moment you hear something…"

"I'll let you know," Dave said and hurried back to his desk.

A message came in from Wilton officer Tom Rayos, whom Sean had redeployed from the Tribol Preserve to Quarry Head Park figuring his officers would be allowed around the perimeter. Sean took his seat and answered.

"Sean, sorry to be blunt, but you're going to be pissed off by this."

"What now?"

Tom said tersely, "We tried to position ourselves near the Quarry Head parking lot, but Frank's given orders to send us away." There was an uneasy pause. "What do you want us to do?"

Sean stopped himself from vocalizing his disgust. "Don't disobey any orders. See if they'll let you stay on the dirt road leading to the park. Offer to assist with crowd control."

"We can still get a view of the park from there."

"Good. Keep me informed."

Minutes later, Dave paged Sean.

"You have news?" he asked.

"Brandon spoke with Henry Winter, who's the director of the Fish and Wildlife Service. It's a good thing you already sent him the material. They're both in favor of making an interim decision to put these reptiles on the endangered species list until they can get more information."

"That's great news. So, what are we waiting for?" Sean asked, his heart beating rapidly at the positive developments.

"They have another meeting to work out final approval, but Brandon believes it will go in our favor."

"When will we know?"

"I'm not sure. He said if the reptiles are declared endangered he will send us a copy of the federal injunction the minute the paperwork is complete. They told me they usually don't make interim decisions, but they're making an exception in this case."

"Let's hope they move their asses. One more thing. The scientists proposed a name for the creature. They called it a Tribolmegasaur. Offer this name to them." Sean handed Dave a piece of paper with the proper spelling.

Just then, Sean's phone beeped, matching the intensity of events clipping along at a fast pace.

"I'm on it," said Dave as he rose to leave.

Sean nodded Dave out then answered his phone.

"Sean, it's Greg. I need to talk to you."

"What's going on?"

"I'm at the university, and I just heard from a reporter who wanted to ask why we were in the Tribol Preserve."

"How did they know? Did someone from the group call them?"

"I don't think so. He said he's with CLN Connecticut news. They had him combing the area when he saw us driving away from the preserve."

"What did you tell him?"

"Nothing yet, because I wanted to speak with you first. Mary Leeds wants to do a live interview with me at the university. I think it could help. Were you able to reach Frank?"

"We spoke briefly, but nothing's changed."

"If he's hell-bent on killing the Tribolmegasaurs, then we have nothing to lose. Sometimes public pressure or exposing a situation can help."

"What if the public's against us?" Sean asked. The truth was that no matter what the opinion was, citizens had a right to be informed.

"They won't be. Tova's available to do the interview with me. She's confident in her ability to handle the media. I've had some pretty good moments on TV too."

"Okay, go ahead. Thanks for letting me know." There was a click as Greg hung up.

Sean worried how the news report would add to the chaos. To increase public safety, he sent additional officers to guard the entrance to the Tribol Preserve.

The phone buzzed again mere seconds later. "Oh man," Sean groaned. "Yes?"

"Mary Leeds on line one," came over his intercom.

"Put her through," he said, remembering their interviews in the past. *Direct and professional.*

"Hello, Sean? This is Mary Leads from Channel Eight."

"Yes, Mary, I heard you'll be speaking with Dr. Mitchell and Dr. Banet today."

"We're heading to the university now." Her tone grew a little more urgent as she said, "Sean, you're being recorded right now. Is it all right if I ask you some questions?"

"I'm okay with it," he said, not surprised at all.

"Great. Can I get a statement from you on what's happening?"

"We've established that the reptiles' home is in the Tribol Preserve in an underground lake. I'm trying to work with the state's police force to get the creatures safely back there." Sean closed his eyes as he said it.

He could tell the news reporter wasn't easily fooled when she spoke. "My sources are telling me the state police are lining up explosives in Quarry Head, which doesn't sound like a way to help return them. I'll be heading there right after the interview. Will you be there?"

They're lining up explosives? His eyes bugged at the revelation. Taking control of his response, he said, "I'll be down there soon. The state officers have jurisdiction. I've ordered my officers to be available as back-up. They're stationed outside the park."

"Does this mean you agree the reptiles should be killed?"

He made his response firm. "I didn't say I agreed with that."

"You mentioned an underground lake. Is this something that was just discovered? What did it look like?"

"Yes, it was just found by Dr Mitchell. I only saw it for a few moments, and it was dark."

"But the creatures were living there?"

"Yes. That's what we're thinking. Dr Mitchell can tell you more about it then I could."

"Is anything else living there?"

"We could not stay to explore it. Now I'm sorry, but you'll have to excuse me. I have to get back to preparing for my meeting with the colonel."

"Would you like to comment more on what you'll be discussing with him?"

"Not at this time."

"Okay, Sean," she acknowledged with respect in her tone. "You owe me an interview later."

"You got it."

Now that he'd found out Frank was setting up explosives in Quarry Head Park, Sean's concern escalated. He opened a street map of the town and committed an evacuation plan to memory. Then he called Officer Rayos for an update. "Tom, tell me what's going on."

Among numerous pauses, Tom fed updates to Sean. "Frank's here with what looks like his entire force. I spoke to a friend of mine from that department, and he told me they were going to use explosives to force the reptiles out of hiding. Uh… they're going to set off the first round any time now, and we know officers have been searching the area with machine guns, but the reptiles haven't been seen. Umm… there's also a group of protesters. You can probably hear them chanting in the background."

Yes, he could hear the chants over the line. "I can't make out what they're saying."

"Right now, they're saying, 'Nothing dead in Quarry Head'.

They're mostly near us at the top of the dirt road but some are protesting on the side of Ridgefield Road. There are reporters here too."

"I'll be there as soon as I can."

"Yes, Chief. Before you go, I also want you to know there's another group of people here who agree with the plan to kill them. It's possible a fight could break out." Tom's voice was heavy with concern.

"Do we have enough officers to handle the crowd?"

"For now."

"Holler if anything changes."

Time was running out.

Twenty
News

The Channel Eight news crew set up their equipment ready to film the interview with Greg and Tova in the large lecture hall of the Biological Science building. News anchor, Mary Leeds arranged for a rectangular wood table and three comfortable cushioned chairs to be set up on the stage. Mary sat at the head, and Greg and Tova next to each other facing the audience.

Greg had cleaned up from the morning exploration in the Tribol Preserve. He wore new socks and a clean T-shirt bought from the school store, both proudly displaying the husky dog mascot. Mary asked her make-up professional not to use any concealer to cover the scratches and bruises on Greg's face and hands.

Invited to listen to the live interview, students, professors, and university staff filled every padded seat in the room. Some stood outside the door, and others went to their dorm room or campus lounge where they could watch it on television.

The camera zoomed in on Mary Leeds, effectively framing her appearance. Sporting short black hair, high cheekbones, and an engaging smile, she appeared sharp, like she had something important to say. After introducing Greg and Tova with her usual finesse, she gave a brief overview of the extraordinary discovery of the new species and Greg's finding of the underground lake. She turned to him and Tova to express her appreciation for them agreeing to this interview on such short notice. Mary paused while he and Tova politely acknowledged her thanks.

It surprised Greg that she had known any details about their exploration of the Tribol Preserve. In a second he realized she probably spoke with Sean before the interview.

She turned to face Greg and Tova, ready to ask the question everyone wanted to hear the answer to. "Now let's get to the events unfolding at Quarry Head Park. You say you want to save these creatures, or should I call them dinosaurs? What would you tell the citizens of the town who are afraid for their safety?"

Tova replied, "If you don't mind, I'd like to answer that. I would just like to clarify that we do not consider them to be dinosaurs. We believe that they're a genus of the large marine reptiles called Plesiosaurs, and Dr. Mitchell has given them the name Tribolmegasaur."

"So, is it fair to say these Tribolmegasaurs co-existed with the dinosaurs?" Mary's pronunciation of the brand-new species' name sounded a little shaky, but she managed to pull it off.

"Yes, they most likely lived out in the ocean millions of years ago and then adapted to the underground lake in the Tribol Preserve over time," Tova said glancing at Mary and then at the audience.

"I want to learn more about the underground lake and how you discovered it, but answer this for me first. Isn't it incredibly dangerous having these giant reptiles so near to a residential area?" Mary turned to focus on the injuries visible on Greg's face and hands, the camera following her cue to do a zoom-in.

"We don't want them to stay in the park either. We want to help the Tribolmegasaurs get back to their natural habitat. As you can see, the reptiles are adapted to their environment under the surface far better than me." He wanted to make it obvious by a tilt of his head and show of his right scratched-up palm that the creatures did not cause his injuries: the exploration of their habitat did. He knew it worked by the chuckling in the audience. "But seriously, police officers are on patrol to make certain the reptiles do not leave the borders of Quarry Head Park, and there have been no further confrontations. We're going to figure out why they left their environment and attempt to safely return them home."

"And then what? How do you know they would stay there?" Mary asked.

"They need a body of water to live in, and this underground lake has kept them hidden for millions of years. Once we figure out what drove them out and resolve the problem, we believe they would continue to live underground, far away from the park as they always have," Tova said.

"In addition, by installing a very strong electric fence around the preserve, we can ensure public safety," Greg added.

"Well that may be one plan for them, but I'm not certain that is what's happening now."

"I do want to ask about the underground lake. Dr. Mitchell, can you tell us how you accidentally made such an important discovery?"

"Just happened to be very lucky. I was searching for anything that would indicate that the reptiles lived there, when I found the opening to a tunnel under a ledge. I had no idea where it would lead, but it was such an unusual passage I had to see where it would go."

"What did you find?"

Beaming at the memory, Greg knew this response would delight those watching the newscast. "Light green water under a creamy white, domed ceiling with cone-shaped mineral deposits hanging down like icicles. This lake was teeming with brightly colored bioluminescent fish. I also saw a waterfall surrounded by golden light. And then it appeared—the creature gliding effortlessly through the water in its very own sanctuary."

"How could you see? Wasn't it dark underground?"

"Yes, but some parts of the cave must have been receiving refracted light through obscure openings on the surface. We also had high beam flashlights. In addition, there were bioluminescent organisms. When you have thousands of them swimming together, they give off a glow."

"That sounds fascinating," said the news anchor, her face expressing a sense of wonder.

"It was."

The interview ended shortly after. A member of the news crew helped Greg and Tova off with their clip-on microphones. Before they left the stage of the lecture hall they shook hands with the newscaster, who thanked them again.

Tova had to leave to go back to New York. As she and Greg parted ways, she expressed her pleasure at the case they presented for the reptile's preservation. He agreed.

A small crowd of people, who had watched the interview, came up to Greg in the hall asking more questions about his morning discovery and the giant reptiles. He spoke with all of them until he saw a group of his students heading briskly toward the exit of the building. Greg excused himself to run after them. He had a feeling…

"Leon, Zoe, Mia," he called some of their names to get everyone's attention.

All seven of them stopped and turned.

"Where are all of you going?" he asked.

"Hey professor, we're going to join the protest at Quarry Head Park," one of the young men replied.

"Wait a moment." He hurried to catch up to them. "You have a right to protest, but I thought the road to the park was blocked."

"We have some friends down there. We're not allowed near the parking lot, but we can go stand where the dirt road to the entrance begins. We want the reptiles saved so we're going to join them," Leon said

"I understand. I've gone to a few protests myself," he said with a smile. "Promise me you'll stay where the police tell you. I want you all to be safe too."

Greg scanned the group to make sure everyone heard him. The students nodded or murmured in agreement. Satisfied, he returned to his lab to collect some data on his corn snake project. The long day finally caught up with him, and he yawned deeply.

Time to go.

Passing the scenic roads near his home, curiosity got the best of him. He made an impromptu decision to drive by Quarry Head Park.

The state police officers, along with a few members of the local police force, kept the crowd far away from the entrance. Mindful of the slow-moving traffic up ahead, he left his car down a side street and walked to the dirt road that led up to the parking area where police officers issued orders to everyone to stand back. There, many of his students in the crowd chanted and waved signs with slogans in favor of saving the reptiles.

Off in the distance, the sounds of machine guns firing made him sick.

He cringed at a great booming noise followed by a massive plume of gray smoke rising from the forest.

A state trooper ran toward him. The expression in his eyes betrayed his fear as he hollered, "Everyone must leave now!"

Three more state officers sprinted from behind, mobilized to move away the crowd. The deafening explosives caused onlookers to wince and cover their ears.

"Oh my God!" shrieked a young woman. "They're out of the park."

Loud bangs, interspersed with sounds of a car crashing into the ground after being thrashed by one of the giant creatures, startled the crowd as they stood, transfixed by the commotion.

"Move quickly," another police woman ordered.

Greg looked for his students. Relieved, he saw them hurrying to their cars.

"There's one in the parking lot," a man yelled. Pandemonium broke out as people screamed and scattered.

He stayed in place while the crowd rushed past him, unable to avert his glance from the oncoming disturbance. A boom resounded as something sinister and massive struck the back of a parked cruiser. The sedan shook as if rear-ended by an eighteen-wheeler.

Before he could process the development, the vehicle flipped over, smashing against the car next to it. A state trooper fired several rounds of machine gun ammunition into the toppled sedan, ripping apart the metal and shattering several windows.

"Shit!" Fear gripped Greg. *Now* was the time to start running.

Before he could command his quavering legs to take flight, the towering head of a Tribolmegasaur emerged from behind the automobile.

Frantic, he turned and darted toward Ridgefield Road. He reached the street safely. Two middle-aged people, a man and a woman, crouched behind an oak tree as they panted.

He dashed over to them. "Are you okay?"

"No. I think it's going to kill someone," the woman said, pointing a finger in the direction of the commotion.

"We saw the creature," the man said, his eyes bugging. "It got out of the park."

Greg also jerked his head about, fearing for his safety as screaming onlookers passed.

Smoke filled the sky, closely following the thunderous bangs of more explosives. Dirt kicked up from the road as the packed crowd ran in a chaotic melee, seeking vehicles to escape. Breaking through the din of the crowd was the piercing sound of an ambulance.

He stayed as close to the path as he could. A police officer hurried toward him. He recognized him from that morning at the Tribol Preserve.

"Step back! Make room for the ambulance," Doug shouted.

"Doug," Greg pleaded. "Frank has to call off this hunt and stop blasting. He's scaring them out of the park."

"You're damn right. Now get outta here," the officer said and ran off in the direction of the danger.

Twenty-One
Hunt

Just outside the perimeter of Quarry Head Park, Officer Tom Rayos called Sean's direct number. "An officer was killed and two wounded," he declared. "It's a disaster."

"Fuck!" Sean squeezed the phone "I'm on my way there now. What's going on?"

"It's the creatures. They're escaping from the park," Tom shouted into his phone. "We've got to do something."

"I'll be there as soon as I can."

Frank's lost control of the situation.

Sean grabbed his jacket and ran out of his office.

"Sean! Wait," came Dave's voice.

Caught in mid-flight, Sean looked back over his shoulder, "Can't! I've got to get to Quarry Head now."

"But, hold on. You got it!"

"The injunction?"

"Yes. A federal injunction. No blasting, no shooting, nothing that can hurt the new endangered species." Dave's face was flushed with excitement.

"All right. Good job," Sean said.

He grabbed the paperwork out of Dave's hands, threw on his police jacket, then ran to his cruiser. With the red and blue lights flashing and sirens blaring, he raced to Quarry Head. Turning into the entrance, he passed an ambulance speeding out.

He gritted his teeth. Ignoring the guards' frantic attempts to wave him off, Sean drove through the yellow barricade tape up to the entrance, leaving the torn ends flapping in his wake. Smoke from the grenades detonated throughout the park clouded the air. However, with his special vision, unfiltered by his corrective lenses, he could see the outlines of images within the fog.

Rushing into the entrance to look for Frank, Sean heard a desperate call for help from deep within the forest. The source was faint, yet unmistakable. Two men from the state police neared Sean, and before they could say anything, he said, "Someone needs help over there." Then he and the two followed the sound.

Another voice cried out, "Help me!"

Sean found Officer Jones among the roots of a mature oak tree, covered in blood. His jacket and shirt were torn, his bullet-proof vest ripped open. Blood gushed out a large rip where the vest had been slashed. The second officer dropped to his knees, wrapping his jacket around the wound. Sean whipped out his phone and called for another ambulance.

"It's a goddamn massacre in here," exclaimed the other state trooper standing behind them.

"Stay with him until the ambulance comes. I have to get to Frank," Sean said.

"Frank's in Zone 1. Over there."

Before the officer finished the sentence, Sean had started racing toward the sector. "Where's Frank?" he demanded.

"Stay outta here," the officer yelled back, going after Sean at first, but fading behind.

Sean sprinted into the clouds of smoke, tracking down Frank's voice as he barked out orders. In the midst of the man-made fog, the outline of a person materialized. *Frank*. Once he reached him, Sean stared into his wide-open eyes. "You have to stop now!"

"Sean! What the hell are you doing here? Get out."

"You're forcing them to scatter and attack. Officers are getting killed."

"Grab him," Frank shouted to his nearest men.

Sean clenched his fists. "I'm warning you. Stay back."

Pain stabbed through his left arm as it was forcibly yanked behind his back, followed by his right. Grunting with fury, Sean twisted and broke free of their hold, using wrestling techniques he mastered years ago. Under assault, he stumbled, until finally he was smashed into the ground.

Swearing, he scrambled to his feet. He grabbed the larger officer's right arm and spun about, causing his assailant to tumble to the leaf-strewn surface.

"This is going to stop now," he yelled at the colonel. "I have a federal injunction. You're illegally hunting an endangered species."

"What the hell did you say?" An irate Frank put up his right hand, signaling to his fellow officers to cease their confrontation.

"They were given protection under the law an hour ago," Sean said, in between ragged breaths. He reached into his pocket for the paperwork and thrust them at Frank.

From the way his eyes bulged as he read them, Sean knew he

had him. *Frank was one stubborn guy, but he wasn't going to disobey a direct order from a federal agency.*

Spewing expletives, Frank continued to scan the documents. Shaking his head in disgust, he refolded the papers along their crease lines and put them into his breast pocket.

"You're making a big mistake," he snarled before radioing his officers. Using a clear, measured voice, he announced, "We're under federal order to ceasefire. The reptiles are on the endangered species list effective immediately. I repeat, cease fire. Return to the perimeter and guard it as per the previous plan."

His message delivered, he turned to Sean with a steely glare. "I'll get you for this," he growled, so close to Sean the colonel's spit sprinkled his face. "Quarry Head is still under my jurisdiction. Now, out of my way."

As Frank stormed by, Sean stood straight, maintaining eye contact. He ignored the blood trickling from his bottom lip, scratched during the tackle.

When the colonel left, Sean drew in a deep breath, then radioed his small crew on crowd control duty by the main road. "Stay on patrol outside the parking lot."

The clouds of dirt raised by the explosions settled. Observing with unaided vision how the golden yellow, orange and red hues of the autumn leaves were all tinted various shades of green and his dark blue uniform a deep shade of violet, he sighed.

Hastening to his cruiser, he brushed the dirt off his clothes. Retrieving a bottle of water from his car, he stood outside and splashed some on his face and hands to get clean. He tended to the cut on his lower lip with an antiseptic wipe barely noticing the sting it triggered.

Driving in a laboriously slow, zigzag motion out of the lot amidst the other police cruisers, he saw Greg waving up ahead. He pulled over and powered down the window. "You okay?"

"I'm fine," Greg said. "I had some students come and protest. I wanted to see that they were safe. Once the blasting stopped, the Tri-megs must have gone back into the forest. What happened? Why'd they stop the hunt?"

Sean leaned back against his seat and raised his left eyebrow, allowing himself a moment of pride. "I bought us some extra time."

Twenty-Two
ROV

Greg could see the worried look on Lee's face as she entered his classroom. At nine fifteen a.m., the chatter of students filled the hallways as they strolled to their first class of the day.

"Greg, is this crisis affecting your... you know," she asked hesitantly, jerking her head to the professor's desk.

"Not really. I still have to arrange for someone to teach the classes I'm missing. I have a teaching assistant who can do it when it doesn't interfere with her schedule, and there's a list of guest speakers I can call on. But the university is, in fact, excited about all the publicity. Their name's been mentioned in the news several times due to my affiliation with them."

"Good."

"Of course, they're fascinated with the possibility of new discoveries on the prehistoric species. They're just being cautious and, uh, hopeful that the progress can continue."

Lee shuddered. "An officer died yesterday. I never thought..."

"That we would be involved in something that would be so dangerous?"

Lee nodded sadly.

"That's our job, though," Greg said, "to help prevent further deaths."

Just then, Mike walked in. "Damn right," he said, his face twisting into a scowl. "Greg, what about your friends who live down the block from Quarry Head? Are they all right?"

"Yes," Greg said with a frown. "I've called them, and everyone is okay."

Lee shook her head. "I hope we can figure out a way to solve this without anyone else getting hurt. We have no idea how many Tribolmegasuars there are, and with all the disturbance yesterday they may try to leave the area."

"Frank acted on his own without any knowledge of how the Tri-megs would respond. We can do better than that."

"I know, I know," she said. "It's a huge responsibility."

"That it is. I know we're up for the challenge," Mike said.

Just then, Greg's cell phone rang. "Hold on to that thought," he said and answered. "Hello?"

"Hi, Greg. Sean here."

"Hello, Sean. We've just started to work on the evidence we compiled yesterday." Then Greg's tone grew somber as he said, "Any word on the injured officers?"

"Fortunately, I'm hearing that everyone will be okay. The state funeral will be taking place this weekend for the man that was killed."

"Can I attend?" Greg asked. Overhearing him, Mike and Lee nodded. Just then, Manny and Tova walked into the room.

"Of course," Sean said over the phone, his voice full of emotion. "It's open to everyone."

"Send me details when you have them."

"I will."

"That was genius of you to appeal to the FWS. None of us thought of that, and we've worked with them before." Greg chuckled.

"Thanks. So, have you come up with anything new yet?"

"We're going over everything now."

"Good, listen, Frank scheduled a meeting here at three this afternoon. That time good for you?"

"Hold on one second," Greg said to Sean and then quickly asked everyone if they could make it.

Lee and Mike eagerly nodded yes, and Tova and Manny indicated they would try to change their schedule to attend.

"Most of us will be there," Greg replied.

"Good," Sean said. "Do you need any information from me, or…" His voice deepened.

"No. It's okay. We're going to go over the scientific facts from our expedition yesterday and write up a detailed plan. The reptiles have given us a number of opportunities to learn about them, and we've done more research to build on what we saw."

"Frank has to consider your input because of the federal injunction."

"Well, we'll make sure everything is airtight this time."

"You do that," Sean said. There was a click as the line was disconnected.

He and the other scientists in the room looked at one another with expressions both weary and resolute. Time to get to work.

"Has anyone heard from Irene?" Mike asked. "It's getting late."

"She rang last night. She should be in any minute now," Lee

said.

"Do you know what she's doing?"

"Yes, she wanted to see how deeply they're blasting for the Route 7 road construction project which is close to the Tribol Preserve," said Lee. "She suspects it may have disrupted an underground water feed, perhaps preventing access to the underground lake and scaring the Tri-megs away from the area."

"An underground lake like the one you discovered is extremely rare," Mike said. "Somehow it's getting enough air to support life. Probably from obscure entrance ways like the one you came across."

"What this means is if we can't find the connection to the underground lake the reptiles will most likely die unless we can create one; and that's practically impossible. There's really no chance of them finding another underground lake nearby," Greg said.

"Unfortunately, I think you're right."

Heads turned as Irene arrived, out of breath. "Sorry I'm late. I was looking into the highway expansion project in Wilton. It's close to the Norwalk River, which could feed into Echo Lake underground. I don't know if they're blasting deep enough to change the course of the water flowing to and from it, but it's a possibility."

"Is there any way we can find out?" Greg asked, eager to begin to formulate a plan of action.

"We need a remotely operated underwater vehicle," Irene replied. "It can be directed to areas in Echo Lake that could be unsafe for divers to explore. If we're right, and there's something preventing the Tri-megs from returning to their habitat, the ROV will enable us to figure out what it is."

"We're familiar with ROVs from our work in the Gulf during the BP disaster," Lee said, looking at Greg.

"Yes, but we didn't operate them," he replied.

"There are technicians trained on that equipment, and I've operated one before. It's the best way to explore underwater," Irene said.

"Excellent," he said, nodding.

"Should we suggest a name for the underground lake? I was thinking we should wait to see how they're connected to be certain they're two separate bodies of water," Lee said.

"Yes. I agree. Let's wait 'til we find the connection and see if they're two distinctly separate bodies of water or connected together as one ecosystem," Irene said.

Greg and the others agreed.

"I have to tell you, I'm fascinated by the glow of light you described yesterday when you came out of the cave," Manny said. "I was wondering about the name of the preserve, how Tribol is such an unusual name. At first, I thought it was a variation of the spelling of the word *tribal*, and the land was being recognized as a site long settled by Indian tribes. But, now I'm questioning if the name refers to some sort of *tribol*uminescent activity. *Light* caused by *friction*."

"Ah," murmured Greg at the clever deduction.

"Yes. That's true." Tova smiled. "It sounds like the fish you saw are bioluminescent. But we have to get in there before we can say for sure."

Irene bobbed her head. "Some of our deep-sea animals like the angler fish or the gulper eel are bioluminescent. The underground lake is almost void of light like in the depths of our oceans so I bet you're right."

"Do you think the lake's always been there?" Lee asked.

"Not necessarily." Manny adjusted his glasses. "This underground lake is truly an amazing phenomenon. Water could have eroded a softer layer of earth under the rock ledges, thus forming a separate lake over time. Or, it could be an extension of Echo Lake, but under the surface as the water in it collected when it reached a resilient layer."

Tova pursed her lips before she said, "Interesting. If there are underground water feeds leading to the Long Island Sound and out to the Atlantic Ocean, that could explain how a Plesiosaur could have survived in these hidden channels. You know, they weren't exclusively a salt water species. Remains have been found in freshwater areas too. It's also possible that the Tri-meg is a genus of a Mosasaur, the marine reptile snakes descended from. I wondered because of its snake-like movement. Maybe it has a double hinged jaw like a snake."

There was a jumble of voices then as all five scientists, including Greg and except for Irene, vocalized his or her opinion.

She chuckled as she held up her hands to get their attention. "Look, everyone. This is a very fascinating academic debate, but we have a job to do, and we don't have much time."

"Right, right," Greg agreed.

Mike spoke. "Since there are so many of these reptiles, I don't think cages are practical anymore. We're going to have to find a way to attract all of them together and have them freely migrate back to the water."

"Why together?" Irene asked.

"They seem to be staying together naturally in Quarry Head Park, and this could help us keep track of them."

"Let's start working on the proposal. It's almost lunch time," Lee said.

The others looked at the clock on the wall with startled glances then everyone scrambled back to work.

"First, let's make sure they can return to the lake," Greg said.

Twenty-Three
Partners

After a busy morning, Sean picked up a sandwich and soda for a late lunch back in his office. All caught up on his paperwork, he heaved a sigh of relief and sat back in his office chair thinking about the next steps. He pushed aside feelings of despair at the multiple tragedies that struck so many people in the park yesterday. Having the federal authorities step in with their regulatory muscle gave him back feelings of optimism and control. Although Sean knew he was doing the right thing for the public, for the scientists, and for the lost creatures who'd discovered a hostile new world, he couldn't help but revel, maybe just a tiny bit, over Frank's about-face.

While Sean ate, a lingering thought came to him, one that had dwelled at the back of his mind for some days now even before the Trimeg crisis broke out and whammed the once-sleepy town of Wilton like a hurricane passing through. Pushing that aside, he recalled how his synapses had lit on fire when he first saw Vanessa. Taking a chance and showing up at her house the other night allowed them to get to know each other better.

He imagined it startled her to see him standing there. The spirited storm that evening heightened his anticipation. *Is she going to tell me to leave?*

When she opened the door a huge gust of wind messed with her hair. She looked even sexier then he imagined. After they'd covered official business, and she invited him to stay, the conversation turned lighter except when she expressed her concerns for the dangers of his job. The truth was, his job somehow interfered with every serious relationship he had.

That sobering fact pulled him back into the present. He looked over the details of the Kenner case. *We've combed the park extensively several times, and let's face it, you would have been discovered by now. So, that takes us back to day one. Where did you go, and why?* He scratched his head.

At a knock on his door, Sean called out, "Come in."

The door opened, and Ryan stepped inside. "I'm sure you're

busy, but is this a good time to go over the Jason Kenner case?"

"I was actually just thinking about the case myself. Take a seat."

"First, do you know if they set a date for Craig Thomson's funeral?" Ryan's tone had lowered.

Sean grimaced. "It's scheduled for Saturday at 1 p.m. You going?"

"Wouldn't miss it."

"Me neither."

Ryan nodded. "How's Ethan, by the way?"

"Much better. I saw him last night. He had some complications that will keep him in the hospital for a while, but they told him he will be able to walk again."

"That's great news. We've all been praying for him."

"Thanks, I know he appreciates the support. So, what do you have for me?"

"From the phone records, I was able to tie Jason to several establishments known for illegal betting. One of the numbers on the credit card statement was from a bar in Milford, 'Handsome Joe's'."

"So, did you go there?"

"I did. These people are *really* looking for him. He owes their bookie almost eight thousand dollars. I didn't tell them I'm a detective. They offered me a reward if I could bring Jason to them."

"Good job," Sean said, knowing that any money obtained would be turned over to the public treasury. "And you said he owes money to other places?"

"Remember the 'Backstreet Bar 'N Grill' in Hartford?"

"Yah, we have a file on one of the owners because he lives in Wilton. I thought they cleaned it up."

"Not exactly."

"Anything connected to Jason?"

"Just that he's into them for six thousand dollars."

"That's fourteen thousand dollars of debt right there," Sean said. "They must have threatened him, too. Make sure the Milford PD gets this latest information. Also, forward the file to the Hartford chief."

"Got it," Ryan said. "So, I also went back through two years of calls and texts, on a cell phone Jason got rid of. I found a few incoming calls from a bar in South Salem, New York, that had been ordered to close for running illegal betting. Sounds familiar, right? I was able to speak to one of the owners of the place, and I asked if he knew Jason Kenner. At first he said he didn't. As it turns out, he did, but only by his initials, J.K. He told me Jason used to frequent the bar. Rumor was, someone was looking for him so Jason stopped coming by."

"This man owes money all over the place," Sean said, shaking his head. "Keep digging in South Salem. It's not too far from Wilton. See if there's anyone there who knows where he is."

"With so many people looking for him you'd think someone would know something, but so far, every lead is a dead end," Ryan said, sighing.

Just then, the buzzer sounded.

"Yes?" Sean asked after pressing the answer button.

"Sean," came Marcy's cheerful voice, "Colonel Gunner is here for your meeting."

Sean's nerves spiked. "The meeting was supposed to be in twenty minutes."

"He's early, and he has two people with him.

Just like Frank not to mention they'd be coming. What game is he playing now?

"Great," Sean said, careful not to show surprise. "What about Greg and the others?"

"They called, and they said they'll be here in ten minutes."

"Show everyone to the conference room."

"I better go," Ryan said.

"See if there's anything else you can get from the phone records. Old friends or girlfriends he could have tipped off. I'll check with you later."

Sean gathered the relevant files and other paperwork including maps, crude sketches, and police reports for the meeting and headed for the conference room.

Here goes. Another round with Colonel Gunner.

"Chief Sean Dermott," Frank said, gesturing toward the two guests. "I'd like you to meet Ms. Karen Grant from the U.S. Department of the Interior and Mr. Henry Winters of the United States Fish and Wildlife Service."

Before Sean could say a word, Henry shook his hand and said, "Chief Dermott, I almost fell off my seat reading the application. Thank you for bringing this to our attention."

Sean breathed a sigh of relief. "Thank you for coming all this way. Please, call me Sean."

"You got it. Are we ready to get started?" Karen asked.

"Dr. Mitchell and the other scientists will be here in a few minutes. Can I get anyone some water or coffee while we wait?"

"No, thank you," she said. "Perhaps if you can take out a map of Quarry Head Park and the Tribol Preserve we can start getting a feel for the geographical areas we'll be discussing."

"Of course," he said, and removed the single topographic map of both areas from the top of his pile of documents. Unfolding the large sheet, he laid it on the table.

Shortly thereafter, Greg walked in with his academic colleagues.

"Ah. Here they are," Sean said and introduced the team of scientists.

Greg walked around distributing the pamphlets his group had put together. After waiting for him to finish, Sean said, "If it's okay with everyone else, I'd like to turn the meeting over to Greg who will provide more information about the reptiles and how we plan to return them to their habitat and still keep our people safe."

Now familiar with the stations audio visual equipment Greg uploaded his presentation so it could be seen on the pull-down screen. He started with the best photos of the Tribolmegasaurs taken from the videos, most of them partial shots, and then his complete sketches of the reptiles. The two federal officers, Henry and Karen, looked on with rapt fascination as the images of the astonishing species appeared on the screen, one after the other.

"Right now, we have aggressive creatures who have been driven out of their natural habitat and therefore are traumatized," Greg explained in the manner of a professor at ease in his classroom. "We have proof they are from the underground lake in the Tribol Preserve, and they need the warmer temperatures, safety, and food supply from that environment to survive."

"You mentioned that you have a plan to get them back to their home and protect them?" Henry asked, looking stern.

Sean hid a smile. *He's correctly putting his job mandate first.*

"Yes, we do." Irene stood. "We need to understand why they left the underground lake, and this will require the use of some underwater equipment so we can go back to Echo Lake and see if there's something blocking their access because we believe the two bodies of water are connected. If we can figure that out, we can reopen the channel and then draw them back to the lake by using light and heat as it was proven this does attract them. With the temperature continuing to get colder they'll be even more desperate for the warmth."

"Are you saying the Tribolmegasaurs used an underground passage to go back and forth from Echo Lake to their underground habitat?" asked Karen.

"That's right," Lee said. "Probably why no one ever saw them before. They have a unique environment under the surface that satisfies their needs. The access to Echo Lake would let them have an additional source of food nearby. It's also possible that in warm weather they may have come out of the water to bask in the sun. They're large, but they are well camouflaged to match the landscape—they could surface and not be seen."

"Then if Echo Lake has food for them, why do you think they left the Tribol Preserve?" Karen asked.

"An underground lake is very unique. It doesn't freeze like other waters will. The creatures would be protected from the elements. The environment may also be supplying the Tribolmegasuars with a specific diet. They may even have access to a larger body of water from there. Our working theory is they need the underground lake in order to survive, and because their entrance to it is blocked they are searching for a new home. We hope to figure it out during the exploration," Greg said.

"Is everything in this booklet?" Henry asked, holding up the paperwork.

"Yes, all this information is in these packets including what equipment we'll need to explore the lake," Irene said.

"I'm going to go over everything you wrote, but I think we have a plan," Henry said.

"I'll be overseeing this, of course," Frank said.

"You will, with Sean and the Wilton Police as your partners," Henry said, pointing at Frank.

"A… of course," Frank stammered.

"Perfect," Karen said, and as if to drive home the point, she added, "We see this as a job for both of you."

"Understood," he said, his voice devoid of emotion. "We can start preparing for the exploration of Echo Lake immediately."

"Good, I'm here to help," Sean said in his most professional voice, addressing the two federal officials rather than Frank.

"Out of curiosity, I've never heard of a lake that's underground. Do any exist elsewhere in the world?" Frank asked.

"Not many, but there are others," Irene eagerly piped in. "There's one by the Yucatan Peninsula in Mexico that is so spectacular that the Mayan's called it a gift from the gods."

"I had no idea."

She smiled some more and looked at Frank. "If you stay after this meeting, I could show you some of those photos on my laptop."

"That sounds temping," the corners of Frank's mouth twitched up, "but I have urgent matters back at the office." He turned to Sean.

"So, anything else to add?"

"No," said Sean, glancing at Greg, then at Karen.

There was a round of head shakes around the room. "Meeting over, then." Frank declared, as he stood to leave.

They all walked outside the building, Sean muttering "no comment" to the reporters sticking mikes in their direction. Just then, he saw a familiar face: Mary Leeds, the Channel Eight news anchor. She walked straight up to him. A multitude of excuses flashed within his mind, none of which seemed right at the moment. *Here we go.*

Twenty-Four
Eventide

Sean took Scout out for their routine evening walk and fed him dinner before getting ready for his Saturday night date with Vanessa. He made sure his home looked clean, with laundry and dishes put away, just in case she wanted to come back with him. Looking around, he approved of what he saw.

Earlier that year, after their break-up when Emily moved out, he decided to stay in the two-bedroom modern style home in Wilton. He felt that living in the community he served would help him understand the people. He also loved the style of the house. It had big windows and high ceilings, very different from the traditional colonials that dominated the area.

Spending extra time in front of his bathroom mirror Sean examined the cut under his lower lip, and the scratches on the rest of his face from the scuffle with Colonel Gunner's officers, all healing nicely. He put in his contacts before dressing to be certain he chose a designer button down that went well with the dark colored slacks he wanted to wear. On first dates, he enjoyed observing the woman's hair, eyes, and clothes in their truest colors. He did not want to deny himself the pleasure of seeing the color of Vanessa's lips, red being the hue that underwent the most dramatic transformation.

With the temperature dropping at night, he grabbed his stylish wool coat and left the house. Based on what little he'd seen of Vanessa so far, he knew she dressed fashionably. He wanted to look his best, too.

Sean parked in front of her home and walked the lighted path to the front door. She greeted him and asked him to wait inside for a moment.

"You look great," he said, catching the details of her low-cut burgundy blouse, complimented by a tight black skirt.

"You do too," she said with a smile as he helped her with her coat.

As they walked to his car, she asked, "Where are we going?"

"I made a reservation for us at a place called Eventide. Have you ever been there?"

"No, but I've heard of it."

"Ethan suggested it when I saw him earlier this week."

"How is he?"

"Much better. And he's really sounding like his old self, which is amazing because this guy has energy like you wouldn't believe."

"You had some wild times together?"

"Maybe a few. I'm not sure you want to hear about them."

"Hmm, I might." She laughed.

"I'm sure I can think of something to tell you over a glass of wine."

"Oh, I'm sorry, but I never drink."

Something in her voice made him pause. "Oh. How come?"

"I never liked the taste."

His instinct told him she sidestepped her true answer, but he didn't press her.

They pulled into the parking lot next to the restaurant, situated on the water's edge of the Norwalk River. He went over to her side of the car, so they could walk in together. When they stepped into the lobby, he thought she looked pleased with the atmosphere as she looked around. The maître-d led them through a large dining area with polished hardwood floors that gleamed, leading to a double-sided fireplace that showcased crackling logs in the center of the main room. Linen cloths covered the tables, and the chairs had rich burnt red leather upholstery.

He offered Vanessa her choice of seats and pulled out her chair. When they sat, one of the wait staff lit two candles in crystal glasses in the center of the table. Vanessa's hazel eyes teased him with ever-changing hues depending on how the candlelight flickered on her lovely face. Even with the sparkle and the cheer, there was something sad behind her gaze; it made him want to understand why. Perhaps it had something to do with her decision to forsake alcohol.

They dined by a large window with a beautiful view of a tranquil river. If they turned their heads just a bit further left, they could savor the sight of a waterfall, beautifully lit in the evenings by strategically aimed floodlights. In the spring and summer, the restaurant's patrons would likely walk along the paths parallel to the riverbank, but at this time of year, few people ventured out into the cold.

Together, he and Vanessa scanned the menu, discussing main courses. When the waiter arrived, Sean ordered a steak, while Vanessa opted for a chicken dish. After she asked for a ginger ale, Sean ordered a ginger beer, a locally crafted lager that had no alcohol.

"What a beautiful night," she said, looking out the window with wonder.

Sean eyed her gold earring, adorned with tiny gemstones, delicate just like her features. While her attention was still diverted by the scenery, he continued to focus on her.

He was bold and infatuated with this lovely vision seated across from him. He imagined reaching out and holding her warm hand on top of the linen tablecloth. Instead, he asked, "It's a little cold outside, but maybe later you'd like to check out the view from the deck? Or if you're up to it, we could walk by the river?"

"Oh, that would be nice," Vanessa said and leaned back in her plush chair, seeming a little uncertain of what to say next. Just then, the waiter arrived with their drinks.

"I've always liked these ginger beers. Do you want to try it?" he asked placing his hand on the glass ready to pass it over.

"I like them too, but that's okay, you go ahead."

He took a drink, letting the ginger taste perk up his taste buds while he thought of something to say to please her.

She spoke first, however. "I don't mean to bring up something sad, but I saw on the news the funeral for Officer Thomson was held today."

"Yes. It was heartbreaking. His wife and child were there, of course, and were devastated."

"I'm sorry. That must've been terrible."

"It was. I can't imagine what they're going through. They have a lot of support. I think hundreds of people came to the funeral, but I can't imagine anything making them feel better right now."

"I know what you mean. I think they can only start to heal with time, but it will never be the same."

After a moment's poignant silence, he changed the subject. "What did you do today? Were you working at your store?"

"Yes. My busy season is about to start. People begin shopping for Christmas after Halloween these days. It used to be more of a rush after Thanksgiving."

"I felt bad when you told me the store wasn't doing well. Will the holiday season make up for it, though?"

"I really hope so. The truth is if I can't show a profit after December, I'll probably have to try to sell it. I hope it doesn't come to that."

She smiled faintly, but Sean could tell that the prospect troubled her.

146

"I bet it's good to be your own boss," he said, adding pep to his voice. "Once in a while I have to report to the colonel of the state police even though I'm a chief. I like it better when I'm in charge." *That was an understatement.*

"They must be keeping an eye on what's happening in Quarry Head Park. Have you been watching the news?"

Sean knew from the tone of the question that Vanessa probably devoured the broadcasts about the giant reptiles along with everyone else. He understood the fascination. "Not much, but I saw a good interview with Greg."

"Who's Greg?"

"Dr. Greg Mitchell. He's the herpetologist I've been working with from the beginning. Watched most of an interview with him and the team's paleontologist by Mary Leeds at Channel Eight online."

"Oh, yes! I saw bits and pieces of that because they replay it. I watched you give an interview too. You sounded so professional."

Sean enjoyed how her eyes lit up when she told him. "I don't usually like giving interviews, but I know they're important for keeping the public informed."

"The discovery at Quarry Head is all over TV. I mean it's not just on the local stations. Everyone's talking about it. I saw a piece on PBS about underground lakes. What do you think you'll find?"

"I'm hoping we find that the two lakes connect and that the reptiles can return to the underground one. Do you know anything about underground lakes or streams? This one was an unbelievable find."

"I know that underground lakes are formed in caves by aquifers, or springs," she said casually.

Puzzled, he tilted his head. "How'd you know that?"

She laughed. "I didn't, until today. I told you, I've been watching the news."

He chuckled. "That's funny, I feel like I'm getting a crash course in geology."

"Do you ever worry about getting hurt?" Her eyebrows narrowed showing her concern.

Here it is. The topic he wanted to avoid.

Surprised that he felt so emotional as Vanessa's anxious gaze bore into his. He answered too quickly, "No." Then he thought some more and continued, "Well, maybe I should be, but I don't think of it like that."

"What do you mean? How else can you think about it?" she asked softly.

"I've been in some dangerous situations, but in the moment you have to stay focused on what needs to be done. It usually pushes out any fear. Besides, if I always focused on what could go wrong, I couldn't do my job."

Vanessa glanced down. "I didn't mean to sound harsh the other night when I said your job made me uncomfortable. My dad had a self-destructive lifestyle that had my mom worried sick, all the time. I saw how it affected her. I'm just worried you'll get hurt or worse. This is going to sound selfish, but I don't know if I could go through that."

Sean figured that whatever Vanessa's dad did had a big impact on her, however, she wasn't wrong that his job could be dangerous, especially now. He answered her honestly not certain how she would react.

"No one knows what's going to happen, and you're right, being a police chief is probably more dangerous than being a salesman. But I'm aware of the dangers of my job, and I guess it's a risk I'm willing to take."

Vanessa nodded but didn't reply. Uncomfortable with her silence, he continued, "In other ways, I'm a pretty safe bet. I don't smoke, or use drugs. I don't drive drunk, and I'm not looking for wild parties. And I consider myself a romantic." This last one made her laugh.

"So, tell me. I can tell you're diligent about your work, but your friend Ethan still seems to be more of the playboy type. How much partying did you and he do together?"

"A lot, but most of that was back in our training days, and we were serious recruits. I think it helped that we were very competitive. It kept us focused on our work." Sean picked up his beverage. Playfully he asked, "What about you?"

"What *about* me?" she looked at him and blinked.

"You know. Am I going to get a call about you causing trouble at a bar or something?"

"Well, you know I don't drink. So, you're not going to get a phone call like that, but is that what you really think of me?" Her eyes sparkled.

"No. I'm just kidding."

As she shook her head and locked onto his gaze, he was confident enough to ask, "Do you want to go someplace after this? I know a dance club not too far away."

"I'm having a really good time, but I put in a long week of work and I was at my store all day today going over inventory. I'd rather not stay out late. We can go to my place."

Hmm. She's inviting me back to her place. Keep your cool. He leaned back a bit, trying not to sound too eager. "I'd like that."

Their food arrived. "This looks great," she said.

More free-flowing topics ensued, such as, what they both had going on for Thanksgiving. Vanessa told him she would join her sister's family and Sean, being an only child, planned to see his parents. In between bites, he basked in her company. Finally, they finished dinner, with nearly empty china plates resting on the table, a fork and a knife idling side by side on each.

Sean's heart beat slightly faster. It was a beautiful night, and he hoped she still wanted to spend some time outside by the water, and so, after paying the bill he asked her, "Shall we take a walk along the path?"

"I'd like that," she said in a breathless tone. "The moon looks so beautiful."

Sean stared out the large window, and Vanessa's gaze followed. The glowing orb set a backdrop for romance.

After putting on their coats they walked by the slow-moving river, watching nature's reflections in the water, Sean interlaced his fingers with hers. A row of evergreens grew along the far side of the river, and the moon cast just enough light to reflect their silhouettes on the dark blue water.

"Are you warm enough?" He checked his surroundings discreetly: they were now in an enclave of trees that blocked off the views of pretty much anyone on the path or from anyone inside the restaurant.

"It's a bit chilly. But let's stay for a minute," Vanessa said, blowing into her cupped hands for warmth and looking toward the water.

He stood behind her and wrapped his arms around her middle, pulling her close. "Better?" he whispered, near enough she would feel his breath on her ear.

She nodded and leaned her head back onto his chest. Aroused by her perfume, he brushed her hair to the side and gave her a smooth kiss on the nape of her neck. Unable to keep his fingers from prying, he undid the buttons on her coat and slipped his hands inside, to rest them on the soft skin of her waist. He locked his warm fingers together around her mid-section.

"That feels wonderful," she said with a deep breath.

Sean moaned. He hated himself for being a gentleman, halting the movement of his hands just below her breasts. *I could... No. Not now.*

She solved his dilemma. Her head brushing against his cheeks, her eyes closed, she placed her hands underneath her blouse, and lifted his hands up to cup her breasts. He gasped as he felt her nipples, taut and firm through her lacy bra.

Unable to restrain himself, he slid his hand under the fabric to caress her delicate curves just enough to inflame her passion. She moaned with desire, and spun around to hold him, face to face. Placing her hands on either side of his shoulders, she pulled him closer and pressed her lips to his.

"You feel so good," he said.

"You do too," she whispered and stroked his thighs, her fingertips still atop the cotton fabric of his pants.

He lost himself in deep kisses. He reached inside her coat once again to explore her body under her skirt. She held him even tighter. Their hips locked together. Gently, he pressed himself against her, and she gasped.

"Sean, Sean…" She put a hand on his chest.

"Ohh…" he moaned, his eyes still closed. "Ohhh," he said, with more emphasis the second time, shaking himself out of the fog of his arousal. "I know, I know…"

"We should stop now," Vanessa whispered, with heavy breaths. Her voice sounded wistful, as if she never wanted the evening to end.

"Yeah," he said, adjusting his belt, while gazing into her languorous eyes. As he fixed the seam of his jacket, she smiled as she assisted him by re-doing the buttons at the top of his coat.

"That was amazing," he whispered.

"I know." Her expression conveyed lingering desire.

"Well," he said looking down at the well-lit path. "We should be going back."

"Okay," she replied, sounding uncertain.

"You said we should stop," he said with an impish grin.

"Did I say that?" she asked with her bewitching smile.

He kissed her once more, exploring her mouth, but kept his hands above her clothes. Again, he merged with her as one, in spirit. After several moments, he released her.

He knew she would not invite him into her house anymore this evening, not now that they had had a chance to satisfy their lustful desires… at least for now. She locked arms with him and leaned in as they walked back to the parking lot.

He drove her home, looking forward to that goodnight kiss.

Twenty-Five
Water

The next week, heavy thunderstorms caused raging water to swell every river and stream in the towns of Fairfield County, including Wilton. Near the train station, the Mill River foamed with white water. Pounding rain created large puddles over the parking lot, forcing commuters to move their cars. Police officers had to re-direct traffic away from the more isolated residential roads overtaken by the downpour.

Secure from the turbulent questions surrounding the Tribol Preserve and Quarry Head Park, Sean sat in his office. Both areas remained heavily guarded. He thought of the poor patrolmen, dressed in parkas, the rain dripping off the brims of their police hats. Bothered that they were still no closer to knowing what caused the disruption to the giant reptile's habitat, Sean browsed the path of the Norwalk River, which ran nearby Echo Lake and the underground lake online. The entry on the chosen website read:

Originating in Ridgefield, the Norwalk River runs through several towns; Branchville, Georgetown, Wilton and Norwalk. It is joined by the Silvermine River, and then it flows into Norwalk Harbor, itself part of a large body of water called the Long Island Sound, an estuary of the Atlantic Ocean bordered by Long Island, New York to the south, and by the land mass of Connecticut to the north.

With elbows on his desk he rubbed his temples thinking: *and then there are underground rivers and springs, which make the trail much more difficult. How are we ever going to figure out what happened to block their access to the underground lake in the Tribol Preserve?*

Interrupted by the intercom letting him know that his expected visitors, Greg and Irene had arrived, Sean closed the site. Marcy escorted them to his office. Their rain jackets were dripping, their hair tussled by the powerful gusts of wind.

"Hi, Greg, Irene, come in. We're having some storm."

"It's not too bad," Irene said. Even the worst of weather didn't distract her from the tasks at hand. "We have some good news. Our

ROV will be here later this afternoon." Both Irene and Greg helped themselves to a seat in front of Sean's desk.

"That *is* good news," Sean said. He could tell she couldn't wait to talk about the equipment. She began speaking the moment he finished his sentence.

"The machine we're getting has video, lights, and a three-function grabber. It will be linked to a boat by a tether and lowered into the water from an A-frame hoist. Frank has made all the arrangements. He said we should be prepared to explore Echo Lake tomorrow morning. It's so much better working *with* him, not against him. He has access to everything."

"Uh huh," said Sean, not ready to hear Frank being portrayed in such a positive way. Especially since Frank didn't provide him with any information about the equipment arriving.

But Irene continued to praise him, "The colonel handled everything so quickly!"

"I'm sure," Sean said, trying to hide his grimace. "Do you know if the path to the lake is finished?"

"Yes. It's ready, and the equipment's being moved there now," Greg said. "Irene's been in contact with him; that's how we know."

"So, this ROV will help us find the hidden underwater passageways?"

"Yes. It will help us see places that may be unsafe to explore in person. Plus, it will automatically collect useful data like the depth of the water, the clarity, temperature—things we will need to know to give a full assessment of the Tribolmegasaur's environment. If any of the giant reptiles remained in the lake, it's best we stay out of the water," Irene said.

"Well, let's go over our plan for tomorrow then."

And they did.

The following day the rain abated, and at last, the sun shone over the late fall foliage. The preserve could not have looked more inviting. The sunlight danced on the water, and the lake mirrored images of its surrounding forest and rocky ledges. Along the shoreline, the prickly brambles swayed, fiercely protecting the area from intruders.

Echo Lake had never seen a motorized craft breaking the calm of the water's surface. Now, that would change. With the stamp of approval from the state's Department of Environmental Protection, a thirty-foot police boat bobbed alongside the makeshift dock. It was a majestic craft, fortified with a marine grade hull and boasting a deckhouse from which the operator could steer the vessel. Sean took a good look at the underwater vehicle, the ROV. The boxy piece of equipment looked sleek, dangling above the deck from an extended boom secured to the stern.

Seven people made up the crew: Frank, Sean, Greg and his colleagues Irene and Manny, as well as two water police officers, Charles Wilkins and Captain Samuel Berg. Additional officers remained on the shore for backup. Frank had limited the number of scientists who would accompany the crew; however, Mike, Lee, and Tova agreed to meet at the university later that afternoon to discuss the findings.

Frank introduced the officers. "Charles has experience operating the ROV. He spent several years doing hydrographic surveying before joining the force. Sam is our captain. When he heard we were exploring Echo Lake, he volunteered for this assignment."

The captain stepped forward. Unlike the stereotypical image of a captain with a white beard and a white outfit, Sam had short dark hair, maintained a clean-shaven face, and wore the standard blue police uniform, but with a cap specifically labeled "Water Police."

"It's great meeting all of you. I've been following the story since the Tribolmegasaur was discovered, and I just had to be part of this expedition," Sam said.

Sam's assistant, Charles, in a similar uniform, chimed in, "Yes, me too. I've spent most of my career on the ocean, but now I'm really interested in what's in this lake."

Irene gazed at the underwater equipment, her eyes wide. "Yes. We all are. Would it be okay if I take a look at the ROV?"

"Actually, let's all board now," Frank announced.

He appeared eager to start the mission. Sean watched him nimbly stepping onto the boat, then give instructions for the rest of the crew to board. When he gestured the *go ahead* signal, Frank gave him the okay to start the engine.

"Untie the ropes," Frank called to one of his officers on shore. And the boat started to drift away from the dock.

Sam steered the craft through calm waters. When they reached the area closest to where Greg discovered the underground lake, Charles dropped the anchor by pressing the button on the switch panel near his place at the helm. Then he released the ROV. Sean observed with anticipation as the machine disappeared under the surface with a bubbly descent. The device hovered above the rocky bottom, and he joined the crew at the monitor to wait for the debris to clear in front of the ROV's camera. White perch fish, darting away from the robotic intruder, flashed on the screen.

Frank asked Irene, "What should we be looking for?"

She smiled. "That's one advantage of cutting off human access to Echo Lake over the last several years. Since the lake bottom's been untouched by man for so long, we'll be looking for signs of disturbance."

"Such as?" he asked, bending to look at the monitor.

"The clues we'll be looking for are any surfaces scraped clean of algae, boulders, or shelves of rock that look out of place. We may see air bubbles from the underground passageway, plus crushed algae or any vegetation that has been uprooted or compacted together."

"That sounds difficult to find," he said in a voice that made Sean wonder if he was trying not to grumble.

"Don't worry. I'm very familiar with this type of environment," Irene said then commented on the aquatic plant life on the lake bottom. "Here we have some common elodea, or as it's called, *American waterweed.* And here you can see the start of an infestation of Eurasian watermilfoil. See the slender stems and feathering leaves? It's actually quite nice if it doesn't invade so much that it's practically all over the lake."

"There's a catfish," said Manny, pointing to the image of whiskers poking out from behind a rock on the bottom of the lake.

"Yes, the ecosystem seems to be thriving. We'll take some water samples to get readings on the oxygen levels and other conditions," Irene said.

"What does that have to do with finding the passageway?" Frank muttered, frowning.

"All scientific information is inherently valuable and has a purpose, Frank," she asserted. "In fact, we've received numerous requests from state and federal environmental protective and regulatory departments to pass on our findings to them since the ROV gives us a special opportunity to find out more about such a fascinating lake."

"Fine, as long as we focus on finding the hidden entrance."

The ROV moved slowly. Charles controlled the claws on the arms by deftly handling the remote controls. It tore off specimens of algae and other vegetation for research. He collected water and mud samples using its hydraulic pump. Crayfish scurried away from the strange invader.

An hour passed, and some of the crew had resorted to idle banter, except for the three scientists, who continued to stare at the screen and write in their notepads.

"Look, there's a snapping turtle." Greg said.

Irene noted the size of the very large brown creature at the bottom of the screen.

"Hey!" Manny sprang to attention.

Sean thought for sure he'd found a clue.

"What is it?" Greg's voice lifted at the end.

"There's something strange about that ledge over there," Manny said, showing them the exact spot on the screen.

Intrigued, everyone, especially Irene and Greg, drew in closer. Sean stood right behind them to view the image of a descending underwater rock ledge at the edge of the lake, with a pile of rock slabs at the bottom. Sean assumed the scientists understood Manny's enthusiasm. It took him a little longer to recognize that the slabs of broken ledge looked different from the rest because they had smooth, clean surfaces.

"There are air bubbles rising from deeper down there!" Irene pointed to the image.

"Can you get us a closer view?" Greg asked.

Charles used the joystick to redirect the boxy metal machine nearer the scene.

"This rock formation does not look natural," observed Manny. "You can see here that the sheen on the rocks near the bottom is darker, and there are some obvious gouges and deep scrapes on the ledge. These marks definitely could not be caused by fish or other crustaceans in the lake." Then he indicated a wedge between two large shelves. "Also, there is dead plant material trapped in there."

Suddenly, Charles cried out.

"What is it?" shouted Sam.

"I saw something large swimming in the water." He gestured to where he saw it.

"Was it a Tri-meg?" Greg asked as he and everyone in the boat turned to look.

Sean's heart raced. He put his hand over his gun and kept it there ready for action.

"I'm not sure. It went back under the surface."

"Can a Tri-meg knock over the boat?" Frank asked Greg. He rested his fingers on the firearm in his utility belt.

"I don't think so. Even if it were big enough, it would not…"

"There!" Charles motioned to a long brown snake that slithered along the surface of the lake causing miniature ripples in its wake.

"False alarm," Greg said. "That's a Northern Water Snake."

Sean let out a deep breath.

"Phew," exclaimed Greg. "It's one of our larger snakes. Sometimes it's aggressive, but if we ignore it, it should leave us alone."

The four-foot snake swam next to the boat for a few seconds, and then disappeared under the surface.

"All right, back to these rocks," said Manny. "Hold on to this view. Because we're close by the shore where Greg found the underground lake, I believe this could be the connection we're looking for."

"Then we're going to have to move these rocks," Irene said. "It's the only way to find out if this is the passageway for those Tri-megs."

"Are you sure that's the right spot?" Frank asked.

Manny nodded.

"I can rig a small explosive into the pile."

Irene turned to Frank with a startled expression. "You can't just set off an explosion underground."

He opened his mouth to respond, but she touched his arm for a moment. With a softer voice, she added, "The aquatic life could be harmed."

"If you use explosives, you would destabilize other rock ledges on the bottom, causing more damage to the passageway," Manny said.

A flash of annoyance crossed Frank's expression. "Then what do you suggest we do?"

"We have to move the rocks slowly, one at a time," Manny said, looking at Charles. "What is the maximum load the ROV can lift?"

"Anything under two hundred and fifty pounds. But some of the rocks I'm seeing look heavier. You'll need an underwater excavator."

Frank mulled over the request then announced, "I can arrange that."

"If you can get us an excavator I know we'll find the opening," Irene said.

Suddenly, something horrific darted across the screen. Everyone gazing at the monitor gasped.

"What is *that*?" Sean asked.

Now the entire crew stared. Tiny strange creatures flashed by.

"I've never seen anything like that," Greg said.

A group of aquatic animals, both mystifying, and grotesque, came in and out of view. They flitted about like wisps of translucent white gelatin. Shaped like long-bodied starfish, but with *arms* more like human limbs, folded back to align with the gliding motion. These arm-like appendages extended way past their pointy tail.

The triangular head, jutting out on top, had two small sockets for eyes. Its mouth had the shape of a downturned crescent. The ghostly creatures soared through the water like stingrays.

For a few seconds, there was silence.

"What are these things?" Frank scowled, his eyes narrowed.

"Let's not jump to conclusions," Greg said, holding up both arms. "We may have just discovered another new species, along with the Tri-megs."

"There's more?" Sean blurted, incredulous.

The odd person out, Irene, grinned as she watched the mystifying images. "They look like very small Ningens."

"Huh?" he said. "What did you say?"

She pointed to the image on the screen. "They look like tiny Ningens. A Ningen's a mythological creature, but people have claimed to see them in the Antarctic, Pacific, and Atlantic Oceans. There was a story about an ROV getting an image of one, but nowhere near here, and the legend is they're much, much larger."

"Again, we can't verify anything," Greg warned the group. "We'll have to upload this video and study it carefully."

Everyone stopped talking and froze, cocking his or her head as if listening intently. This continued for a few more seconds, then they glanced at one another with startled glances appearing too nervous to say what was on their mind.

Sean volunteered first. "I think I just experienced something odd."

"Me too," admitted Greg. Several of them gazed at Frank. While he appeared ambivalent, he did not reveal his thoughts.

"Okay," declared Irene. "I'll say it. I distinctly felt that something in the lake cried out for help."

The others murmured their agreement.

"Not that it was spoken, though," she said. "More like a wounded animal crying out."

"I felt it too," Greg said. "Very sad, very needy."

Charles jumped in. "I definitely experienced something in my mind. I thought it was from the water, but then…" His voice grew low as he said, "I wasn't hearing anything. It wasn't through my ears… It was telepathic."

"I've never experienced anything like that," Manny said.

"Can you imagine what it will be like to study them?" Greg asked.

The scientists began talking all at once, discussing the strange new animals, the still elusive Tri-megs, and the underground lake.

Frank cleared his throat. "I think we've done what we can for today," he asserted. "It's time to head back. Charles, bring up the ROV."

Sean understood that just because Frank had to work with him it didn't mean Frank would confer with him on every detail. His senior position as an officer of the state gave him more access to personnel and equipment then he had. While they continued to make progress toward finding the creature's home, Sean felt letting Frank take the role of leader made sense for now.

The crew settled as they headed to the shore. The boat touched the small dock, and Charles jumped out and tethered it to the cleats. Greg, Manny, and Irene spoke about going back to the university and meeting up with the other three scientists to discuss their findings.

"Do you think you'll be able to have the excavator here tomorrow?" Sean asked Frank.

"Yes, there's one not too far away in Bridgeport that was being used for bridge repairs. I'll have it brought over."

"Good."

"Not for the people who need the bridge."

Sean nodded, uncertain if Frank was joking. Before he could reply, Frank turned and headed for his vehicle.

Twenty-Six
Panic

After reviewing several files in the familiar comfort of his office, Sean could not help but recall the fresh lake breeze, the swaying motion of the police water craft, and the blips of bizarre aquatic sightings on the modest-sized monitor. Enjoying this quick break, he called Vanessa to confirm their plans for the evening.

Sounding eager to talk she asked about the exploration.

"We made a lot of progress. I'll let you know all about it when I see you, but what if I told you I saw a talking fish?"

"I might say I'm busy tonight," she answered, laughing.

"Okay, this fish wasn't quite talking, but I could hear it."

"Well, what did it say?"

"Umm, I think I'll tell you about it later before you change your mind."

"Smart," she said. "I'll see you at seven."

"Can't wait."

Sean grinned while hanging up. Ryan walked into his office, shaking his head. "I'm sorry Sean. I'm not finding anything that helps us find Jason Kenner. It's like he vanished."

"Nothing else came out of the phone records?"

"When he first moved to Wilton, he called a local Gamblers Anonymous number."

"Did he ever go?"

"They're meeting tomorrow. I can talk to the person in charge. If he went there maybe he confessed that he was thinking of leaving town. That might finally give us a clue. I'll check it out."

Before he could reply, the officer at the front desk paged him with an urgent message.

He snatched up his phone as Ryan quietly stood by. "Go ahead."

"Chief, we have a 9-1-1 from 210 Gray Rocks Road. The homeowner's saying there's a giant reptile in her pond. She gave her name as Betsy Ivanov."

Sean's nerves tightened. Desperate to prevent another major

catastrophe with the Tribolmegasaurs, he resolved to set things right. "I'm on my way."

He knew from his familiarity with the town that Gray Rocks Road ran alongside a reservoir.

Running to his cruiser, Sean retrieved his transmitter and called for Ann and her colleague, Officer Eddie Langer, to follow as back up. She responded immediately. "We're on our way, Chief."

Sean pulled into the half circle driveway of the residence. Inside the open doorway, he saw a woman in a business suit pacing. Apparently, she'd felt nervous and wanted to see them the moment they arrived.

Typical for this location, the four thousand square foot, stately colonial style home had a three-car garage and approximately two acres of land. The leaves and branches that came down in the ferocious storm the day before had not been cleaned up yet. The grounds on the estate looked natural and well-suited for the reptile, but he wondered how it could have left the park despite the tight police patrol on the outskirts.

"I'm Chief Sean Dermott. Can you show me where it is?" Sean said calmly.

"Finally," Mrs. Ivanov exclaimed, hovering between being polite and being unnerved. "I came home from work and saw it in my backyard. It's dangerous! Is anyone else coming?"

Fortunately, Ann and Harris had arrived, pulling up behind his car.

"Actually, my back-up is here. Can you show us where the reptile is?"

The resident seemed somewhat consoled by the addition of the two other officers. "Yes, come through the house. You can see it from the back window."

Sean, Ann, and Harris passed through the front hall to the living room. The marble floor gave way to gleaming hardwood floors—a testament to the skillful blending of nature and country-style living common to the area. Outside, past the patio and the manicured lawn, a natural area with towering evergreens and deciduous trees graced the yard. A small pond sat in the west corner.

"There," said the shaken resident, pointing to the right side of the property.

Sean and his officers peered in that direction. Partially hidden under the water's surface, he saw the long brown mouth of the Tribolmegasaur.

"It's not moving," Ann whispered.

"Good. Let's check it out," Sean replied, his adrenalin spiking.

If they're getting out we're in trouble. Fuck!

He nodded to Ann, and she made almost no noise opening the back door, her gun drawn and aimed at the creature resting just below the surface of the water. Harris followed just a few steps behind, his firearm also at the ready. They gradually approached the pond's edge where the reptile lay submerged. Ann and Harris stiffened, and Sean tightened the trigger.

Cautious, he walked two feet closer, his shifting viewpoint finally brought him relief. "Hold it, put down your guns!" he commanded. He holstered his weapon and walked up to the spot.

Ann joined him at the water's edge. A large rotting tree trunk had fallen into the small pond, and sat mostly submerged, except for a portion with a lengthy branch. The jutting structure resembled the long mouth of the reptile. The reversal of danger had been so dramatic, he almost laughed at the sight. He gave his team a knowing glance, then walked back to the house to talk with the homeowner.

Mrs. Ivanov seemed conflicted after she witnessed the evidence of the false alarm. "They could get out of the park, you know. If not here, I know we're going to find them somewhere else."

"We'll do the best we can," he replied.

"Maybe you should've killed them all when you had the chance."

Holding back his unfavorable reaction, he said goodbye, though she still managed to muster enough grace to thank him for coming out right away.

Before Ann opened the door to her cruiser, Sean said, "I want you to doublecheck that there've been no other calls like this. Call the Ridgefield, Norwalk, and the Weston PD, too."

"Are you worried people are starting to panic?"

"Not yet, but I want to stay informed. With the news of the Tri-megs all over the media we're going to have more citizens who are scared, like that woman," Sean said, cocking his head toward the house just behind them.

"She seemed very nervous about the Tri-megs, didn't she?"

"She's not the only one," Sean muttered, his jaw tense. "We have to get them out of the park and back to their home before more of the public turns against us."

Twenty-Seven
Tribol

In her store, Vanessa showed Sean the latest in handmade placemats woven in tasteful earth colors that just arrived today, but he couldn't resist. He leaned over and kissed his gorgeous date, their lips pressing together briefly. "You look beautiful," he murmured, as if in a dream. The scent of her perfume infatuated him, and he couldn't stop nibbling at her neck.

"Sean," she cried out, a broad smile raising her cheekbones as she pushed him away playfully. "Let me close out the register, and we can go."

She had stayed late at her shop packaging some online sales. They agreed they'd go to dinner in town and a movie at the Wilton theatre, both within walking distance.

"Sorry," Sean confessed, unable to wipe the smirk off his face. "I couldn't help it."

"Well, we'd better get going, or you'll undress me right here," she whispered. Even as she said it, her complexion took on a pinker tinge.

"I would *love* that," he whispered back, his lips barely touching her earlobe.

Shooing him off, she walked to the cash register and tallied up the sales. Business continued to improve during the holiday period, but not at a rate that would cover her debts. Her smile faded.

"Is everything all right?" he asked.

"Oh, yes. I'm just feeling stressed about finances. I don't even want to think about it."

"The store looks amazing. I'm surprised things are slow," he said, peering around. The interior of the store appeared warm, and inviting, with plenty of merchandise.

I have some savings I could loan her, but... we've only just started dating. What if she refuses my offer, or worse, gets angry at me for taking pity on her? Plus, if we break up before she pays me back, that would be awkward.

"It hasn't been good for a while so it all adds up. I think I made a big mistake spending so much money to renovate it."

A flash of inspiration popped up in his mind. "More people have been coming to town with the Quarry Head situation. That should help."

"That's true. I'm hoping it leads to more shoppers. I've noticed the restaurants seem a little busier and there're more cars in the parking lot."

"Now that I think about it, Ethan made some comment about the town becoming the center of attention over the discovery."

"He could be right. I'm staying positive." Vanessa locked the register and turned off the lights.

Sean put his arm around her on their way out and glanced back at the storefront. The picture window remained illuminated with a charming Thanksgiving scene. The side table, next to the white birch chair, displayed a crystal dish filled with gourds surrounded by three cranberry-colored candles in different sizes.

"I'm going to come back and buy some candles for my home. It's the type of thing I've always liked but just never got around to buying." When he said that, he imagined making love to her by candlelight.

She smiled. "How about if I give you some of my favorite candles, and in exchange you buy me dinner?"

"I'd like that."

Once across the street, he led her into the gourmet hamburger restaurant for a sit-down meal. The place offered a wide variety of options: take-out, fast meals ready within minutes, or more complex dishes that took longer. They selected the middle option so they could enjoy eating inside, but still finish quickly enough to catch the 8:30 movie they both wanted to see. For both of them, Sean ordered two cheeseburgers, sweet potato fries, and ice water at a table next to a window.

"Are you going back to the Tribol Preserve tomorrow? My assistant Jenny, who thinks you're very cute by the way, said she heard on the news that you're exploring Echo Lake again."

A smile twitched on the edges of his lips. "Have I met Jenny?"

"Not yet. She's seen you on television. You're becoming a celebrity."

"Maybe I should go into acting?"

"No. The town needs you," Vanessa said, grinning. "Jenny's been a real friend to me, especially when Jason first went missing."

"I'm sorry we haven't been able to locate your friend. Ryan keeps giving me updates, but there's just no lead as to where he might be."

"I know you're trying. This sort of thing happened with Jason once before. When I finished college, we lost touch for years. But of course, this is different because no one seems to know where he is—he's officially missing."

"It bothers me. Usually when someone has friends and family who care about them they don't just disappear. I assure you we haven't given up."

"You know, I don't blame you. As long as the case is open, that's all I can ask."

Sean still felt like he failed her. There had to be something he missed.

"What about tomorrow? Are you going to Echo Lake?"

"Yes. First thing in the morning," he said, letting go of his frustration over the Kenner case for now.

"Isn't it dangerous? I mean the reptiles are living right there."

"They could be, but I'm relying on a team of professionals. They're beginning to understand the nature of the Tribolmegasaurs. That will help us identify what's dangerous and what isn't."

"Are any of the scientists, uh, you know, around your age and pretty?" she asked, her eyebrow raised.

Sean chortled. "You're not jealous, are you?"

She shrugged. "I don't know, maybe."

Her gaze appeared thoughtful.

The cheerful server placed their meals in front of them. When the young man walked away, Sean leaned over and said, "You have nothing to be jealous about. All I can think about is you."

Looking up, she smiled.

They started eating, but she stopped suddenly and said, "Hey. I think I let you off the hook about something."

"What did I do?" he asked, pretending to hide guilt he didn't have.

"It wasn't anything you did; it's what you said. I think you mentioned earlier you were talking to a fish?" she said with a gleam in her eyes.

"Okay, okay, I'll tell you about the fish, but you have to listen with an open mind."

"I promise."

"Well, we went out in the boat and dropped a machine called an ROV to the bottom of the lake where it could take videos and samples underwater. We could immediately see what it was filming," Sean marveled at the memory. "The diversity of species we saw was amazing. But our main goal was to find the opening to the underground passage. Everyone was certain the access had somehow been blocked, and that's why the Tri-megs left the area and are roaming around the park. Then Irene noticed that there were plants crushed in a pile of boulders. Some of the rock surfaces were scraped clean, and our geologist, Manny, said it's possible we found an area that had recently collapsed."

"So, that's where you think the opening is?"

"Yes, we should know for certain tomorrow. Now here's where we saw the unusual fish." His voice took on a tinge of excitement. "They were like wispy ghosts with just sockets for eyes. Like a white smooth starfish with long droopy arms."

"What do you mean? It's something no one's ever seen?" she asked, puzzled.

"I think so. It was definitely weird. Plus, it was like they were communicating with us telepathically, crying out for help. It's not just me though. Everyone else on the boat said the same thing."

"That sounds unreal, but I can believe it."

"You can?"

She nodded. "I think animals have some kind of sixth sense. Remember I told you I had a dog I used to walk in the park with my mom and sister? This dog would bark when my mother got off the train from work, miles away. We used to test it. When we heard the barking, I'd call my mom, and each time I did she had just arrived at the station."

"Yes, but I have to admit hearing their voices in my head caught me off guard," he said.

Sean noticed Vanessa looking past him, and he turned to see what had caught her attention. Leaving a table behind him, a frail, elderly woman strolled toward them. Her striking green-and-purple patterned ankle-length dress and long gray hair made her stand out. At the table she'd departed, a grinning elderly bald man, presumably her husband, still sat.

When she reached their table, she looked at Sean and said, "May I sit for a moment? I have a story to tell you."

"Please, have this seat," he said, standing to assist her. He politely pulled out the chair for her and pushed it in when she seated herself.

"I'm Rose. You're the police chief who's been talking about these creatures running around," she said when Sean returned to his spot. She had a twinkle in her eyes, which were such a clear, pale blue he questioned his vision for a moment. "I would like to give you some history of the area."

"We'd like that. I'm Sean, and this is Vanessa."

"Hi, dear," Rose said to Vanessa. She gazed at each of them. "You're not in a hurry, are you?"

"Not at all," Vanessa said graciously, leaning forward as she placed her folded hands on the table.

Rose smiled. "My great, great, great grandparents lived in Wilton in the 1700's. They were farmers and worked on a small plot of land not far from Echo Lake."

"Really?" he said, encouraging her to go on. The connection to Echo Lake intrigued him.

"The soil was not very good for farming because it was rocky, but they loved the land, and they intended that their children and grandchildren would live there. They believed that the forests had magic and passed down stories about people seeing huge reptiles with fins and long necks in the water." Her eyes sparkled as she spoke fondly about her ancestors.

"Then in the 1800's the quarry opened, so they could produce millstones from the bedrock. The activity caused much of the wildlife to disappear, and these huge reptiles weren't seen again. Eventually the farmers, including my family, moved even further away from the lake. I grew up with these stories, and I always believed there was something still living in the water."

"You were right," he said, fascinated.

"Turns out I was. You know, as time went on the stories were told as folklore, but thanks to my imagination, I believed they were true. Giant reptiles with fins!" She smiled with delight.

"You seem to know a lot about the history of the area," he said. "Can you tell me anything about why it's called Tribol Preserve? Seems like an unusual name."

"Yes, I can. I was told that some people believed there was a species of very small crabs that lived on the rocks in the lake. They would scratch the ledge with their pincers, and every time they touched the rocks, there would be some sort of burst of light. In the dark, it was very easy to see them."

"Wow!" Vanessa looked at Sean as if to check his reaction.

Rose nodded, beaming. "These crabs were very special too, because the story is they would also glow at night. The legend is these crabs would light up the lake."

"I would love to see that," Vanessa said, nearly whispering.

Rose's expression turned sad. "But the land suffered many floods, and the rock ledges that sustained the crabs started to chip easily since the sediment was unstable. Over time, the tiny crabs disappeared. My parents told me the name Tribol came from the light created by the crabs pricking at the rocks. Triboluminescence is the word scientists used to describe a sudden glow of light that happens when materials are crushed or ripped apart."

"Yes," Sean remarked. "That's what happens if you pull two pieces of duct tape apart. We used to do that when I was young to see it spark."

The elderly woman nodded. "That's right. *Tribo* is Greek for rubbed or friction. And *lumen* comes from the Latin word for light."

"So," Vanessa said with an eager tone, joining in, "You just combine some letters, and come up with the word Tribol."

Rose smiled. "I love the part about the crabs lighting up the lake. However, most other people don't know about them and say the name is based on the light that shines from the gneiss."

Sean and Vanessa looked at each other in puzzlement.

"You know, gneiss, the textured rocks with the banded pattern."

"Oh," Sean and Vanessa said in unison. He still didn't recall hearing the rock's name before, but the explanation satisfied him.

"Yes. In the 1800's when the rock was quarried, its shiny patterns were widely admired. Did you know that gneiss comes from the German verb *gneist*, which means to spark?" She paused for a second. "To me, the name Tribol came from the association with those special crabs that died out. However, most people think otherwise."

Enthused over all the revelations, Sean couldn't think of any more questions. "Thank you for sharing this with us."

"My pleasure," she said as she stood. He walked her back to her table.

"What an interesting lady. How cool to have stories from over three hundred years ago," Vanessa said when he returned.

"Yes, I've always wanted to know more about Echo Lake and the preserve."

"What time do you have to be there tomorrow?"

"I have to be at the station by seven in the morning."

"Maybe we should see the movie another night. I don't want you to be tired."

"Don't worry. Let's finish dessert then we can decide." He'd already ordered the restaurant's specialty to share, warm chocolate cake with melted chocolate and caramel topping. They'd been so engrossed in Rose's story they'd barely touched the dish.

"Do you like it?" he asked of the cake.

"Yes, I have a terrible sweet tooth."

"Here, let me help you."

The server had strategically placed three fresh strawberries on the side of the plate. Sean dipped a strawberry in the melted chocolate and held it to Vanessa's lips. She opened her mouth, slowly. After he placed the sweet berry on her tongue, his own mouth watered as he watched her bite into the luscious fruit.

She closed her eyes and took in a deep breath. "If we skip the movie, you can follow me home."

Sean leaned in closer. "Let's go now."

Twenty-Eight
Brace Yourself

The next morning, a naked Sean awoke under pristine linen covers, grinning as he glanced at Vanessa's arm lying over his chest. At once, flashes of their sexual passion flipped through his mind re-igniting his desire. Last night, when she had called out his name at the height of their intimacy, the sensation of ultimate pleasure coursed through his body, leaving him deeply satisfied.

He moved away, easing her arm onto the mattress so he would not wake her. Drawing up his pants at the side of her bed, he admired how the waves in her long brunette hair cascaded over the side of her delicate face and graced her toned back. Finding it difficult to suppress the urge to spend more time with her in bed, he finished dressing, so he could get back to his house and change into his uniform for work.

Today they hoped to uncover the hidden passageway to the underground lake. Sean arranged for two of his police officers to escort Greg, Manny, and Irene into the Tribol Preserve where he would meet them and the rest of the team at Echo Lake.

Everyone involved with the exploration arrived in time to watch Frank waving in the driver of the truck towing an underwater hydraulic excavator up to the temporary dock. This orange-colored machine consisted of a boom, an arm, and a deep tilting bucket with teeth on the rim. To power it to drive over the lake bottom, an electrical umbilical cable connected it to a control panel stationed on the deck of the police boat, much like the ROV. However, the excavator's more powerful frame and substantially larger attachments enabled it to dig through the lakebed and to lift heavy rocks.

"Right there," Frank said, and the driver jumped out of the vehicle to unhitch the large underwater machine from the trailer.

Like the rest of the team, Sean wore a heavy jacket and carried a packed lunch in preparation for a full day on the lake. He also had a stainless-steel thermos of coffee under his arm—something he found practical for long hours on cold shifts. Greg warned everyone about an upcoming cold snap. If they didn't get the Tribolmegasaurs back to the underground lake soon, the freezing temperature would probably kill them.

Frank said a few words before they boarded the vessel. "Good morning. I want you all to meet Officer James Bailey. He works with me in the state department and is an expert operator. James, this is our herpetologist Dr. Greg Mitchell, our aquatic ecologist Dr. Irene Stone, and our geologist Dr. Manny Laurence."

James shook hands with them. "It's a privilege to work with all of you. I've seen some of your interviews on TV, and I'm fascinated by the discovery of these new reptiles."

"We're glad to have you with us," Greg said.

"Must have been hard to get this excavator to the lake," Manny said, eyeing the large machine.

"An effort, but well worth it. It's exactly what we need for this job because it's equipped with a backhoe and rock breaker bucket," James said.

"Good thing it was available," Sean said.

James headed for the vessel. "I'm going to join Charles onboard and get the system up and running."

Yes. Sean remembered Officer Charles Wilkins, the water police officer who handled the smaller ROV yesterday.

While Charles set up the equipment he'd be operating, James worked on the system for the underwater excavator which included similar devices: a monitor, keyboard, and joy stick for controlling the machine's movements. Clutching their bags, the three scientists boarded then seated themselves next to the screens.

"Colonel, we're ready when you are," said Sam, standing behind the steering wheel.

"Let's head out," Frank said and gave the order to his officer on shore to untie the vessel.

Without any fanfare, Sam piloted the boat away from the makeshift dock. Working the control panels, James commanded the excavator to roll straight into the shallow water at the shoreline. Sean looked on as it submerged.

The watercraft charted a path for the excavator, which trailed behind onto the lakebed, connected by the electric umbilical cord. The strong winds made the water choppy, causing many of the passengers to secure a hold on any available support, such as the railing surrounding the boat.

After several minutes of careful navigation, he steered the vessel to the coordinates of the underwater pile of rubble below the sheer rock ledge they spotted yesterday. When the boat reached the desired location, he dropped the anchor. Now the ROV needed to be deployed.

He shifted the vessel into neutral so Charles could lower the machine. These two sophisticated pieces of equipment would work together in tandem. Charles would continue to manipulate the smaller ROV, while James directed the larger machine.

The underwater excavator had its own optical scanners; however, the ROV gave a broader field of vision.

When the ROV reached the desired depth, everyone watched the monitor as Charles grasped the joystick to send it toward the location they believed to be the opening to the pathway of the underground lake.

The debris from the motion settled enough for Manny to assess the situation. "There's a thick slab of rock on top of the pile, but I can't tell exactly how big it is. As Irene said, most of the rocks are covered with algae and lakeweed, but this piece is oddly clean, as though it's just recently been exposed to the water. I think what we're looking at is a very large section of ledge that broke off. You can see how the Tribol Preserve has many cliffs and hills." He gestured to the rough horizon. "This lake follows that same land pattern. Under the water there are jagged ledges like those we see in the preserve. Depending on how the ledge broke off, it could've shattered shelves of rock as it fell, which would explain the pile we're seeing."

Sean thought about what Manny just explained and how the landscape came together. With a content sigh, he appreciated the continuity of the terrain and that time had carved its changes, creating wonder.

The scientists pointed at the screen and discussed the best approach. When they came to an agreement, Frank gave the order to begin digging away at the pile.

For about ninety minutes, the team watched the scene repeat itself on the monitor—a giant metal monster crawling on eight-foot long tracks over the murky lake floor and a large metal bucket firmly scooping rocks and carrying them away, repeatedly. The motion of the machine kept most of the fish away. Occasionally large clumps of aquatic plants wedged between rocks would be set free, and they would swirl in the water, floating away out of sight.

By noon, the crew took turns leaving the monitors. Sean ate his packed lunch, while keeping watch over the water. He stayed on his feet more than the scientists. They remained seated and took quick breaks to stand and stretch or rub their legs. By mid-afternoon, with no end to the digging in sight, Manny suggested they use the rock breaker to split some of the larger boulders to speed up progress. Sean agreed right away, and Frank gave the thumbs-up.

Using the underwater video camera, James selected some of the big rock shelves the excavator could remove without disturbing the rest of the pile.

Suddenly, the largest wedge on top shifted slightly. Irene moved closer to the monitor. "Look, there's a current," she exclaimed, turning to the debris flowing away from the space. "Now, let's expose more of this area. I think we found the opening we're looking for."

"Yes," Manny shouted.

"I can see bubbles flowing out from that spot," Greg said.

"The slab's moving down, and it's bringing more rocks behind it!" James could not find the center of gravity to hold up the huge shelf, and even if he could, the avalanche of boulders coming down with it would have crushed the machine. As he commanded the bucket to retreat, the giant wedge and massive rocks tumbled toward them pushing a huge volume of water aside as it all dropped to the bottom of the lake.

"Hold on!" yelled Frank as a swell of water rose up before the vessel.

Abandoning the controls, James and Charles, who were the first to see the miscalculation, retreated to just behind the cabin while Sam desperately attempted to turn the bow of the ship toward the incoming swell in order to stabilize his boat. The crest of the massive wave broke over the deck, rocking the craft. The crew grabbed onto anything stable they could find. Unable to secure a position of support, Irene crashed to the deck, sprawling across the wood as water smashed into her body.

Frank let go of the guardrail and dashed to grab her around the waist. Another huge wave struck, tilting the boat toward its port side. They stumbled backward together until his rear hit the side of the vessel. He let go of her just as he was about to tip over, head first, into the lake. Leaving his secure spot, Sean ran to Frank and grabbed hold of his right arm, keeping him safe on board.

The boat lurched with sudden, violent movements as the shaken crew tried to hold on. Greg lost his balance and fell away from the rail he held onto into the turbulent current of icy water still percolating on the deck. His pants legs and footwear soaking wet, he pulled himself up safely. "I'm all right."

"Check the crew," Frank said to Sean when he steadied himself.

"Are you okay?" Frank asked Irene as she took off her coat and rolled up her shirt sleeve to examine a newly emerging bruise on her left arm.

"Yes. I'll be fine," she said, her teeth chattering. "It's just sore right now." She smiled at her savior. "Thank you for catching me."

"I'm glad you're not badly hurt."

Ignoring them for the moment, Sean asked, "Greg, how are you doing?"

"I'm fine, too. Nothing's broken," he said, twisting his wrists and flexing his ankle.

Frank radioed his officers who were waiting at the shore and told them they did not need additional help at this time.

James found some towels downstairs and handed them out to everyone. They weren't enough to fully dry off their damp pants, socks, and shoes, leaving them shivering in the cold weather.

"Let's get on with it," Frank ordered the crew. "With the temperature dropping, I'll give us a few more minutes, but then we'll have to go in."

"You're right, Frank. Let's continue," Irene said.

"I'll need to assess the damage to the excavator. I think the rock fell on it," James said.

"I think the ROV can still help with that," Charles replied.

The accident had left the excavator partially crushed and its video camera destroyed, rendering it unusable. Fortunately, the ROV's camera continued to work. After patiently waiting for enough debris to settle, Charles navigated the machine around the pile of crushed rocks on the lake bottom. He succeeded in having the ROV approach what they all hoped would be the opening of the underwater passageway.

Sean held his breath, viewing as the ROV hovered over the rock slabs and into an opening. The image of a tunnel came on the screen.

Irene broke the silence. "We have a passage."

"Is this the path to the underground lake?" Frank asked.

"I think so," Greg said, sucking in an audible breath as the ROV continued down the tunnel.

"Hey!" said Charles, reading off the data from the console. "It's now more than a hundred feet below the lake bottom."

Everyone cheered, Sean along with them. They had found the underground lake!

Charles continued, "I'm going to send the camera out on its tether to give us views all around."

Clear, light green water appeared, a very different color from the serene deep blue of the lake calmly lapping away at the hull of the boat. "Wow!"

Irene laid her hand on the crook of Frank's arm. "I told you we would find it."

Excited, Sean leaned in to get a better view, the biting cold from the wind temporarily forgotten. "Amazing," he said with a wide smile. He stared at the monitor, anticipating the unveiling of the underground world.

"There! I see fish. Do you see that school of fish glowing?" Irene asked. "They look like ocean-dwelling lancelets. Do you see the streaks of neon blue on their backs?"

"Yes, I see them. Look over there," Greg said as hundreds of pen-size beams of light darted about through the enchanting water heading in thousands of different directions.

"Look," Manny said. "There are a bunch of creatures scurrying about at the bottom. Charles, aim the camera over there."

Once again, the underground lake yielded more of its magic, as dozens of oval-shaped glistening crustaceans scuttled along casting a bright green glow.

"They're crabs," Sean said with awe. *Wait until I tell Vanessa.*

Confused gazes focused on him.

"How do you know?" Greg asked, his eyebrows raised.

"An old lady I met last night in a restaurant told me," he said, dazed.

"I'll zoom in so we can get a better look," said Charles.

Everyone crowded in toward the monitor, watching the spectacle.

"Absolutely amazing," Irene said. "I could watch this forever."

Suddenly the screen went dark. *Is the equipment malfunctioning?*

"Hold on. There's nothing wrong with the camera," Charles said.

"Look!" Irene jabbed a finger at the monitor. The hue of the screen brightened, as if a shadow had lifted.

Sean gasped as mottled scales skimmed along the monitor, so close he felt he could practically reach out and touch the giant creature gliding by the camera lens.

It was Greg who first identified them. "It's a Tribolmegasaur."

The creature was sleek and graceful as it slowly swam across the monitor, in contrast to Sean's still-fresh memories of its cousins' rampage across the forest floor. A school of glowing, gleaming, ghost-like tiny shapes followed, and this time, he recognized the Ninjen-like fish, intriguing in their magical appearance.

By now, he could see that although the scientists remained engaged in the findings their clenched jaws and shivering limbs betrayed their exposure to hypothermic conditions. He glanced at Frank, who didn't need prompting.

"We have to go back and get some dry clothes," he ordered. "At least we can turn up the heaters in the cars to warm up."

"Th-th-that would be so wonderful," Irene said, her teeth chattering.

The team briefly discussed the need to reinforce the passageway to the underground lake. The scientists spoke about gathering to analyze the findings. Chilled to the bone but warmed to the heart, Sean went home content and fulfilled.

The passage way to the underground lake had been found. The question that remained to be answered was this: could the displaced Tribolmegasaurs be led home?

Twenty-Nine
Press

Back at his office, Sean yawned and looked at the time on the bottom right of his computer. Nine forty-seven p.m. He stretched his hands above his head to shake off the fatigue as he read the police incident reports filed for the day.

He groaned when he realized he'd forgotten to ring Vanessa. *Damn.*

She'd left a voicemail for him around 4:00 p.m., asking him to contact her.

"Oh, man," he said to no one as he picked up his phone and dialed her number. While waiting for her to answer, vivid flashbacks of heated arguments with Emily raced through his mind. Back then he also worked long hours, causing them to fight over missed calls and thwarted plans.

"Hello, Sean," came Vanessa's voice at the other end of the line. Her tone sounded flat, not her usual warm, upbeat self.

"Hi. How are you?"

"I'm okay."

"I got your message. Sorry I didn't call sooner. I haven't had a minute since I got back to the station."

"I understand. I know you're busy."

"Would you believe I actually saw the luminescent crabs the lady at the restaurant told us about?"

"No way!"

"Yes—I couldn't believe it. When I saw them, I thought of you right away."

"Really? You'll have to tell me all about it. But you must be exhausted now."

The tone of her voice softened the more they spoke. They made plans to have lunch together the next day, and his heart ached with anticipation as he hung up.

Turning down his street, on his way home, Sean thought fondly of his dog Scout. Whenever he came home, Scout ran to him with boundless energy, tail wagging. To help compensate for these long days when he couldn't get home until late, he'd installed a "pet door" so Scout could leave the house to play outside in the large fenced in backyard.

That night, when Sean walked into his house, Scout jumped up and down with delight, panting heavily and running about in frenetic circles. In turn, Sean prepared a bowl of dog food for him and filled another dish with fresh water. Just before bed, he tossed a stuffed toy through the hallway for Scout to fetch. Sean relaxed for the first time that day.

Wait! Ethan's press conference is tomorrow.

Finally, after weeks of being in the hospital with complications from the attack the doctors agreed Ethan could be discharged with extensive rehabilitation on an outpatient bases and a visiting nurse.

The press conference was being held at Norwalk hospital. Sean had to go, to show support for his best friend, plus the media would likely have questions for him and Frank, who also needed to be there to represent the state police.

Can I make it back in time for lunch with Vanessa? But Ethan's interview was not something he would miss.

The next morning after a walk around the block with Scout and his usual breakfast of cold cereal with milk and a glass of orange juice, Sean started his work day at the station going over details on the department's budget. He left for the conference with plenty of time to see Ethan before they discharged him.

"Hey, how are you today?" he asked once he arrived in Ethan's room.

"Hey, Sean!" Ethan's face brimmed with happiness. "Not too bad, thanks."

Gone were the dark circles under his eyes and the pale color of his skin. He sat on his bed, freshly attired in the Connecticut State Police uniform Sean picked up from his house a week ago. Thanks to strategic clips of the scissors and some handy sewing, Ethan split open the left pant leg to accommodate the cast on his leg.

"When did the doctors say you'll be on your feet again?"

"Not for a while. I'll have to use this for now," Ethan said as he grimaced, jabbing at thumb at a wheelchair resting just a few feet away from him.

"Uh huh."

"They're sending a physical therapist to my house three times a week." He tapped his right leg with his hand, demonstrating that infectious energy Sean had always recognized. "But I should be able to ditch the wheelchair in a few weeks and just use crutches."

"And?"

"Um, I should be able to walk on my own again in a couple of months, that's what they say." He shook his head. "Way too long. I'm setting a three-week goal." He winked.

Sean laughed along with his optimism. "I bet you'll make it, just don't overdo it. Do you need any help getting home?"

"No, thanks. My parents are picking me up. My mom's been cooking a lot. She wants to leave me with one of her homemade lasagnas and a pot roast. She even offered to stay over if I need help, but the social worker arranged for a home health aide to come in every day for a while, so I told her not to worry."

"That was nice of your mom. When can I drop by?"

"How about this Sunday? The Giants are playing the Saints. I was thinking of having some friends over. Why don't you bring Vanessa?"

"We'll see," Sean said, his voice trailing off.

"Hey, what's up?"

"Nothing, she could be busy that day."

"Sean. What's going on?"

"Okay, okay," Sean muttered.

A slender nurse with a well-toned figure walked into the room. Ethan straightened up in the bed, "Yes, Kelly?"

"Sorry to interrupt, gentlemen," Kelly said. "Your supervisor called, and he stressed that you be downstairs at quarter to eleven, so they can set you up."

"Yeah, yeah," he said, shrugging. "I'll be there."

"Gotcha," Kelly said, as she walked away. Sean didn't have to glance at Ethan to know he was watching her shapely behind as she left.

"Okay," Sean said, stepping toward the wheelchair to assist Ethan.

"No, Sean," Ethan said, waving dismissively. "Come on, out with it."

"With what?"

"Vanessa, of course."

Sean glanced around the room, making sure no one was within earshot. "I think I'm going to have the same problem I had with Emily. The other day I forgot to ring because I was busy. Today I'm supposed to meet her for lunch, but it doesn't look like I'll be on time, and I can't bring myself to break the news to her. And we've only just started dating."

"She's going to have to get used to it. That's the way our work is."

"She told me at the beginning she didn't feel comfortable with the danger factor. I don't think she'd considered the unpredictable hours. Isn't this just going to be an excuse to break it off?" Sean held his breath, afraid of the answer.

"How the hell should I know?"

He winced. "Let me put it this way then. Do you think it's fair to ask someone to put up with this bullshit?"

Ethan's answer left no ambiguity. "Sure!"

Sean laughed. Ethan had a way of cutting out the crap and getting straight to the point.

Kelly returned to the ward, with an orderly in tandem behind her. The attendant walked up to Ethan to assist, but he refused his offer. Instead, displaying the nimbleness of the athlete he once was, he grasped the bars on the side of his bed and propped himself into the wheelchair.

With a smile, Kelly said, "Paperwork's all done. You're free to go."

"Thanks. Maybe I'll come back and visit you," Ethan said with a raised eyebrow and a boyish grin.

"Go on. Get outta here," Kelly said in a sly tone, grinning.

The attendant tried to steer Ethan downstairs, but the patient just kept on thrusting the wheels with his own hands, so the orderly gave up and followed from behind. Ethan wheeled himself into the elevator and turned himself about, displaying his mastery.

The doors opened on ground level, revealing the lobby. Sean gaped. Bright beams of light shone from the perimeter of the room. Thick cables snaked on the speckled concrete floor, held down with black duct tape. Lined up side by side, representatives from the different media outlets waited: numerous reporters with all their cameras and microphones.

Knowing some of the reporters would already have started filming, Sean set his mouth in a grim line to reflect the solemn mood.

Reporters with camera crews rushed over to Ethan when he wheeled into sight, and a noticeable murmur arose from the crowd. The attendant walked away from the scene and waited by the sidelines.

"He's pushing himself," one male voice rang out.

"Mr. Roberts, Mr. Roberts," a female voice beseeched.

A stern-looking Colonel Gunner stepped in and held his hand up at the oncoming crowd. "Please restrain yourselves," he commanded, looking every inch an authority figure. "He's recovering, and he needs his space."

A collective groan escaped the reporters. Reluctantly they all backed away.

Frank spoke to Ethan, with his back to the media. "How are you feeling this morning?"

"Better every day," he said.

"Sean, glad you could make it," Frank said, in an unemotional yet sincere tone.

"Wouldn't miss it," he replied, noting the civil greeting.

At that point, Sean deferred, walking away from Ethan and joining the crowd of onlookers.

Once Ethan rolled up to a spot near a microphone that had been lowered enough to match his seated position, Frank took command.

Standing straight, he began, "Thank you all for coming today. We've arranged this question and answer session, because many of you have expressed good wishes for an outstanding detective who demonstrated courage in the line of duty." He paused and looked at Ethan with the faintest trace of a smile. "Detective Ethan Roberts."

There was a prolonged period of applause. Frank held up his hand after a few seconds and everyone quieted. Then he walked away, signaling that the reporters could begin.

Sean watched the press conference, fascinated with Ethan's poised answers and the press' hunger for more information. He gave his account of what happened in Quarry Head Park the day of the attack, when they discovered the first Tribolmegasaur. The reporters barraged him with further questions. After the formal conference, the press formed scrums around Sean and Frank.

Sean's own band of reporters peppered him with the same line of questions he'd been answering for the past several days: the impact of the Tribolmegasaurs on the safety and calm of the town of Wilton, the steps being taken to restore public order, and the expected timeline for when the reptiles would finally be removed from the park.

The moment the relentless zoom lens of the outsized television camera veered away from his composed face, he glanced at his watch. *Damn!* 12:25 p.m. He rushed to his car, knowing he'd run out of time to say goodbye to his friend. Ethan's parents were with him, and his supporters waited to shake his hand.

Sean fretted as he drove, but kept within speed limits as he hurried back to Wilton. After twenty minutes, he arrived at the well-decorated shop.

Hiding his concern that Vanessa would be annoyed, Sean

attempted a brave face as he walked in the front door. Jenny greeted him from where she stood behind the counter.

"Hello. You must be Sean," she said with her trademark smile. "I recognized you right away from the television interviews. Vanessa's told me so much about you."

"Hi. It's nice to meet you, too. You must be Jenny," he said with a smile.

"Yes. I've worked with Vanessa since she took over the shop."

"I'm glad we got to meet in person."

"Me, too. You're even better looking than on TV." She grinned. "But I'm sure you're not here to see me. Vanessa's in the back."

"Thank you."

When he walked into the office, Vanessa got up from her desk. He shut the door and pecked her on the lips. "Sorry I'm late. So where do you want to go?"

She stepped aside to show him the fold-out bridge table where she set out lunch. "I hope you don't mind. I already picked up turkey and corned beef sandwiches. We can split each in half and share if you like both."

He grinned with appreciation. Drawing her into his arms, he kissed her more, but stopped sensing her aloofness. "This is perfect. I'd like some of both. Thanks."

"Luckily, it wasn't the kind of food I had to keep warm while waiting for you," she said with a distinct edge in her tone before they took their seats.

"I'm sorry. There was a press conference for Ethan. He was just released from the hospital. I couldn't miss it."

"That's great news. I'm so glad he can go home, but couldn't you have taken two minutes to let me know?"

"I can't always let you know."

"Why not?" she snapped, her face showing a brief flash of anger.

"Sorry," he said, holding up his hand. "What I meant to say was, of course, I'll try." He took a bite of his sandwich. "I guess when the press conference started, there were so many people around, it was hard to leave because everyone knew I was there."

"Oh." She sighed and put her uneaten sandwich back down into its container. "You're very close with Ethan and the officers you work with, aren't you? And you have a huge responsibility as chief of our town. Our people depend on you. Maybe I'm getting in the way." She folded up a napkin to wipe her fingers, her expression solemn.

"No, not at all," Sean protested, aghast. He moved his chair closer to hers and held her hands. "I want to tell you something very important."

"Mmm hmm. Go ahead."

"This has happened to me before. My last girlfriend kept giving me ultimatums. Like I had to call her at certain times, and so on. It never worked. I told her I wasn't going to change, and after a while she got tired of it and just packed up and left."

"I remember you telling me, but maybe she had a point. It's not fair to leave someone waiting. Maybe she was worried."

"What I'm trying to say to you is, I will do my best to always make time for you, but like you said, I'm a cop, like it or not. Sometimes something may come up, and I won't be able to call. Times when there's an emergency or an incident that needs my attention."

"I understand. I appreciate you being honest with me. There's something I think I should tell you too."

Sean had no idea what she had to say, but the color left her face, and her demeanor turned somber. "What is it?"

"I know you were late because of work, and I understand your commitment to your friend. It's just going to be hard for me to handle a relationship where I'm not counted first."

"But, Vanessa…"

She held his hands tighter and looked into his eyes. "I've had my own problems with relationships. I'm going to tell you something I don't tell many people."

It took her a moment before she continued.

"My dad's an alcoholic. He wasn't a very good father. Over and over he made promises about quitting, but he never followed through. My mom spent most of her time caring for him."

"That must have been hard for you," Sean said. *That explains the sadness behind her eyes. And she trusts me enough to share it.*

She nodded. "I'm still recovering from all the ways his illness hurt me, and I'm coming to realize it's affecting my relationships. Foolishly I've chosen to date men who were selfish. My last boyfriend relocated for work without even discussing it with me. He assumed I'd just leave my store and go with him. What I'm saying is, I understand your dedication to the force, but if you can't make me a priority too, I just don't know if I can handle it. In fact, I know I won't be happy."

His heart ached as he observed the tender yet bittersweet look on her face. "I'm sorry to hear about your father. Is that why you don't drink?"

"Yes. I don't like the smell, and I'm glad you haven't ordered anything with alcohol when we're together. I know I'm being unfair, but that's how I honestly feel."

"I understand."

"My father still drinks, and now it's even worse. He's suffering from many health problems, and he hasn't worked for several years."

"You have to believe me when I say, I'm not like them. I mean, your father, and your last boyfriend."

"I know. That's why I want to try."

He exhaled with relief. "I'm glad you told me." He pulled her closer. Her skin felt warm against his. As they hugged, he savored the realization once again that she was all he needed, right now. "I have something I need to tell you too."

"You're not going to tell me your mom's an alcoholic?"

"No."

"What is it?"

"It's something you can't tell anyone. Not even your assistant Jenny. I don't want anyone to know."

"You're scaring me. What is it?"

"I'm color blind."

"What? How can you be and still do your job?"

Sean told her about the accident and about how the special contact lenses allowed him to continue seeing normally and how they let him return to work when he passed the vision test. She caressed the left side of his face. With tears in her eyes, she promised she'd never tell.

After their confessions, their conversation flowed, as if the weeks they'd known each other had been years. He told her more about the press conference, and they spoke about where they would go on Saturday night. Time flew by, and he apologized for having to leave.

"Come here," he ordered with a smirk after he stood to put his coat on.

She rushed over, and he moved in to plant a long, deep kiss on her lips. She moaned, placing her hands on his shoulders as she drew him in closer. Passion and desire enveloped Sean, vanquishing any lingering doubt.

"I'll call you later," he said.

"Yes," she said, closing her eyes as his lips touched hers. Arm in arm they he walked her to the door, enjoying every last second before he had to leave.

His heart was heavy with longing as he drove off in his car.

He glanced at the road ahead and breathed in Vanessa's perfume which had lingered on his shirt, a subtle reminder of her alluring presence. He smiled, and everything seemed brighter.

Thirty
Back to the Nest

"We will be starting Operation Back to the Nest at 8:00 a.m. on Wednesday," Frank announced in a booming voice from the front of the conference room at the Wilton Police Station.

Sean stood at his side. All the people involved in the Tri-meg crisis attended the meeting: the police officers, both state and town, who had been enlisted inside the park, and the six scientists: Greg, Lee, Mike, Manny, Tova, and Irene. Every seat in the crowded room was taken; some officers had to stand in the back.

A pro at delivering detailed presentations, Frank aimed a laser pointer at the wall, where a projected map displayed both Quarry Head Park and the Tribol Preserve. He deftly pointed out the current locations of where the Tri-megs had been found and their destination, Echo Lake.

Everyone nodded.

"We're going to try to get the reptiles home, one day at a time. We have three secure resting areas for them equal distances apart. These stops will help us keep the Tri-megs together, and there's a better chance of getting them to go where we want them if they're traveling in shorter distances." As he spoke, Frank aimed the laser beam at the three resting spots marked on the map. Everyone craned their necks, looking on.

He cleared his throat. "Once the Tri-megs reach the third site, we'll set up lights and heat lamps by the shore of Echo Lake. We'll use the same equipment as last time, but we'll need two sets. Moving the apparatus to these areas meant we had to clear paths for the trucks. We tried to widen the existing trails within the park, but we also had to clear new paths."

Proud of the plan they came up with, Sean listened to Frank. Whatever his personal feelings for Frank, he had to grudgingly give him credit for coordinating most of the clearing and securing the equipment needed to undergo this well-organized operation.

"The first site will be relatively close to the entrance where the creatures were seen," Frank continued. "We're hoping they all gather together and will stay under the heat lamps and lights throughout the night. Then, the next morning we turn off that set of equipment and turn on the second set of equipment already stationed closer to Echo Lake, and so on."

"If we have only two sets of equipment, how do we spread it among three sites and Echo Lake?" a state officer asked.

"Excellent question. Since we can't disturb a resting site when the Tri-megs are there, we'll move equipment from the empty area to the new one when they're sleeping. Our team of scientists have concluded the reptiles are diurnal, meaning they'll be active during the day."

"Got it. Thanks, Colonel."

Officer Ann McKay spoke. Folks turned to look at her, probably remembering she sustained an injury during the first encounter with a Tri-meg. "You believe the reptiles will gather and stay by the equipment to avoid freezing, and in this way you'll work them back to Echo Lake. Do you think they'll simply swim into the underground lake once they're back?"

Lee raised her hand and spoke with excitement in her voice. "Exactly. It's where they lived for possibly over a million years. They should instinctively try to return to it if we get them close enough."

Frank spoke again. "The passageway between the bodies of waters has been reinforced to prevent a collapse in the future. We've also installed a monitoring system along where they're connected so we can watch them any time once they return."

"That's fantastic!" Irene said.

The buzz in the room grew at this news. Sean, too, hoped for a time when he could access this view even from his office.

Frank continued to speak above the chatter and immediately the group quieted. "The surveillance cameras are being put up throughout Quarry Head Park and the Tribol Preserve, so we can track the giant reptiles. Since there's no electricity in the area, we're going to use a solar powered system."

"Will one computer screen be enough?" asked Greg.

"I've arranged for a larger mobile office, and I'm working on having three monitors."

After many more back-and-forth questions with the audience, Frank turned the meeting over to his weapons specialist. "Sergeant Tent is going to go over the plan to motivate the Tri-megs to move toward the heated zones."

Sergeant Tent came forward. "Just like last time, we will be using dedicated channel walkie-talkies. I will have a team of officers with me. The operation will begin with a round of explosives in a targeted area to get the Tri-megs moving away from the entrance of Quarry Head and toward the Tribol Preserve. Where we set off these explosives is based on the information I've been receiving from Greg's team. Frank will give the warning before we begin. During this time, anyone in the field will take cover and no one can leave the mobile office."

Localized and controlled blasting based on scientific information. The way it should've been done originally.

Sergeant Tent paused then asked, "Any questions?"

No one spoke.

"Thank you, Tent," Frank said from the side. "Greg, can you come up here to answer some questions? I have one myself."

"Sure thing," Greg said, stepping up.

"I reviewed the method you came up with to document the number of Tri-megs we're tracking. Could you say a few words about that?"

"Yes. We will take a freeze frame snapshot of each Tribolmegasaur from the surveillance film and then put the pictures in a Dropbox file, which you can all access via your computers. We will label the reptiles T-meg number one, T-meg number two, and so on."

"What's your best guess as to how many Tri-megs there are out there?"

"We can't be certain, but we believe there are at least five. We have head-to-tail photos of two of them, a partial picture of a third, and we think we have descriptions of two additional ones. We have approximate lengths on the two caught on video. One is roughly twenty-eight feet long and the other is about fifteen feet long. This information is now in the computer file you will all now have access to."

"Good," Frank said. "The officers assigned to the mobile office will inform every one of the status of each reptile."

Sean jumped in. "We're going to have to finalize the plans for the barricade around Echo Lake, so we can protect the public, just in case the Tri-megs don't return to their habitat like we expect them to. Do we have any more details on the electric fencing?"

"We're almost done," Frank answered. "There will be two layers of protection: the eighteen-foot mesh fence and then a lower fence of highly conductive wire running along just in front. Voltage at a rate of one pulse per second will be sent through each barrier. This is enough to keep them contained, but will not kill them."

The officers in attendance started murmuring. From the chatter generated, the mood seemed positive and upbeat.

"One final thing," Frank said appearing serious. Again, the attendees quieted. "Everyone will sign out with the officer stationed in the mobile office before they leave the park, and anyone not in uniform will be escorted to their car by a police officer. Any further questions?"

Silence filled the room. Sean felt a sense of pride.

"All right, let's go do our jobs. The whole world will be watching."

Thirty-One
Chilled

The night before the operation Sean slept blissfully, alone in his bed, drifting in and out of an erotic fantasy.

"I want you," she whispered in his ear. The image of Vanessa snuggling up next to him naked seemed so vivid.

"I want you too," he said in this dream.

With raw desire, he pinned her to the sheets, his knees planted on the mattress, straddling her. He heard her gasp as he planted wet kisses down her neck, her breasts, and curves of her figure. Thoughts of physical pleasure swept through his mind as he eagerly explored her body, and she his.

Ring.

Rudely woken by his alarm, he stayed in bed for just a few more moments, savoring the erotic afterglow.

But soon, a queasy feeling struck his stomach. The dangerous job of rounding up the Tri-megs was now at hand. He remembered the state funeral for Officer Craig Thomson. Thought about Ethan, sitting in a wheelchair, his stoic gaze as he faced the television cameras at the hospital.

Sean shook his head and went on with his morning routine. He dressed in a freshly pressed uniform and wore a bulletproof vest. At the end, he also put in his corrective contact lenses.

Scout followed him down to the kitchen. After letting his dog out in the back yard, instead of going on their usual morning walk to save time, he fed him and put down a fresh bowl of water before pouring a bowl of cereal for himself.

He drank the last sip of orange juice straight from the carton, thinking about how worried Vanessa sounded when they spoke on the phone last night. "Will you be safe and stay in the mobile office the entire time?" she'd asked.

"No," he'd said, knowing his reality vastly differed from her own. He rationalized her question was based on a hopeful wish. "I have to be outside, particularly in the beginning when we're first finding them."

"Well, if you're not home in the evenings, who's going to take care of Scout?"

He'd never thought to ask for anyone's help. "I don't know. I was going to leave extra food and water."

But she offered to come and feed Scout in the evening, and Sean wanted her around.

He finished his breakfast and gave Scout a treat before leaving the house. Lustful memories of his erotic dream flashed through his mind as Sean made his way to Quarry Head Park. Only after seeing a police car on patrol did his focus shift back to work.

He entered the park, experiencing an overwhelming sense of déjà vu. Stark, bare branches of the trees contrasted against the somber gray morning sky, as the advent of winter loomed over the splendor of autumn.

Danger lurks here. We have to restore safety. Suddenly, all the hours of effort with Frank, with the scientists, with the media, entered his mind. *All this painstaking work put into planning, and it could all come crashing down at any one moment.* He went over the details in his mind again and again, making certain he didn't miss anything.

Recently the beautiful park had taken on the appearance of a construction site within the one acre where the police, scientists, and technicians had mobilized their resources, working as a dedicated team. He walked over to Frank, hearing frost crackle under his boots. He could see his breath in the frigid air. The mobile office, bulldozers, and heat lamps obstructed the view of the woodlands.

Frank greeted Sean heartily. "It's looking good. One last check of the first two sites, and I'll give the order to start the equipment. Let's grab a motor bike and check out the set-ups."

"Right, Frank," Sean said.

He reveled in grabbing the handlebars and hearing the roar of the engine. Strapping on his helmet, he reminisced about his experiences with Frank. If they got the Tri-megs back home, Sean wondered if the colonel would continue to send his officers to oversee his work like before. Some federal department might have a say in that too. He did notice that ever since he saved Frank from going overboard on the boat, the colonel scrutinized his work less.

Together they rode down the first cleared trail.

After stopping and looking over the equipment, Frank said, "It's set up properly. Let's check out site two."

Sean looked up at the now-quiet lights and heat lamps that towered over his head, knowing they would be switched on within the hour. They took off, continuing to the second resting area.

A few minutes later they crossed a stream, their dirt bikes splashing water about. Soon after, they arrived at the second resting site. Sean stood with his bike and took off his helmet. He took in a deep breath, admiring the hills covered in dense forests.

This second resting area had the same equipment as in the first and looked just as impressive. He walked around with Frank giving everything one last inspection. After a few minutes he told Frank everything looked good. They roared off on their motorbikes, the dirt kicking up as the wheels spun.

Once at the mobile office, Sean parked the bike nearby and joined the large group now milling about in front of the building, about half a mile from the main parking lot. Four of the six scientists—Greg, Lee, Mike, and Irene—were present, as well as the combined forces of town and state police.

Motioning for everyone to gather, Frank looked over the group and shouted out in his best megaphone voice, "This is a historic day. You've all worked hard. Now let's start operation Back to the Nest."

Everyone knew what to do and hurried to their designated positions.

"Okay, then. Here we go," Greg said as he joined his three colleagues as they entered the trailer.

Outside, Sean and Frank returned to the first resting spot. "Greg, we're ready for you to turn on the equipment," Sean said on his radio transmitter.

"Right away," came Greg's voice. "The program's up, and I'm starting the generator, two heating units, overhead lights, and heat lamps."

Inside the floodlit area, perspiration formed on Sean and Frank's foreheads after five minutes.

"Everything is working. It's hot as hell here," Frank said. "Now, I'm going to have Tent start blasting inward from the perimeter. No one is allowed to leave the office until further notice."

Sean traveled back to the trailer to check the monitors. When he entered, he saw each of the three screens displayed images from all over the park, ready for the scientists to hunt for views of the elusive Tri-megs.

Greg had just checked the temperatures at the site.

"The heaters are set to ninety degrees, and with the lights and heat lamps we should be able to keep the area as high as seventy-eight degrees, depending on the outside temperature and wind. Right now, it's holding at seventy-five degrees."

Sean nodded. "I could feel the heat back there. Seemed to be working."

The controlled blasts sounded off in the distance, reassuring him the operation was going as planned. He looked through the window at a huge puff of gray smoke hovering over the canopy of the trees. Soon, they would find out if the Tri-megs would appear.

Hours passed. An incoming transmission from Frank sounded impatient. "We're not seeing any movement from the reptiles. I'm going to have Tent blast the area again."

"We might not be close enough to them," Greg replied. "The Tri-megs haven't been seen recently. They may have moved somewhere else in the park."

"I'll have Tent set off explosives further away from the entrance to try to cover more ground," Frank said.

The day went on, with still no sightings of the Tri-megs. Sean ached inwardly from the stress of no progress.

Finally, at around four o'clock, daylight started to fade. Frank radioed for Sean to meet him in the mobile office. "Where are they?" he demanded with a scowl.

"We think we need more cameras by the small pond that's about a half mile away," Greg replied.

Sean waited for Frank's response, itching for a course of action after the day's lack of progress.

"Why?" Frank asked.

Irene's lips curled into a charming smile as she spoke directly to him. "Since they're marine creatures, the most likely place for them to be if they stayed in this area would be that pond further west. We suspect they will be searching for another underground lake environment within any body of water they come across. Right now, there's hardly any video surveillance there, so it's important to set more cameras up."

"Why didn't I know about this before?"

"We're doing our best," Lee said. "We just thought of it now. None of this has ever been done before."

"Fine," the colonel said, still frowning.

"I'm staying," Sean said.

"As for the rest of you, come back here at eight a.m. tomorrow morning."

With a bustle of activity, and a din of chatter, the scientists signed out with state trooper Dale Chapman. Police officers carrying machine guns escorted them to their cars. Officer Chapman would wait to be relieved.

While Frank made the necessary arrangements, Sean had a

moment to himself. He walked to a quiet area with large boulders, sat then called Vanessa. With no real progress and chilled by the cool air, he was restless.

"Hi, Sean," she answered with enthusiasm, but he could still sense her concern. "I've been thinking about you. Are you safe?"

"Couldn't be safer. We haven't seen them yet."

"I'm sorry. Are you able to go home now?"

"No. Not 'til later. We have to set up more surveillance equipment."

"Okay, I'll go to your house and take care of Scout."

"I appreciate it. I can't stay on the phone long. I just wanted you to know I'm all right, and the first free evening I get, I want to be with you."

"I want to see you, too," Vanessa said, sighing.

They spoke for a few more minutes. After they said goodbye, Sean looked out at the horizon at the setting sun. An orange glow covered the mountains. He wished he could share the moment with Vanessa.

He stood and slowly let out a deep breath. *Back to work.*

When he entered the mobile office, Frank looked up from his seat in front of the monitors next to Dale. "Hey, Sean. Not a very productive day."

"No, let's hope these additional cameras make a difference," Sean said, taking the chair beside him.

"Watch this. I'm going to switch those cameras over to night vision," Frank said.

It took a moment for the program to start. Sean, Dale and Frank looked on.

"Now that's a good system. The images couldn't be much clearer," Frank said.

"Impressive," Sean said, recognizing that the night vision views looked similar to the hues of greens he usually saw with his unaided vision. "Can we bring up Echo Lake yet?"

"No. It was up, but then there was some technical trouble. They're working on it."

An officer knocked on the door and entered. "Colonel, the path has been cleared, and we're loading the equipment on the truck now."

"We'll be right there," Frank said.

Sean zipped up his jacket and put on his gloves before stepping back into the chilly air. The full moon provided some much-needed light as he and Frank joined the driver.

The truck descended a gentle hill to a cleared area. Sean

jumped out of the vehicle and helped the driver unload the solar panels.

Hours were spent overseeing a crew clearing trees and installing the new cameras in positions that would allow unobstructed views of the pond. Sean gratefully snacked on a packet of trail mix he kept on hand and a bottle of water he'd put in his jacket pocket. More than half of the local and state police officers had gone home, but a skeleton crew of stand-by officers remained. Along with their subordinates, the chiefs made certain the surveillance equipment worked properly. The truck driver took them back to the entrance where they returned to the mobile office to clock out.

Exhausted, he drove home. When he approached his house, he noticed Vanessa left a light on for him. He stepped inside, and Scout showed his delight by jumping up and down before running up to him.

"Good boy, Scout," he said, patting the dog's back.

On the way to the kitchen, he noticed that the dog food bowl had been used and the water bowl freshly filled. On the kitchen counter he saw a note in Vanessa's beautiful handwriting.

> *Sean,*
> *I fed Scout and let him run in the backyard.*
> *We both miss you.*
> *Vanessa*

"I'm jealous," he said, glaring playfully with crossed arms at the panting dog. "You get to see her, but I don't."

Thirty-Two
Romance

Sean woke up alone in bed. Sighing, he longed for another evening with Vanessa. He peered out his window, staring at the faint glow of dawn.

After a very quick morning walk with Scout, he found himself back at the front entrance of Quarry Head Park. Scientists walked over to the mobile office, taking measured steps and frowning.

Sean joined them and asked, "What are you talking about?"

"Mostly the weather," Greg said. "You see we were concerned that the cold could kill them, and we're still worried about that. Hopefully they found a protected area where they're trying to keep from freezing."

"That's right," Lee said. "Although it's quite cold today, they're predicting unseasonably warmer weather for tomorrow. When the temperature rises, they'll be more inclined to come out and bask in the sun."

Frank walked over from nearby. Hearing some of their discussion he asked, "What are you suggesting? The additional surveillance cameras are up. Are you ready?"

"We're just as eager as you are to find the Tri-megs and get them back to their home, but we think today is just too cold for the reptiles. Tomorrow's weather is supposed to be sunny and in the mid-fifties. We're thinking nothing will happen until then," Greg said.

Intense frustration showed on the colonel's face. After asking several more questions, the scientists' collective expertise seemed to convince him they were right. "I'm very disappointed we're wasting resources today, but let's move on. We'll be back to start at eight a.m. sharp tomorrow morning."

Knowing that he had fallen behind in his paperwork, Sean returned to his office. Normally he liked a cool room temperature, but after days of working outdoors in the cold, he cranked up his office thermostat, welcoming the heat. He imagined making a cozy fire in his living room fireplace and making love to Vanessa on the rug.

With the arousing reverie still fresh in his mind, he called her at the shop. She sounded happily surprised to hear from him and just as eager to make plans to go out for dinner after work.

For the next few hours, he pored through his briefing notes, gave out assignments, approved the dates for the free CPR classes offered at the high school, and worked out a tentative schedule for the other community programs his department offered for December.

He also read over the latest update on the Jason Kenner file: "...Kenner moved twice in the last three years, and there are no decisive leads as to where he might be. Kenner's status on the National Missing Persons System is updated weekly. The owners will take possession of the house he's renting on December 15th..." Sean sighed. *We're no closer to finding him.*

His phone rang, and when Frank's number appeared on the screen, he saw his plans for the evening slipping away.

"Two of the surveillance cameras stopped working, and I'm making arrangements to have them repaired right away. I need you to meet me at Quarry Head," Frank said.

"Now?" Sean asked, repressing his feelings of dismay.

"Yes, now. We're starting again tomorrow morning. It needs to be done ASAP," Frank said, ending the discussion.

Disappointed, Sean phoned Vanessa right away.

"Is everything okay?" she asked.

He could tell by her tone she knew a second call from him after setting a date wasn't good news. "I just spoke to Frank, and I have to go back to Quarry Head. I don't know how long I'll be there. I'm not happy about it, but you know…"

"Oh, no. What's going on?"

"Some equipment malfunctions. I'll probably be there most of the evening. I feel so bad about this."

"You don't have to apologize. Although, I was looking forward to seeing you."

"I was too. Oh, man!"

"I understand. Don't worry, I'll go to your house to take care of Scout."

"I appreciate it. Are you finding everything okay?"

She laughed. "Yes, you have a terrific dog. He's making me miss having a pet."

"He's a great dog. I'm glad I found him."

"Be safe tonight. I can't help being scared when I think about you out there."

"I'll be fine. Listen, there's still no news on Jason. I found out that the owners of the house have the right to take back possession of it on December 15th. Ryan already contacted Jason's family to pass on the message. I just wanted you to know."

"Thanks for telling me. Maybe I'll call his mom and see if I can do anything to help her. I just can't believe no one has heard from him."

"I'm sorry. It's frustrating for me. I wish I had better news for you."

"Me too. But you have enough on your mind right now with the reptiles in the park. Focus on that and be safe."

It continued to bother him that Jason's file remained opened. Sean signed off on the last report and left to meet Frank at Quarry Head.

Driving past the entrance to the town center on his way to the park, he felt the lure of knowing Vanessa was just a minute away in her store. Acting upon an impulse, he turned the car around and pulled up at Annabel's Flower Shop. With no time to spare, he ran into the store and purchased a bouquet of red and pink roses.

"For someone special?" the woman behind the counter asked with a pleasant smile.

"Very."

Hurrying back to his car, he drove down the block and turned into the parking lot. Tucking the beautiful assortment under his jacket, he waved hello to Jenny. Moments later, with a grin on his face, he spotted Vanessa near the back of her shop, stacking boxes of Christmas cards on a shelf. With no one nearby, he snuck up behind her and gently brushed her hair to the side, so he could kiss the back of her neck.

She jumped and spun. Her eyes lit up when she saw him standing in front of her. Without uttering a word, she grabbed his hand and led him to her office. "What are you doing here? Did your plans change?" she asked, her eyes glinting.

"No, I just couldn't wait any longer to see you, and I wanted to bring you this," he said, holding out the bouquet.

"Oh, they're so beautiful!" she said, her gaze brimming with delight.

Putting his hands around her waist, he tugged her to him, away from the open door. She dropped the gift on the desk and wrapped her arms around his shoulders.

"I need to be with you," he said, kissing her.

"I want you too."

"I only have a minute," he said, caressing her body.

"That's not enough time," she whispered, closing her eyes.

It's really not, he thought, stirred by the feel of her body pressed against his.

"I'm going to have to go," he said, still running his fingers through her hair and down her back. "But the next day I'm free I'm going to come get you and carry you back to my house."

"Promise?" She smiled.

"Yes."

"I love the flowers. Thank you."

They slowly kissed, and she stroked his chest.

He held her hands and kissed her again, letting each one linger. "You don't know how hard it is for me to go. But I have to."

The last thing he saw was her flirtatious smile. *Oh boy.*

He drove the short distance to Quarry Head Park where he met up with Frank in the mobile office and together, they went with the technical team to remove and replace the faulty cameras. It took several hours to repair and rewire both units. He glanced at Frank, who despite being over twenty years his senior, still managed to display stamina under pressure.

Finally, around eleven p.m. they finished the job. Frank ordered the crew to head home, ensuring the officer stationed in the mobile office continued to check that all the surveillance equipment continued to work properly through the night.

Ready for some rest, Sean left the park, hoping Vanessa had left him another note.

He walked into his home pleased as always with Scout's high-spirited greeting. When he strolled into the kitchen, Sean smiled seeing another page from his notepad with her lovely handwriting.

Sean,

You made my day. I only wish we had more time together.

I love my flowers. I'm keeping them in my bedroom—where I love to think of you.

Vanessa.

Chuckling he walked over to his well-padded couch. Blissfully he rested his head on the soft cushion. Scout, his tongue hanging out, jumped onto Sean's chest and licked his face. He laughed and pushed him away just enough so he could pat his dog on the back.

They both fell asleep right there.

Thirty-Three
Basking

Greg gazed at the screen in front of him. Another new day, and already several hours had gone by. This time, though, temperatures seemed more accommodating; he did not clasp the seam of his old wool blend coat as tightly this morning as he had the past two days. In fact, he felt warm inside the mobile office, so he took off his jacket, comfortable in just his frayed dark blue sweatshirt. The day did not start with Tent and his crew blasting. The scientists felt the Tri-megs would come out naturally to bask in the sun, so they convinced Frank to give them a chance to do just that.

"Nice weather," Lee said as she looked out the window. The sun shone brightly overhead.

"Yes, if the Tri-megs don't rouse themselves today we may start worrying they didn't survive that cold snap when the temperature went below freezing," Mike said.

After this sobering thought Greg resumed his monitoring work in silence.

On the screens, live feeds of the usual New England wildlife—chipmunks, squirrels, and woodpeckers—came into view. Rays of sunshine filtered through the tree branches, reflecting off the rippled surface of the small pond in Quarry Head.

Frank's voice broke through on the radio, stirring Greg out of his trance. "It's been hours," he barked. "I'm having Tent's team get ready to set off the explosives."

"Hold on. I understand you want to start now, but the Tri-megs should be coming out sometime soon since the sun's nearly at its peak. Please just give it 'til noon."

"You have fifteen minutes." Frank didn't sound convinced.

Suddenly, a slight shift of the office caused Greg and some of the others to hold onto their seats or the desk for support.

Lee shuffled her feet in response, and the other scientists straightened in their chairs. Alert, Officer Hendricks radioed Frank right away about the sudden disturbance. Aaron, the lead computer technician, glanced over the equipment, his neck craned.

"What was *that*?" Irene asked, her voice alarmed.

"Could it be a Tri-meg?" Tova asked, rising from her seat to cast a frantic glance at the others.

"It could be," Greg said, holding his hands up as he attempted to stay calm and calculate his next step. "Don't move. I'm going to aim the video camera toward the office."

"Can the Tri-megs break in here?" Aaron asked.

"No, I don't think so," Lee said. "They most likely will not attack. They become aggressive if they feel threatened, but that's not the case here."

"I agree," Mike added. "I think if that was a Tri-meg right next to us, it would be trying to bask against the wall here. The outside surface of this office can get quite warm, after all."

Greg frowned. "I can't see anything right next to us. The camera doesn't zoom back that far. Frank?" he called into the transmitter.

"Yes?"

"We think there's a Tri-meg next to the office. Tell everyone to stay away—we don't want anyone to get hurt."

There was a pause. Then came Frank's heightened response. "What?"

"Just check it out from a distance, please. We think it's attracted to the sun's warmth on our walls outside."

The other scientists' eyes grew wide as Frank swore over the sound system. "Don't move! Everyone, hold your positions."

The scientists all paused, looking at one another.

"No one is to come within a five-hundred-yard perimeter of the mobile office unless I say so," he commanded. He then spoke staccato-style on his radio, laying out his orders to assorted officers including Sergeant Tent.

Within minutes he spoke again, addressing Greg and the others in the office. "First, let's verify it's actually there. We never intended for the cameras to point straight at the office," Frank said. "I can't see the office from where I am even with the binoculars. I'm going to get closer."

"Wait. Give me a minute, and I'll see if I can see it." Greg put the transmitter on his desk and walked up to the window and propped himself against the wall. He gasped at the sight of the gigantic creature right below him.

In its resting position, the Tri-meg's back nearly matched the height of the windowsill. From his line of view, he could only see the top of the body. His gaze traced the contours of the scaly creature all the way up its long tapering neck to its head planted against the warm wall. He watched the rise and fall of each breath. Enchanted with the magnificence of the specimen before him, he continued to study it.

"Greg," Lee urged, "Can you see it?"

"Yes," he whispered.

At long last. A Tribolmegasaur had appeared.

The others dared to stand atop their chairs after bringing them over, just a little closer.

"Beautiful, isn't it?" Lee said, her features soft and mesmerized by this wonder of nature.

"Anything further, Greg?" came Frank's impatient voice.

Greg returned to his seat. "Sorry!" Clutching the transmitter once again, he continued, "Well, it's hard for us to see all of it, but it's definitely lying against the office."

"I have my field camera," Mike said, walking over with the device in his hand. "I'll take a picture for the file. This one can now be labeled T-meg number one. If we get a better view, we can compare it with the ones already on record."

"I see more creatures on the screen now," said Irene, pointing to the monitor.

"What did Irene just say?" Frank's voice came in.

Lee sat back away from the window, and Greg brought over the walkie-talkie to Irene and stood behind her, marveling at yet more Tri-meg sightings in the grid of images on the monitors.

"Hello, Frank," Irene spoke in quiet tone. "We were right about the pond after all. I see one under the surface of the water, with its fins splayed."

Greg darted back to his chair to sort out images of the giant reptiles spotted to date. Having received training on the program he navigated the commands on the computer screen and started clicking away. "I've downloaded the photo Mike took of our Tri-meg by the office—that's T-meg number one. The one Irene found in the pond is now labeled T-meg number two for the record."

"Look at this ledge," Lee exclaimed in an outburst.

Greg's eyes widened. Two Tri-megs lay peacefully together east of the pond. Their bodies neatly hidden against the shelves of rocks by the surrounding fallen leaves.

"T-meg number three and T-meg number four," Greg said, beaming with pride. Clipping out two separate frames of the reptiles, he labeled them accordingly and put them into the electronic file.

Frank's voice boomed in over the radio. "Perfect. After two days, they finally show up. Okay, I'll order the blasting so we can encourage these animals to go straight ahead to the first resting site."

"Go ahead, Frank. We don't see any other Tri-megs, although I think there could be at least one more."

"All right. Everyone at the ready. We'll start the explosives now."

Minutes later, booming thunder rocked the ground, causing the team inside the mobile office to jump despite the heads up. A second later, movement rocked the entire structure. Greg and the others inside stumbled, but recovered quickly. Greg snapped a photo of the Tri-meg before it sped away.

Irene scanned the screen. "Hey," she exclaimed. "The Tri-megs by the pond are gone!"

"Everything okay in there?" Sean's voice came over the radio.

"Yes, Sean," Greg answered, holding up the transmitter. "The Tri-meg at our office is gone, and the two by the ledge have taken off in the right direction."

"Excellent," Frank responded. "Now, steady. Greg, try to keep an eye on them as they move."

"Will do," he responded, hopeful. Yet, he wondered why no one saw T-meg number two from the pond on any of the monitors.

Then came Sean's voice, "Greg. There's one still in the water."

He brought up the video recordings and found T-meg number two with just its head poking out of the surface.

"I can have Tent scare it out," Frank said.

"I guess we have no choice."

Frank met Tent in the mobile office. Greg and his team gave their professional input on the plan to move T-meg number two toward the resting site.

On the monitor Greg observed a short, flax-haired officer climb the ledge and place dynamite near the pond. *Where was Tent?* He understood, nodding. Clearly, the commander of the explosives project would supervise the work from a safe distance. As the officer wedged the explosives between the boulders, T-meg number two emerged above the pond's surface and slithered onto the shoreline, in close proximity to the human victim. The giant creature braced itself on its four flippers and reared up, over twelve feet tall. The officer, his mouth wide open, jumped down the rocky surface and scrambled to take cover behind a crop of boulders.

Tent's commanding voice cracked. "Ready to blast—now!"

A booming sound broke out.

Greg gripped the desk so hard his knuckles turned white as he watched the Tri-meg dive back into the water. He held his breath as he hoped the Tri-meg would leave the pond and join the others.

At the sound of a second explosion, the skittish Tribolmegasaur surfaced, slithering side-to-side into an area of tall pine and spruce trees.

For a moment, the office was quiet until Sean's voice broke in. "Did you see the Tri-meg leave the pond?"

Greg took in a deep breath. "Yes, Sean. It's going in the right direction."

He settled back in his chairs, taking a sip of cold water from his water bottle to release his pent-up anxiety and get back to the task of tracking the Tribolmegasaurs.

Time ticked by slowly as he waited for another glimpse of the reptiles on the screens.

And as he began to worry that the creatures were now lost and nowhere near the resting area they'd established for them, Irene said, "I see one approaching camera seven."

"There's another one behind it now," Tova declared, leaning over her shoulder.

"How are we going to keep up with them? We'll never be able to have them all in view simultaneously," Lee said.

"That's right," Greg said. "All we can do is review more sections of the park on the monitors as they go by and hope to make more sightings." The first ever chase of prehistoric reptiles, he noted with trepidation.

Two of the Tri-megs had been spotted again, in the zone of camera twelve. Determining that the quarter-mile benchmark had been attained, Greg agreed with Frank's decision to have Sergeant Tent set off another round of explosions to make certain the reptiles did not return to the pond, but instead would continue toward the "prize" that the humans had painstakingly erected for them.

Step-by-step, the recurring strategy continued. Controlled blasts in strategic locations. New views of the Tri-megs captured on cameras further ahead. More rounds of explosions, all herding them toward the heat and basking lights generously waiting at the first resting stop.

"The sun's going down and the temperature's dropping. They're so close to the resting area now," Irene said.

"That's right. We shouldn't need to stress them out with more blasting. It's time to cross our fingers and pray that they'll reach the area on their own," Lee replied.

Greg notified Frank to hold off on the use of any more explosives.

"Well, that is the mother lode," Mike said. "They'd be crazy to give it up all that wonderful heat."

"We hope," Lee added.

Mike paced back and forth keeping his gaze on the monitors; Lee bit her lip. Everyone in the office remained silent. Time passed. Hardly blinking, Greg stared at the screen in front of him.

And then Irene cried out, "Oh my Lord! There they are."'

Thirty-Four
Warmer

The Tri-megs had arrived at the first stop on their way back to their home.

Sean could hear Greg's excitement over the radio. "All right! That's T-meg number three, and next to it is T-meg number four."

Their lengths each estimated at twenty feet, these two Tri-megs sat together on the ledge. Both had a distinguished rust-orange streak to their scales, whereas, T-meg number three displayed this robust color on its head. T-meg four displayed this hue on its long neck.

Excitement in the area was palpable. Fingers danced on dozens of smartphones in the area at the top of the dirt road to the park, where reporters learned what happened. They called their stations to alert them of the breaking news.

The moment he had a chance, Sean reached out to Vanessa. Thrilled, sharing the news with her infused into him a warm sense of bonding. She thanked him for being thoughtful enough to check in, signing off with the sound of a kiss.

When the sun set, the two leaders Sean and Frank strolled inside the mobile office. Gazing at the three screens, the five scientists didn't turn heads as they entered.

"Do you think they'll stay together through the night?" Irene asked.

"I'm not sure. In their habitat underground they may sleep together in dens for warmth. If that's the case, they should stay together," Greg said.

"Hey, guys." Lee's eyes were wide. "I see two more Tri-megs in there. It looks like we have T-meg one, the smallest one that was against the office this morning, and I believe the other is nearly twice its size, possibly T-meg number two from the pond."

Everyone gathered around Greg's monitor to watch the Tri-megs approach their companions and lie down next to each other under the warm glow of the heat lamps and overhead lights.

"What do you suggest we do now?" Frank asked Greg, glancing out the window at the sunset.

"We all agree a few of us should sit tight and watch the area overnight. We have four in view and we believe there is a fifth."

"But you're not certain."

"No, but from the field reports we went over the descriptions of every Tribolmegasuar that's been seen from the first one that attacked Ethan and Ann to now. Seems that the one from the first siting is still out there. Judging by the estimated size at least, but it's hard to be one hundred percent sure."

"How will we find the missing ones—if there are any?" Frank asked.

"It's very cold out, and the heat at the site is working to attract them. If there are more, they may be nearby. Or maybe we can find them in another area with the surveillance cameras."

"That's a lot of maybes." He frowned.

"I know. I don't like that either. Most reptiles are solitary creatures; however, when temperatures drop they all need to find warmth. What we've created at these sites is something like an above ground hibernaculum, an area where they can gather that is protected from frost and freezing temperatures. I'm fairly confident that if other Tri-megs are nearby, they will join them."

"Well, there'll be officers on the monitors 'round the clock. We'll have to be diligent."

"I'll be happy to stay longer, at least until 10 p.m.," Greg said, "so I can continue to try to find any others."

With his condition, Sean knew he'd be the best at spotting the reptile, especially at night. "I'll stay too."

"Okay, you can all stay as long as you want, just make sure you sign out with the officer on duty when you leave."

"Thanks, Frank," said a grateful Greg.

"I see it just switched over to night vision," Sean noted as everyone turned back toward the screens.

During the evening, one by one, the team members signed out with the officer in charge. Sean stayed on patrol outside. He discretely removed his contact to give himself the advantage of seeing better in the dark and deciphering camouflage. After some time passed, he went back into the trailer to sit with Greg.

"It's getting late, but before I go home I'm going to do one more complete scan of the grounds with the surveillance equipment," Greg said.

"I'll take a look with you. Any more thoughts on where any others could be?"

"If there're more, they most likely found spots warmer than the near freezing outdoor temperature. I've been looking at the rock ledges. They may have retained some heat from the day's sun, although not for long."

Sean stared intently at the monitor. "Can you put camera thirteen on the full screen?"

"Sure." Greg clicked on the view of a spot approximately five hundred feet north of the resting site. It consisted of a hilly area with a rock outcrop, much like what he just described.

"There!" Sean pointed to the monitor. His gaze steady and laser-focused.

"What?" Greg asked.

"Can you see the white oblong spot, in the bottom left corner? I think that's the eye of a Tri-meg," Sean said, viewing it clearly.

Greg squinted at the screen while Sean waited. Leaning back, he whistled. "You found it!"

Thirty-Five
Dreams

Two days later, while Vanessa unpacked more Christmas ornaments for sale at her store, she thought about how the town seemed busier. There were certainly more people shopping. The winter holidays usual brought in additional customers, but that was not the only reason. Just as Sean predicted, hundreds of out-of-town reporters, scientists, and government officials scheduled meetings in Wilton to discuss the Tribolmegasaurs. In addition, a large number of curious tourists streamed into "Tri-meg Town" because Quarry Head Park was only minutes away. Some of these visitors stopped into her shop and bought something as a token of their trip, or picked up a last-minute gift.

She wondered if the near-constant saturated news coverage of the reptiles would result in Wilton becoming a regular tourist destination. In the back of her mind she thought about commissioning souvenirs with Tribolmegasaur on them or even having figurines of the creatures made, but she purposely waited, knowing that the reptiles still presented a grave danger, and she would not capitalize on that.

From what she'd heard on the radio and from phone conversations with Sean, Operation Back to the Nest continued to be a success. After two frustrating days of no sightings, the authorities found five Tri-megs and had been successfully corralling them through the park using the rest stops. The radio news announcer breathlessly told a captive crowd that tomorrow they would reach the third resting area, the final one before returning to Echo Lake and their underground lake home. All over the country and especially in Connecticut, people followed the developments as enthusiastically as they would the Super Bowl or the Olympics.

Other than his romantic stop at her shop to give her those gorgeous flowers, Vanessa hadn't seen Sean in over a week. She tenderly attended to them, changing the water every day to ensure they'd last as long as possible.

While taking care of Scout, she started getting used to Sean's house, absorbing his presence when she walked through the front door and picking up tiny clues about him, the man. The pile of takeout menus in the corner of the kitchen counter, along with the almost empty refrigerator...*probably not a cook or maybe he just doesn't have time*. He liked to hang his jackets and sweatshirts on the banister of the stairs. She found junk mail and magazines, one on men's fitness, on the small kitchen table. A small dish on the kitchen counter had a few keys and an expensive looking flexible fitness band in black.

Each time she passed the front hall, she gazed at the adoring photos of him posing with his parents at his graduation from the police academy. *He probably had more attention from them being an only child.*

Still at her shop, she finished writing a last-minute order and then drove to his house. *Poor Sean.* Putting in so many hours at the park, in addition to his regular duties as police chief. For a moment, she thought about running over to his office and clearing up his paperwork, but laughed at the idiocy of the idea. He did appreciate that she left some blueberry muffins from the bakery in his refrigerator. *When would he have time to shop?*

Soon the work to lure the Tri-megs home would be over. Then she could have him back.

He must have realized he would not be home before dark and left a light on in the entrance. Scout ran over to greet her with his tail wagging. "Good boy," she told him and bent over to stroke the happy dog's furry head and back.

"Okay, boy, it's okay," she said as he started licking her face. "Let's get you out for a walk."

She turned on the kitchen light to get his leash from the drawer and found a note Sean left for her on the counter.

Vanessa,
The reptiles are moving closer to Echo Lake.
It's amazing watching these giant creatures but I'm hoping we can get them home soon.
Last night I dreamed we were at your house again.
It's been too long since I've had you in my arms.
I miss you.
Sean

Holding the paper to her breasts, she sighed, daydreaming about their intimate night together. She gently touched her fingers to her lips remembering his deep passionate kisses and the ecstasy she felt when he caressed her naked body.

She closed her eyes, only to have Scout's barking jolt her back to reality.

"Sorry, boy, here we go."

The light of the moon cast a soft glow on the streets as she walked Scout down the quiet road. She enjoyed looking at the star-filled sky, but felt a chill at the back of her neck thinking about Sean being in Quarry Head Park with the Tri-megs lurking about. Deciding to cut short her walk, she tugged at Scout's leash.

"Come on, boy," she said. "You can run around the backyard."

When they walked back inside the home, she felt calm again as she watched Scout romp about in the well-lit, fenced-in yard from inside the warm house before calling him in for food.

He quickly ate, then walked to the front door and slumped down on the floor, as if dejected about his missing master.

I miss him, too. She left Sean a loving message.

Sean,
I've been following the reported sightings of the reptiles.
Please stay safe.
I had fun with Scout. We both miss playing with you.
You can tell me about your dream when we see each other and I'll tell you about mine.
Vanessa

Thirty-Six
Fog

Sean woke up five minutes before his 7:00 a.m. alarm. He hadn't tried to call Vanessa last night because he worked later than usual, and he thought she would be sleeping. When he read her note that said she fantasized about him too, he could not stop thinking about her.

He peered out his window at the threatening rain clouds across the sky. After getting ready for work, he put on a heavy jacket and took Scout for a short walk.

Checking the weather on his laptop at his kitchen table, he read the forecast: late day thunderstorms and heavy fog with the possibility of freezing rain. He finished breakfast and put his rain gear in a bag. Before leaving, he wrote to Vanessa.

Vanessa,
If you're here and the weather is bad, please consider staying over. I don't want you driving home in a bad storm and I'd love to find you in my bed!
Please be safe.
Sean

Light rain showers were starting to fall when Sean arrived at the park. Greg and his team, Mike, Lee, and Irene showed, eager for Frank to begin the morning meeting. Everyone gathered outside the mobile office.

"Good morning," Frank said, squinting as the rain hit his face. "The five Tri-megs stayed at the second resting area through the night. The equipment from the first site has been transported to the third location. Sergeant Tent's team has positioned explosives on three sides of the preserve leaving the third resting site as the only safe place for them to go. I've instructed two additional officers from my department to patrol Whitmere and Wildflower Road. These streets border the Tribol Preserve. I want the surveillance cameras for that area up at all times—that would be cameras twenty-three, twenty-four, and twenty-six."

"Can we wait until they start moving on their own before we use the explosives? There was so much blasting the past three days they might get used to it, and we definitely don't want that," Greg said.

"That's fine. Radio me when you want to begin. For now, we'll turn off the heat and lights. I'm assuming they will start to move in the next hour or two?"

"Yes, they should be waking up soon."

"If everyone's ready, let's take our positions," Frank said.

Curious, Sean went to the mobile office to see the Tri-megs on the monitor. He stood in front of the screen, watching the reptiles huddled under the now-powered down heat lamps and lights, the cold moving in. The colors of their scaled bodies blended with the mustard yellow and burnt orange patches of the fallen leaves, symbolizing solidarity with the earth. *Unbelievable.*

All three computer monitors had the video images of the entrance to the Tribol Preserve on the bottom row of the screens, just as Frank had ordered.

Everyone assembled around the desk, focusing on the images, making idle talk. In the meantime, Sean waited more than half an hour for the Tri-megs to signal their awakening.

"Look, they're moving now," Lee exclaimed, the urgent sound of her voice alerting the others to take heed.

Two of the reptiles lifted their heads.

"I'll radio Frank," Greg said. "They're looking for warmth again."

Motivated, Sean left the office to patrol outside with Ann. Together, for two hours, they surveyed the area, keeping in close contact with all the team members at work.

"One of the Tri-megs may have separated from the rest," a worried Greg said into the radio. "It's T-meg number two. I'll let you know when we pick it up on the monitors again."

The rain clouds intensified, darkening the day. Soggy leaves made the muddy ground slippery under Sean's boots. Streams of water poured out in torrents in front of his police chief cap visor.

"Sean," Greg radioed, "I think you better come in."

"On my way," Sean said, directing Ann to pair up with another officer on patrol.

When he entered the mobile office, he placed his dripping wet raincoat on the hook by the door and put on a spare jacket he kept in a bag in the corner. He glanced at Greg's screen, catching a glimpse of the missing Tri-meg, now lurking near Wildflower Road.

"There," Greg said, pointing to the image. "That's T-meg number two, and it's too close to the street. You think you can get it back on course?"

"Yes. It's a job for Tent. I'll call it in." He placed the call.

"Careful," Greg said, as Sean put on his rain gear.

Handling his motorbike, Sean had to be mindful of the wet terrain, especially since tree roots, boulders, and broken branches, filled the area.

After several minutes, he halted upon an elevated point that gave him a view of Wildflower Road in case he could spot the errant Tri-meg. A rapidly moving light in the distance alerted him to the presence of Sergeant Tent on a motorcycle, giving the signal that more blasting was imminent. Plugging his fingers into his ears, Sean braced himself as a grenade exploded about fifty yards away.

After about ten minutes, he heard Greg's enthusiastic commentary on the radio, "Hey, guys! It worked! T-meg number two was caught on video back in the preserve."

He heard some cheers in the background of the transmission.

The sun set, and crosswinds emerged, scattering rain in every direction. The drops coated the lenses of the video cameras. That, combined with the fog that rose from the ground, made viewing the surveillance footage extremely difficult.

He returned to the mobile office just in time to here Irene announce that T-megs number one and three made it to the warmth of the heat lamps and lights at the third resting area.

"That's a relief. I was wondering if this storm would affect their behavior," Sean said.

She turned to him with a smile on her face. "We were too, but they seem to be finding the heat just fine."

"There's T-meg number five. I'm switching to the night lights. It's already too dark to see," Greg said.

Just then, Frank strolled in, drenched and bursting with tension. "All Tri-megs accounted for?" he snapped.

"Not yet. Right now, there are only three at the site. We're missing T-meg number two and T-meg number four but that doesn't mean they're not nearby. We can barely see anything on the monitor. The rain's too heavy, and the fog's too thick," Mike said.

"There!" Sean turned to see Lee pointing at the top left side of the screen and said. "I see them now!" she said. "There are two next to each other by those fallen branches."

Sean glanced at the monitor, spotting T-meg number two, the largest one in the group, and T-meg number four, the one with the dark orange color on its long neck.

"Thank heavens they've all reached the resting area," Irene said.

"That's it for now, team. For everyone's safety in this weather I'm suggesting you call it a day and rather return early tomorrow," Frank said, looking satisfied.

Sean waited until the scientists had been safely escorted to their cars by an officer from the state police.

"Okay," Frank announced to a small gathering of town and state police officers who remained and assembled in front of him just outside the mobile office. "We're very close to the end. The Tri-megs are all accounted for, and tomorrow we should be able to get them back to Echo Lake and from there, we can only hope they will find the restored access to the underground lake."

Sean, standing right beside Frank, felt exhilarated. *Then they will be back in their home!* There would be many things to do after the operation, including overseeing projects to secure the Tribol Preserve so no Tri-megs could leave the area. He already had meetings with conservation specialists and government officials regarding not only the Tribolmegasuars, but also the other unusual creatures in the underground lake on his calendar.

"It will be another late night tonight," Frank declared. "We have to move the heat lamps and lights from resting site number two, to as close to Echo Lake as we can. Once they're there, I'm certain they will head for the water."

Perfect!

Frank rattled off a short list of names, including Sean's. "If I called your name, you're with me. Let's go." He led the group to where a truck would take them to the second resting area where they would strike the equipment and move it to the shore.

He and Sean chatted briefly as they set off.

"Frank," said Sean, "I must admit, I'm feeling good about this. Now that the Tri-megs are so close to home, we may be able to declare the operation a success tomorrow. Although anything could still go wrong. We're just so close."

"I know." Frank grinned and patted Sean on the shoulder.

He smiled to himself.

The crew worked a few hours in the dark, securing all the equipment and readying everything for the next day. Through a clearing in the forest, he could now see Echo Lake just a hundred yards away.

Exhaling a deep breath, he closed his eyes and inhaled the

scent of the water. As the fog shifted, for a few brief minutes, moonlight shimmered on the surface of Echo Lake. In the dark of night, the lake looked enticingly beautiful.

Now, the last heat lamp shone. It's brilliant light, pierced the haze and the night sky. Frank ordered it off, and nodded to Sean. "That's it. Let's go."

He rode on the back seat of the truck to the mobile office, at which point Frank signed out and Sean remained. The rest of the small nighttime crew also headed home. Now only he and the officer assigned to the mobile office, Daniel, worked in the trailer. After lingering about inside the self-contained unit for several more minutes, so Sean could unwind by watching the images of the five Tri-megs huddled together, he signed out with Daniel.

Sean tugged his hood up over his head and hurried over the muddy ground toward the parking lot. He glanced around, admiring the silhouettes of the pines against the night sky and all the details of the forests with clarity, having removed his contact hours ago. After five minutes of following the path, he suddenly heard a brushing noise. Turning to see what made the sound, his instincts provoked him to draw his gun. He held up the weapon.

What was that? A vice-like grip of tension caused his throat to run dry. Mustering his confidence, after all, he had been trained to detect, avoid, and escape dangerous situations, he moved backward from the sound as quietly as possible.

In a flash, he saw with clarity, the tail of a Tribolmegasaur slithering through the bushes, only yards away.

Terror seized him.

The sound of his own feet trampling through the soaking wet leaves sounding unnaturally loud to his adrenalin-heightened senses.

He braced for action, planting one foot ready to propel him forward, his firearm raised ready to fire.

The creature turned and slithered toward him with faster speed than he could muster. It swung its neck around and wrapped its powerful jaws around Sean's chest. The reptile's teeth, like daggers, pierced into his bullet-proof vest, the vice-like grip relentless. He screamed from the fierce pain. The creature tightened its grip and rammed his shoulder against the jagged boulders on the ground as it carried him off.

Pouring rain muffled his call for help and the clouds of fog on the ground offered no hope of him being seen. Sean could feel his ribs cracking as he gasped for air. Fighting to remain conscious he heard his radio and phone shatter on a rock ledge. Struggling, he managed to aim his gun at the giant animal. Convulsing with intense spasms, Sean pressed the firearm into the reptile's thick muscular neck and compressed the trigger.

Blood from the scratches on his left shoulder ran down his arm. The bulletproof vest gave just enough protection to stop the creature's teeth from tearing into his flesh, but now it pressed on his damaged ribs further constricting his ability to breathe.

Man and beast dropped to the ground. The giant reptile recoiled and released the steel-like grip of its jaws.

In shock, Sean rolled over and down a steep incline. The forest floor shook as the massive Tribolmegasaur tumbled down the eight-foot ledge after him.

Trembling, now on his knees, he held his hand to his bloodied chest.

The reptile's dark red tongue darted in and out of its mouth as it neared its prey.

He collapsed to the ground, unconscious.

Thirty-Seven
Instinct

The roads in town were flooded from the downpour. With her fog lights on, Vanessa drove slowly to Sean's house around 8:30 p.m. after another busy and profitable day at her store. Cheerful she smiled, listening to a catchy rendition of *Jingle Bells* on the car radio.

Even with her umbrella up, she had to run to the front door to avoid getting soaked. Finding the note Sean left for her on the kitchen counter, she picked it up, curious. She beamed when she read that he wanted her to stay over.

Scout followed her through the house, wagging his tail. She let the excited dog out in the backyard, but he returned drenched after only a minute. She used some paper towels to dry him off before feeding him dinner.

Looking outside through the large window in the entrance, she watched the trees sway in the wind. A branch fell from a tall maple, startling her, but only for a second. The rain pounded against the house. The fog had made her drive through the storm even more difficult, and it could still get even thicker. Concerned about being able to see the road on the way home tonight, she decided she wanted to stay over anyway. It took her only moments to work it out. *If I leave in the morning by eight, I can still go home and get ready for work.* She couldn't wait to feel his strong sexy body under the covers. *I'll stay.*

Wondering if she should find a movie on television downstairs or go up to his bedroom, she glanced at the digital clock display on the stove which read 9:45 p.m. She smiled thinking of putting on one of his T-shirts. He certainly wouldn't mind. He might even like that. So, she went upstairs to try to find one.

As she opened the top drawer on the dresser, she heard a noise from the front entrance. Having owned a dog when she grew up, she recognized the source right away. Still on the inside of the house, Scout pawed repeatedly at the front door.

Sean's home! Her spirits rose, and she practically ran down the stairs.

There, she saw Scout, whimpering and scratching away. She

frowned. *Sean doesn't need me to open the door. It's his house. So why didn't he just walk in?*

Puzzled, she looked out the windows, trying to see if his car was in the driveway.

Scout looked at her with sad eyes and cried out some more. Then the dog paced over to the same spot and pawed at the door again.

"I get it," she told him. "You want to go out, don't you?"

He just stood and whined.

Using a voice she would use with a three-year-old, she walked off to the kitchen, saying to Scout. "Come on, you can go out in the backyard."

But he wouldn't follow. She halted in mid-stride.

Maybe I need to light up the backyard.

Once in the kitchen, she flicked on the light switch. The backyard lit up, thick raindrops, illuminated in the glow, appeared. This only heightened her distaste for the raging storm and did nothing to encourage Scout to go outside. *Maybe you don't want to go out in the rain... but what's bothering you?* He ran to her but now sat howling at her feet.

"What is it, boy? Go out," she said, encouraging him by standing in front of the open door and waving her hand.

The wind whipped in blowing Sean's note off the counter onto the ceramic tile floor. She quickly shut the door, picked up the precious piece of paper then tucked it into her pocketbook on a chair next to the kitchen table.

Scout ran to the front door hallway and started howling again. Vanessa was worried. *Maybe he's hurt.*

Bending next to Scout, she examined him for any cuts or scratches, but found nothing to indicate an injury.

"There, there, Scout," she said, trying to pet and soothe him, but he just wouldn't be consoled.

Whimpering, the poor dog flattened himself against the floor and laid his head down. She had to try to reach Sean to ask what could be wrong with Scout.

The call did not go through, and Scout's odd behavior escalated. Now, he jumped up putting his front paws on the door and started snarling.

Oh my gosh. He's going crazy! Something's not right.

Vanessa called the police station. "Hello, I'm Vanessa Strauss. I need to speak to Chief Sean Dermott. Are you able to reach him for me?"

"Chief Dermott isn't here. Can I help you?" the officer replied.

"I know he's working at Quarry Head Park, but I'm house-sitting for him, and there seems to be a problem with his dog. Can you give him that message?"

"I'll ring over there and see if he can return your call."

She thanked her and left her phone number with the officer.

Several minutes later the phone rang, and Vanessa quickly answered.

"I'm sorry, Ms. Strauss, it's Officer Gallagher, we just spoke? I'm afraid I couldn't reach him. They said he left the park forty-five minutes ago."

"Did he stop by the police station on the way home?"

"Not that I know of."

"Do you know if he had another assignment?"

"I don't know, sorry."

Vanessa's heart raced, thinking of all the stores that were now closed. She glanced at her phone for the time—10:15 p.m. "Then something *must* be wrong. He would be home if he left that long ago.

"You have to tell them something is wrong." Her voice was urgent and pleading.

"Maybe he stopped somewhere on his way?"

"I know something's not right. Tell someone in the park that he did not make it home. Please." She made sure her insistent tone left no room for ambiguity.

"Okay, I'll pass on that message."

She couldn't even wait a minute. She looked up the phone number of the Connecticut State Police to contact Ethan. The officer who answered said she would relay the message.

Minutes later, the phone rang. "Vanessa, it's Ethan. What's going on?"

"Ethan, I'm sorry to bother you, but I think something's happened to Sean. He never made it home from the park. It's been almost an hour since they said he left Quarry Head, but I'm at his house, and he's not here," she said barely taking a breath as she spoke.

"Okay. There must be some explanation. I'll contact them over there and find out what's going on then let you know."

She could not sit still. She paced the living room. The phone barely rang before she answered.

"I told my colonel you were at Sean's house and that he did not make it back. He confirmed Sean signed out at 9:26 this evening and his car was still in the parking lot. Now they…"

"They have to look for him," Vanessa cried before Ethan could finish.

"They are. Frank's mobilizing a search. He's the best we have. Don't worry, we'll find him."

"Thank you. I'm so glad I reached you."

"You did the right thing. I'll ring as soon as I find anything out."

She walked over to the couch: *stay calm, breathe.*

Starting to feel sick she lay down. Scout jumped up next to her and quietly laid his head on her legs.

~ * ~

Frank spread out the members of his search team at intervals of twenty yards and had them use their handheld floodlights to comb the path from the mobile office, where Sean last checked out, to his Jeep in the parking lot, which he did not take home.

Thick fog shrouded the damp forest floor. Frank paced the area with Officers Dana Langley and Jake Heath. Dana shone a flashlight in one direction and cautioned them, "There's a big drop there. I'm going down."

"We have you covered," Frank said, as he and Jake stood guard and flooded the crater with light.

Then Dana carefully descended the eight-foot ledge. Not a moment later a yell from her. "Oh no!"

"What is it?" Frank yelled from up top.

"Officer down! I'm calling an ambulance."

"I'm on my way," he responded and told Jake to bring in the others.

Frank scaled down the rock shelf and found Sean prone, covered in blood, unmoving. Hopping into a squatting position next to him, Frank placed his index and middle finger on the side of Sean's neck to check for a pulse. The remainder of the search crew converged on the spot. The party took turns clambering down the shelf, forming a semi-circle in the dark holding out their flashlights.

"He's breathing," Frank said with relief.

As soon as he spoke, Sean's chest underwent a sudden spasm, alarming Frank. "Sean, can you hear me? Sean, it's Frank. Can you hear me?"

Sean slowly lifted his head and squeezed his eyes closed even tighter before opening them. "I can hear you. It's my chest," he said, buckling over. He moaned in between forced, shallow breaths, as he struggled to speak. "My ribs hurt like hell."

Immediately Frank helped remove the torn protective vest and put his jacket over him to keep him warm.

"The Tri-meg! Where is it?" Sean asked, his eyes wide open.

Despite plodding, jerky movements, he unfolded into an upright position and reached for the gun by his feet.

Dana quickly braced her arm across his back.

His eyes alert, Frank shifted side-to-side, checking for the sign of any reptile poised to attack. He heard members of his search team gasp.

"There!" Sean turned slightly, wincing.

Frank looked on to see the Tribolmegasaur, stiff as it lay on the ground. The huge, glistening creature looked every piece a museum exhibit, once a living, breathing specimen born from thousands of generations that linked it to its prehistoric ancestors, those who did not survive the cataclysmic event that had savaged the planet. And now it, too, had perished.

Thirty-Eight
Peacefully

The phone rang at Sean's house at 11:43 p.m., and Vanessa immediately answered. "Yes, tell me," she said before Ethan could talk.

"They found him. He was attacked, but he's going to be okay. They took him to the hospital—"

"What hospital? I'm going to see him."

"Norwalk. But wait. I don't think he'll have to stay there."

"How do you know?"

"From what the paramedics told me, he needs stiches on his left shoulder, and they'll do an MRI to check for a concussion. But unless it's a really bad one they won't keep him overnight for that. They're also pretty sure he has some broken ribs so they will do an X-ray to see the damage and then, if he has the all clear, an officer will take him home. I really believe he'll be home in a few hours."

She could hear the sincerity in Ethan's voice and recognized that he wasn't worried about Sean's injuries which reassured her. "Then I'll call to see if I should wait here for him."

"Good idea."

The reality of Ethan's news struck her anew. "Oh, my God! One of the reptiles went after him?"

"Yes, I'm afraid so."

"How could that happen?" Anger tensed her shoulders. "I thought everything was under control."

"I did too. Look, just wait there until Sean comes home. He'll tell you what happened."

She took in a deep breath then exhaled and said, "Thank you for everything you've done."

"Of course. It's a good thing you realized he was missing. He could have been out there alone for a much longer time. Sean's my best friend, so you know…" Ethan paused, and she sensed that he didn't feel comfortable expressing his emotions.

She looked at Scout resting quietly in the center of the room. "I'm just glad he's safe. Ethan, thank you for helping me."

"Speak to you soon."

The moment they said goodbye, she looked up the number for Norwalk Hospital. The attending nurse told her Sean had just arrived in the emergency ward, but as Vanessa wasn't family, she couldn't provide any further details. She did offer to pass on a message to him though. Vanessa thanked her and asked her just to let him know she would wait at the house.

For the next hour she reluctantly curled up on his couch trying to rest, hoping the comfort of being in his home would soothe her, but the cold reality of the attack on Sean struck at her psyche, preventing the peace of mind she sought. After another half an hour, she turned on the television to distract her while she sat beside Scout, stroking his ears and neck.

At 1:35 a.m., a beam of light from the headlights on a vehicle caused her to stand from the sofa, fully alert. Scout thumped his tail on the floor. Sean had arrived.

She ran up to the door and opened it, then dashed outside. "Wait, I'll come help you," she hollered to the officer emerging from the driver's side of the cruiser.

"That's all right. Just wait there," the officer replied as he went to the passenger side to open the door for Sean.

"It's okay," he said as he stood from the car with caution.

The officer walked with him up to the entrance. He carried Sean's prescription for painkillers which he handed to Vanessa, then he expressed his admiration for the chief and asked if he could do anything else for him.

Sean thanked him for his help and told him he would be fine.

Once inside she embraced him with care, aware that he must be in a great deal of pain. She helped him upstairs and pulled back the sheets on his side of the bed.

"Wait for me," he said, heading into the bathroom.

"Of course." She paced, trying to calm herself.

She found a white T-shirt in his top drawer. Slipping out of her dress, she pulled on the oversized shirt and eased under the covers, still too restless to do more than continue to steal glances at the washroom door, wondering when it would ever open.

Fifteen minutes later, he emerged with a towel around his waist. She fought to hold back tears at the cuts and bruises on his upper torso, arms and legs, now freshly washed. The congealed dark, red blood still visible deep underneath the wounds betrayed the severity of the attack. On his left shoulder a bandage covered a cut that required twenty-two stitches. He unfastened the knot on his towel, causing it to slip to the floor. He eased himself under the sheets, his back resting against two pillows propped up against the headboard. Careful to not jostle the bed she eased up beside him.

"What happened out there?" she asked, caressing his arm.

He told her about the attack, but she could tell he softened the more disturbing details.

"That must have been terrifying," she said, but Sean had already closed his eyes.

She watched him to make sure he looked comfortable. Exhausted herself, she saw how calm he looked, deploying rhythmic breathing, and knew everything would be all right.

His eyes were still closed when he reached for her hand. She cuddled up to him, and drifted off to sleep.

Thirty-Nine
Autopsy

At 11:37 p.m., Greg's phone rang. His lids still half-closed, he reached toward his nightstand and answered. Judy turned away from him in her sleep and curled up on her side of the bed.

"Hullo?" he replied in a drowsy voice.

"Sorry to wake you," said Frank. "Normally I wouldn't call at this time, but this is an emergency."

He now had Greg's full attention. Sitting up straight, he wondered if the mission was now in trouble and why? "What is it?" he asked in a clear voice.

"I need you to do a dissection of a dead Tri-meg, and I need this done before we re-start the blasting tomorrow, because I'm concerned about the safety of our officers."

Now Greg knew he wouldn't go back to sleep until the questions swirling around in his head were answered.

"You found a dead Tri-meg?" Judy's voice rang out. In the dark, he turned and held her hand to acknowledge her presence. "How? Where?"

Frank took a second longer to respond. "It attacked Sean…"

"Dear God!"

A gasp from Judy told Greg she'd overheard.

"He was found a short distance from the trail leading back to the parking lot, but he must have shot it before it could do worse damage to him. He has bruised ribs and wounds on his shoulders and chest, but should make a full recovery."

"Thank God he'll be okay," Greg said. He frowned. "Of course, I'll do the dissection, but what exactly are we looking for?"

"It's not one of the five we've been tracking. This is a sixth Tri-meg. Maybe you can find something that will tell us why it didn't migrate with the others."

"Like if it was wounded or maybe sick. Yes. I can do that. Where is the Tri-meg now?"

Frank cleared his throat. "I'm standing in front of it as we speak. I've ordered our flatbed trailer, and we're getting ready to lift it out of here. Do you think you could do the dissection at the university? Is it equipped?"

"Yes, it is. I just have to arrange with the dean of my faculty and get his permission."

"When can you do that?"

Greg closed his eyes so he could think out the next steps. "Not until tomorrow, when I can call his executive assistant. I don't have his home phone number."

"That's fine. In that case, I'll have it stored inside the Wilton Firehall overnight where it'll be hidden from public view. Then, when you call me with the go-ahead, I'll have my men bring it over."

"That's perfect, thanks." The Tri-meg wouldn't fit in a regular laboratory, but the university grounds had several warehouse-sized spaces. *Yes.* It could work. He would find a way to make it work for this opportunity of a lifetime.

"Then we have a plan," Frank said.

After exchanging more phone numbers, they hung up.

"You get to examine a Tribolmegasaur at the university?" Judy asked.

"Yes. I'd be more excited if Sean didn't get hurt, but this is amazing," Greg said. "Excuse me, I have to call Mike and Lee."

"At this time of night?" she asked with surprise, but Greg was already out of the room and scooting down the stairs before she finished.

Mike and Lee shared Greg's enthusiasm. They agreed to meet him at the university at 8:00 sharp the following morning. Then, about an hour later, with nothing further that he could do, Greg checked in on Judy, whom he found sleeping once more. He joined her in bed and was soon asleep himself.

At 7:15 that morning, he already had a light breakfast, dressed, and showered and was ready to meet his colleagues on campus. He spoke with Tova, Irene, and Manny, who'd received messages earlier in the morning about the incident with the Tribolmegasaur and Sean. Tova planned to come to the university but they would start without her. When he arrived, Mike and Lee waited in the lobby for him along with the security guard.

"Does anyone have an update on Sean?" Mike asked.

"Yes. He was released from the hospital last night with bruised ribs, as well as some cuts and bruises. I don't have any more specific details," Greg said.

"Thank goodness he'll be okay," Lee said.

"I can't believe we're going to be able to dissect a prehistoric creature." Mike's wide-open eyes gleamed with intrigue.

"If we can make everything happen," Greg said, grimacing as he thought of all the complex logistics involved in such a sudden and complicated undertaking. Working the phones, he corresponded with several departments all at once: the Dean of the Faculty of Biological Sciences, the Plant and Operations Department, and the External Affairs Department. The dean wasn't in yet, but he followed the developments by phone and gave approval where needed.

All the interdepartmental staff worked together. He called Frank next who advised Greg not to answer calls from the media, as he hoped to secretly transport the huge prehistoric reptile to the university. They agreed; there would be no public notice, thus preventing throngs of awe-struck spectators seeking a peek at one of the world's most earth-shattering find. Frank said he would deploy several officers to block off public access to the grounds where the Tri-meg would be delivered.

With everything in place, Greg called upon two of his doctoral candidates, Nika and Drew, to tag along. They packed several kits of dissection tools into Greg's car. Knowing the standard forceps and scalpels would not be big or strong enough to get through the outer layer of the reptile's scales, he brought a special medical saw from his home. The bright-eyed students also organized video cameras and wired laptops for recording the dissection. Then they all drove together to the designated warehouse on the university grounds.

A massive sliding door framing them in the background, Greg and his team excitedly awaited the arrival of the body inside the cool air of the enormous warehouse. A huge tarp of cellophane covered the ground to prevent spillage upon the underlying cement floor.

"Best to do this as soon as possible," Mike said. "The Tri-meg will start to give off a foul odor."

Just then they saw the giant metal door slide upward, and they heard the rapid beeping noises characteristic of utility vehicles backing up.

"It's here," Greg cried out.

"Wow," Mike said with awe as the vehicle with the dead Tribolmegasaur backed into the space.

The giant creature had been loaded by rolling it onto a sinewy canvas edged with brass rings. This meant that Frank's officers could position the carcass by crane. Maneuvering the joystick, the operator of the hoist lowered the prehistoric marvel to the floor, in close proximity to the first scientific team ever to get their hands on a fresh specimen descended from an era that pre-dated mankind by millions of years.

And there it was. Approximately two tons of reptile body mass, all enclosed in glistening thick scaled skin, the color closely matching the earth from the forest floor. Greg was overwhelmed at seeing such a majestic being right before his eyes.

The Tri-meg's still-damp body lay sprawled on its back, ready for examination. Long, triangular teeth emerged through the parted jaws. Yellow eyes with thin, jet black, diamond-shaped pupils, now lifeless, glared back at the group.

Inside the arch of its neck, the bullet from Sean's gun lodged deeply under the skin. Blood had poured out the hole and dried down to its midsection.

Strange. As Greg lifted the special dissecting saw from his home, more like a slender meat cleaver, he noticed a protrusion in the wider bottom third of the Tri-meg's body.

"I say we start here," he said, tracing the bulge with his tool. "Something may be blocking the Tri-meg's digestive system, and it seems the most pronounced here."

"Agreed," said Lee.

Mike nodded.

Greg's interns carried over the box that contained some of the other tools he might need for the dissection. Everyone put on a lab coat, rubber gloves, and a surgical mask.

Pressing down firmly on the area to be opened, he made a clean, straight line with the massive blade.

Though the skin split at the cut, very little blood poured out. Rather, a horrid, putrid smell wafted out and savagely assailed olfactory nerves.

"Jeez," said Lee, covering her mouth with a medical cloth. Her eyes watered.

The insides parted, and the tips of the bones of a human hand thrust out. Decaying muscle tissue and pale gray skin, clumped among the exposed bones, presented ghastly, mind-searing images to anyone unfortunate enough to witness it.

Lee gagged.

"Oh, my lord," Mike murmured. "It's a person."

She turned her head away, shocked by the sight. It was so revolting, Greg and the others stepped back, stupefied.

"Was that actually a human in there?" exclaimed the lab assistant Drew facing the opposite side of the room with his hands over his eyes. Nika nodded slowly.

"Afraid so," Greg said, still not daring to glance back at the Tri-meg yet. He noticed the others kept their gazes away from it, too.

"I'm sorry," said Drew, his face ashen. "I-I can't go back to this. I think I may throw up." He shuddered, still not looking at the creature.

Lee turned to the students. "That's okay, we never expected this. And we certainly wouldn't ask you to continue."

"You may go," Greg said, feeling unnerved himself. "Please do not talk to anyone about this. We'll need to wait for someone from the police department to advise us on what happens next, especially out of respect for the deceased. If you need to speak to a counselor, there are some excellent ones at the health center, and they'll know to keep this confidential."

Drew nodded, fidgeting, seemingly unable to stand a second longer. Covering his mouth, he darted out through the door of the sizeable warehouse.

In a soft tone, Greg said, "Nika, I think at this point you should go, too. I respect that you want to continue, but we're going to have to stop and contact the police now anyway."

Nika looked tense but said, "All right professor, thank you," and hurried out.

Mike glanced at his two colleagues. "We better contact Frank."

"Agreed," Greg said. "I'm sure we'll have to wait for the police to get here. I'll let him know now."

Within twenty minutes of speaking with Frank, Wilton police officer Brydon Frey arrived on the scene, equipped with a camera and notepad. "Show me," he told them tersely.

As Greg approached the carcass, Brydon took dozens of photos and closely examined, but did not handle, the protruding body parts of the dead human victim.

"Do we have your permission to carry on?" Greg asked.

"Yes, in fact, I need you to separate the victim from the carcass. Then we'll arrange for our own autopsy with the medical examiner. I have already called for the coroner."

"Very well," he muttered.

Everyone put on surgical face masks before he swallowed nervously and continued his dissection.

He pressed down on the reptile's body just under the first incision and continued the cut. The partially digested remains of a human leg could be seen through a slimy film that defined the inside of the Tri-meg's digestive membrane. Detective Frey continued snapping away with his camera, while Lee shuddered, and Mike averted his gaze for a moment.

Greg withdrew his scalpel, shaking his head in sadness. "It's clear to me why this Tri-meg did not migrate with the others. It was severely injured by ingesting this human victim, which also may be part of the reason it was agitated enough to attack Sean. Tri-megs are not able to ingest prey as large as a human."

Lee paled even further. "And what do you recommend we tell Frank?"

"We let him know the results so we can continue with the operation."

Forty
Devoted

Vanessa woke, and turned to the serene face of a sleeping Sean. *Mmm, such a rugged, handsome man.* His normal skin color had returned. The pallor of his face last night flitted through her mind. She shuddered at the memory.

If Sean takes time off as a result of the injuries, maybe I can ask Jenny to cover for me at work, so I can help him. She slowly turned to get out of bed.

"Hey, where are you going?" he asked, as he opened his eyes, startling Vanessa, but in a good way.

She sat back down beside him, comforted by how much better he looked. His eyes were sharp and inquisitive once again. "You're up. I thought I should let you sleep. How're you feeling?"

"A bit uncomfortable, but the painkillers will help. You stayed with me," he said and set his hand on hers.

"Of course. What else did you expect?" she said, adoring his touch. "I could stay and bring up breakfast, if you want?"

To her surprise, he started kicking the blankets off and sat straight up. "I'm going to get up now, too. I'll be able to watch the operation from the mobile office."

These words sent a chill through her body. "Come on. You have to rest," she said, her heart beating faster.

"If I don't go, I'll miss out on what could be the most rewarding part. They're almost back to the lake."

A flash of realization struck her. His devotion to the plight of the prehistoric specimens and the safety of the town meant he simply had to see it through, attack or no attack. And now, with his moment of victory so tantalizingly close, it would be cruel to snatch it away from him. She knew what she had to do, but as the truth dawned on her, she just couldn't relent. She looked at him through watery eyes.

"Please, don't go," she said. A tear trickled down her cheek.

"Please, let me do this," he said gently. "I love you."

For a moment, she stayed still. "You do?" she murmured.

He tugged her closer. "I do. I love you," he repeated, kissing her face and her tears.

"I love you too."

"I know it's hard to understand why I have to go. I would think the same thing if I were you."

"I know," she said, wiping her eyes. "You have to do this."

"Thank you for understanding me."

She loved him and knew nothing she said would change his mind. "What about your injuries?"

"I'll stay in the mobile office, so I'll be able to sit and take it easy, and I can leave if I get uncomfortable. We've got over fifty police officers there, so I'm sure I'll be well protected." He laughed.

She forced a smile, seeing him wince just a little. "You better."

"Last night…how did you know I was hurt?"

She looked at Scout, curled up at the foot of the bed. "He knew."

"*He* knew I was in trouble?"

"You wouldn't believe it. He was scratching at the door and howling. He was running all over, jumping up and down. Like he went haywire."

"Good boy," he said, and the dog, shamelessly seeking attention from his master, jumped up onto the bed and licked him all over his face. Sean protected his chest with his hand.

She patted Scout and said, "Let me take him out this morning."

"Maybe we can walk him together," he said. "But I think I need just a bit longer in bed. I like the way my shirt looks on you."

"It's my new lingerie," she said, as he lifted it off her. "So, you said you love me huh?"

He looked at her and smiled. "Yes. Now, let me show you."

Forty-One
Golden Sun

The previous day's heavy rain left the ground in the park muddy with debris and fallen branches. From his home Sean called the officer on duty in the mobile office for an update on the Tri-megs. He was told they were at the third resting site, basking under the enticing heat lamps, snug and warm in their artificially warmed island. All five original Tri-megs stayed in the resting area together

The weather was bright and sunny, seemingly a sign of a favorable outcome for the mission. By the end of the day the lost Tribolmegasaurs, Sean hoped, would be at the last heated area by the shore of Echo Lake and then return to the underground lake, where they'd lived for millions of years.

Due to the autopsy of the dead Tri-meg in the morning, he learned Frank had delayed the operation, content to let the five accounted-for-Tri-megs bask some more under the heat lamps. The giant reptiles moved around but stayed together, seemingly happy with their artificial blanket of warmth.

Sean's brief chat allowed him to thank Frank for finding him. Their initial uneasy working relationship finally seemed to have sorted itself out, and Sean smiled when Frank muttered, "I owed you one."

Before they got on the phone, Vanessa had convinced Sean to rest at home a few hours longer. He felt upbeat, knowing this plan would please her.

By eleven a.m., he had arrived, and opened the door to the mobile office. Everyone turned and then exclaimed in surprise as Sean walked in, a sly grin on his face. In the crowded room sat the six scientists, Aaron, Frank, and two others Sean recalled: Henry Winters from the U.S. Fish and Wildlife Service and Karen Grant from the U.S. Department of the Interior.

"Sean," Greg and Lee shouted.

Frank held up his hand, still maintaining his gruff exterior. "Look, everyone, he insisted. He said he's not going to miss seeing the Tri-megs home, but not to worry, he's relieved of all his duties. All he has to do is watch."

Sean looked at the crowded conditions inside and joked, "Looks like you had the same problem saying no to everyone else."

"How are you feeling? Are you in much pain?" Greg asked.

"It's bearable, but I had to be here."

"We heard everything. I can't believe you made it. You're lucky to be alive," Lee said, smiling.

"Thanks," Sean said, grimacing as a spasm of pain stabbed him on his side, but his optimism soon drove the discomfort away. "What happened at the autopsy? Do we know why the Tri-meg didn't go with the others?"

"Well..." Frank said, making a face as he turned to Greg.

Greg looked down and cleared his throat. "Um, Sean, if you haven't heard, it may be a shock to you. We found a body inside."

It didn't take Sean more than a moment to surmise. "I'm guessing it was Jason Kenner."

Saying the name out loud only made it worse. He experienced a new round of profound grief, picturing himself telling a distraught Vanessa about the death of her childhood friend.

"Probably," Frank said, averting his gaze.

Greg added, with a solemn expression, "We can confirm it was a man. The medical examiner will only be able to tell us the identity after the autopsy is complete and possibly through DNA or dental records. I'm afraid there was a lot of deterioration."

Sean shook his head as dread gnawed within the pit of his stomach.

Frank snapped to attention then announced, "Okay, everyone. We're going to get started. Sean, I've given strict instructions that the officer outside the door is to shoot you if you try to join us in the field." He winked, lightening the mood before heading out.

Sean was cajoled and directed to sit in front of the center monitor. Aaron turned off the heat lamps and lights at site three and started them up by the lake.

Robbed of the blissful warmth, one by one, the Tribolmegasaurs started moving.

"I'm notifying Frank. Here we go," said Greg.

On the horizon, smoke from the explosives filled the air. Everyone appeared to know the drill. The Tri-megs, hour after hour, flashed briefly on selected surveillance views on each of the three computer screens. This time, they seemed aware that home was close by. They darted through the forest faster and faster, amazing Sean with their true speed.

"I don't think they are going to stop," Greg said. "Something seems different about their pace."

"What are you saying?" Sean asked.

Mike spoke. "I think Greg's right. Their movement is different, faster. I think they are heading straight for the water."

"Look here," Lee said, indicating a Tri-meg that came into view even closer to the heating units showing no sign of slowing down.

Irene stood from her chair. "There! There's another one."

Some held their breath, and for a moment, the room became eerily quiet.

"Only five hundred feet until Echo Lake," Greg said, pointing at the monitor.

A fascinated Sean leaned forward in his chair.

Frank's baritone voice boomed into the mobile office through the radio, "That's it. I'm coming back to the office."

"They're now at two hundred and fifty feet and closing," Greg stood, shifting from foot to foot.

A few minutes later, Mike rose. "Here they are!" The five Tri-megs appeared near the shore of Echo Lake, passing the heat lamps and lights. They continued to slither, lapping down the final distance with increased tempo.

"One hundred feet to go." Greg did a jig as everyone else laughed.

Just then, Frank strolled into the office. Everyone was now on their feet, their seats forgotten.

"Come here, Frank. We think you should see this," Sean said.

Five magnificent finned Tri-megs, the colors of brush and earth, slid onto the gravelly shore of Echo Lake. As the first one submerged into the water, its terrestrial-toned scales disappeared from their view. Reveling in the newfound freedom of their natural environment after weeks trapped on land, they swam gracefully away.

"They're beautiful," Lee said in hushed tones.

Sean nodded. *It's time to close the door on Operation Back to the Nest and be proud for what we've done.*

"The press should be watching this," he said. "They've been waiting on the main road."

"I agree," Frank said, inviting only five, pre-selected members of the media into the mobile office due to the limited space.

Sean sent messages to Vanessa and Ethan telling them he was safe, and the Tri-megs were on their way home. Ethan replied, *Great job; I'm watching this on the news right now* and Vanessa said almost the same but added, *I love you.*

Frank announced, "It's time to show the world who these Tri-megs are and what we fought to save."

"Now switching on the feed to the underground lake," Greg said as he clicked on his keypad.

The new underwater images on the screens enthralled Sean and he could tell the others felt the same. Dozens of glowing Ningen-like fish swam across the camera view. A rush of excitement swept through the room.

Everyone cheered and hugged one another as all five Tribolmegasaurs continued to glide effortlessly through the water passage back to their home in the underground lake.

Sean walked outside the mobile office, feeling the need for fresh air and to connect with the forest that had been his working environment for some time now. The golden sun on the horizon signaled a new beginning: the dawn of mankind's newfound knowledge of the Tribolmegasaurs.

Acknowledgement

Ivy Keating: Special thanks to Cassiel Knight and CBG, Jo Huysamen our editor, Ginger Moran my writing coach, and Alan Lebowitz who said writing is spiritual.

About the Authors

Motivated by nature's mysteries and the complexity of human behavior, Ivy Keating writes science fiction and fantasy novels exploring the relationship between mankind and the natural world. A master's degree in social work helps her explore the depths of her characters and the repercussions of their actions. Inspired by the landscape of New England, she wrote *Camouflage*.

Scott Spotson is a Canadian novelist who excels in imagining scenes of intrigue and adventure within ordinary lives, then pulls together various plots to create a compelling story. He loves hiking and cross-country skiing in the national parks of Canada and was delighted to take part in *Camouflage*, believing this work of fiction a fitting tribute to nature.

Ivy and Scott love to hear from readers. Connect with them at:

Website/Blog
www.ivykeating.com
www.scottspotson.com

Twitter
https://twitter.com/ivy_keating
https://twitter.com/ScottSpotson

Facebook
http://www.facebook.com/IvyKeating/
http://www.facebook.com/SpotSpotson/

Instagram
https://www.instagram.com/ivykeating/

We hope you enjoyed *Camouflage*. If you did, please write a review, tell your friends, or check out the other offerings from Ivy and Scott as well as other authors at Champagne Book Group.

~ * ~

For notice of sales and special deals, visit Champagne Book Group at (http://www.champagnebooks.com) and sign up for our newsletter, including chances to get advance copies of releases before the general reader public does.

www.ingramcontent.com/pod-product-compliance
Lightning Source LLC
Chambersburg PA
CBHW032040240626
47154CB00003B/1012